SWEETEST
TABOO

SWEETEST TABOO

YOLONDA GREGGS

ARABESQUE

BET★ BOOKS

BET Publications, LLC
http://www.bet.com
http://www.arabesquebooks.com

ARABESQU   **74178393**

BET Publications, LLC
c/o BET Books
One BET Plaza
1900 W Place NE
Washington, DC 20018-1211

All Kensington Titles, Imprints, and Distributed Lines are available at special quantity discounts for bulk purchases for sales promotions, premiums, fund-raising, and educational or institutional use. Special excerpts or customized printings can also be created to fit specific needs. For details, write or phone the office of the Kensington special sales manager: Kensington Publishing Corp., 850 Third Avenue, New York, NY 10022, attn: Special Sales Department, Phone: 1-800-221-2647.

First Printing: November 2005
10 9 8 7 6 5 4 3 2 1

Printed in the United States of America

To my daughter whom I am in wonder of everyday.

ACKNOWLEDGMENTS

My Jehovahjireh—my provider. You are more than enough for me.

I'd like to thank my editor, Demetria Lucas, and the BET family for taking a chance on me as unpublished author and guiding my career in a positive direction. It'a been a great experience so far!

Lenie, thank you for sharing your difficult experience with amnesia. Your honesty is invaluable. And you were a great boss!

To my brother, Scotty, and my sister-in-law, Yolanda: thanks for your assistance with police procedure and the critique and helpful feedback!

I have to thank you, Lisa Burnette, for your enthusiasm and support. Your praise for this work encouraged my daily.

I want to send a special thank you to everyone who offered feedback for the title of my newsletter, *Notes in G-Minor*. You're all automatically on my mailing list for life. ☺

And to award-winning author, J. B. Daniels. Thank you for the advanced quotes for my first book, *Honor's Destiny*. I hope to one day be in a position as an author where I can help a new writer on the first leg of her journey.

PROLOGUE

Dressed in black with a cap lowered over her eyes, Cai McIntyre slipped into an unguarded back entrance of the hospital. No matter where she went from one coast to the other, hospital security sucked.

The maternity ward was on the third floor. She'd scoped out the place earlier, waiting for her parents and Nic to leave. This wasn't the time for a family reunion. She had to get to Florida ASAP, which meant she had about fifteen minutes to get in, get out, and be on her way.

Reaching the door to the stairwell, Cai crept inside and took the stairs two at a time, her footsteps stealth, lithe. Her job as a child-finder required quick, unobtrusive movement. Success or failure had a direct impact on a child's fate.

She pushed on the heavy door on the third floor, heard the squish of soft-soled shoes on tile and waited. She shouldn't be here, and she knew it. The media presence that dogged her sister's footsteps could spell disaster if they ever linked Cai to Honor, the model who couldn't seem to retire no matter how she tried. The news of the birth of Honor's baby had created frenzy, and Cai couldn't afford to be connected to her.

But she'd promised to come.

The squishy sound faded and Cai pushed on the door again. With a quick glance to her left and right, she headed for Honor's room. Cai paused outside the door, closed her eyes and took a deep breath. Honor and Mia were going to try to reach out to her, to draw her into them emotionally. She had to resist. She'd come too far to quit now.

Cai slipped inside, then released a sharp, frustrated sigh. Mia and Honor were sound asleep—Mia on an orange leather recliner and Honor in the bed. Damn it! They'd promised to protect the baby. Anyone could sneak in and snatch her away.

A shudder tore through her chest as she struggled to breathe. *Relax.* Fate wouldn't be *that* cruel.

Her gaze latched onto the baby in the bassinet located between Mia and Honor. Instant tears crowded Cai's eyes and a little of the pain in her chest eased. Only a little. Why had she ever agreed to come? She'd known it would hurt like hell.

Cai took a hesitant step toward the baby, half-turned, then quickly stepped up to the glass cradle. She touched the baby's cheek, her balled fist. Her eyes opened and Cai's insides melted. She was so soft and warm, beautiful with Honor's trademark auburn hair and the McIntyre girls' copper eyes.

Cai scooped the baby into her arms, captivated by the perfect weight of her little body, her sweet baby scent. She was long. Would probably be tall like her mommy, Cai thought, smiling. "So you're Nicola. We've been waiting for you."

Cai brushed her lips across Nicola's little fingers, counting each one the way she had with her baby, Ashanti Naja. That little girl had come into the world with Cai's black hair and matching heart-shaped birthmark on her left thigh and her daddy's everything else. She and Jason had fallen in love with her at first sight, and Cai had spent three glorious days learning about the new life that had forever changed hers. Naja was an African name. It meant stoic and strong, which Ashanti would have to be until they were together again.

Cai kissed the baby's cheek and placed her back inside the bassinet. She looked at Honor sleeping so peacefully. After battling anorexia, she had thought she would never have children. But here she was, a mommy. Common sense dictated Cai leave without waking her but the part of her that still craved human contact stopped her.

She bent over Honor and tugged on one of her riotous curls like she used to do when they were kids. People used to mistake her for her famous sister, but Honor had an innocence about her, a softness Cai no longer mirrored. Years of martial arts training had honed her body and her mind. Her emotions? Now that was another story.

Honor's eyes fluttered open and Cai slid onto the bed beside her. "Hey, brat," she whispered.

Honor bolted upright and threw her arms around Cai's neck for a quick hug. "What took you so long?" she said in a low but excited voice. "And it's Mrs. Morgan now, thank you very much."

Cai smiled. Wife and motherhood had only added another striking dimension to her sister. "You'll always be my bratty little sister."

Honor's smile faded a bit, and she glanced at Nicola. "Did you see her?"

"She's beautiful."

"You okay?" Honor asked softly.

Cai looked away. *No*, she thought sadly. She wouldn't be okay until her Ashanti was home, which would be soon. When Cai was eighteen, a woman posing as a nurse had kidnapped her daughter from the hospital. She'd been desperate and powerless, hoping, praying the police would find her baby. At twenty-seven, she didn't need their help. Yesterday, she'd gotten her first real lead and she'd find her daughter herself. "I'd better go. I shouldn't have awakened you."

Honor latched onto Cai's arm with both of her hands. "Don't leave. You should be with us, your family. We can share her, Cai. Nicola's just as much a part of you as she is me."

Cai thought back to the day she'd made a similar offer to share her daughter, once she found her, when Honor thought she couldn't conceive. Emotionally, Cai was drained and it would be so easy to give in, but that just wasn't an option. "I know, honey. But . . . it's . . . easier this way."

"Hard to hate when you're surrounded by love, huh?" Mia stood, stretched and walked the short distance to the bed. Sliding her arms around Cai's neck, Mia held her longer than Cai liked. "It's good to see you, stranger."

At five-three Mia was five inches shorter than Cai and Honor, but she was the oldest and didn't mind playing the role. Cai shouldered her way loose. "You two act like you haven't seen me in years when we were all together for Honor's wedding."

Honor's lips twisted. "We haven't all been together since Mia—"

"Cai," Mia interrupted, glaring at Honor, "You arrived five minutes before we walked down the aisle and you left early."

The problem with the truth was it couldn't be argued. Her work kept her busy, and as a result, she was in and out of her family's lives. Mostly out. "I have to go."

Mia tipped Cai's face up to hers with a finger beneath her chin. "I love you. We all do."

Driven by guilt, Mia could be relentless.

Gently pulling her hand away, Cai sighed. "I know."

They were waiting for Cai to respond with a similar sentiment, but she couldn't open the door to let love in because she might let the hate out, and she needed the hate to survive. "I'll be in touch." With one last look at Nicola, Cai started for the door. "Take care of my niece. You promised, Honor. Don't leave her for a minute, not even a second."

Honor brushed away a tear from the corner of her eye and Cai groaned inwardly, her regret complete. "We'll keep her safe. Don't worry."

Cai opened the door, hesitated, then walked out. She stopped in the hallway, resisting the urge to go back inside. They didn't understand right now, but everything would be the way it was once she found her Ashanti. It would.

Rounding the corner, Cai lowered her cap over her eyes again so she wouldn't be recognized. The sight of the stout RN at the nurse's station renewed her earlier irritation and she stopped to write a list of their security problems and suggested changes. The weary looking woman peered at her skeptically until she saw her initials—BHV.

A frustrated press had dubbed her the Bounty Hunter with a Vengeance because of her unorthodox methods of retrieving stolen children. They didn't like the fact that she kept her identity a secret, but there were aspects of her life she never wanted publicized. Running off to Vegas to marry an older man when she was eighteen and having a baby ten months later were two of them. Her husband abandoning her shortly thereafter was third.

The elevator opened, drawing Cai's attention and she glanced up, right into the eyes of Chastity McIntyre, her mother. On her worst day, Cai could outfox the best reporter, but Mom? Never. Noticing the nurse, Chastity remained silent. Cai was tempted to let the doors close without boarding, but Chastity crossed her arms in a way that said, "I wish you would," that had her trudging toward the box.

The elevator closed behind her and bounced into motion as the two women faced off.

"Of course I knew you'd come," her mother began.

Cai chuckled as she pulled her mother's arms around her waist. Yeah, she'd known her mother's radar would pick her up . . . and maybe a part of her had wanted that.

That home-again feeling, like a leech sucking its victim dry, began to invade her limbs, and she released her mother. "Hi, Mom."

The strongest of the McIntyre women, Chastity still looked hurt by the swift release. "How long are you staying?"

"I'm on my way to Florida." Normally she kept her family up to speed on her cases, but she didn't want to get their hopes up if her lead didn't pan out.

Her mother removed Cai's cap and combed her fingers through her hair like she used to do when Cai was a little girl. "I wish you wouldn't push yourself so hard. You look so tired, baby."

Cai let her head fall to the left and her mother withdrew her hand. If they would just stop trying so hard, she could breathe whenever she came home.

The elevator stopped and the doors parted. Feeling

close to tears—and she hated that feeling—Cai pushed
and held the Door Open button. "I'll be fine, Mom."

"Will you?" Her mother hesitated, which was unusual
and sent shivers of alarm up and down Cai's arms. "I'm
not sure if I should tell you this but . . . Jason called."

Cai's finger slipped off the button and the doors
began to close. "*Jason*? Why?"

CHAPTER 1

"Hurry up, Mel! We have to go!" Christopher St. Clair shouted from the kitchen. His daughter's room was on the other side of the house, so he could only hope she'd heard him.

He grabbed a bag of ice from the freezer and dropped it on the floor to crush it. The commander of Keesler Air Force Base had ordered a mandatory evacuation for all active duty personnel as a category 4 hurricane approached the Mississippi Gulf Coast. Forecasters were predicting it'd hit Biloxi tomorrow, which was also being evacuated. In the meantime, rain and heavy gusts of wind were clearing a path of destruction.

Chris dumped the ice into the cooler and set it on the floor by the door leading to the carport. He hadn't planned to leave until noon, but a neighbor had come by minutes ago to tell him the road outside base housing was already flooding. He feared two more hours of the lashing rain would render it useless.

On his way through the living room, Chris glanced out the window and stopped, struck by the majestic beauty of Mother Nature's temper. Smiling faintly, he stared at the rain "dancing in the wind," as Kimmy would say. She loved rainy days and would be in her element.

Even now, he could picture his wife out there, twirling around with her arms outstretched, her face lifted toward the sky. *All that vitality gone in one tragic, senseless moment.*

No! He cut off the thought before it could lead him any further into despair. One year had passed since her death and he still missed her . . . so much.

Melana strolled into the living room carrying a pink and white duffle bag. She'd pulled her shoulder length black hair into its usual ponytail and was wearing blue jeans over her long legs.

"I've been ready for half an hour, Daddy," she told him in her usual sedate manner.

He eyed her bag with a raised brow. "What do you have in there?"

She shrugged. "The usual stuff."

Chris chuckled. "The usual stuff? We've never gone to a shelter before."

"The usual *girl* stuff," she informed him, as if she were stating the obvious.

Why was he bothering? Melana was the most organized, practical nine year old he'd ever met. Everything in its place was her motto, and, as a result, he never had to tell her to do . . . well . . . anything. She was always punctual, never in a hurry. It was funny because he and Kimmy were the total opposite.

Over the last few days, Melana had read every hurricane preparedness pamphlet and article she could find and had, if true to her nature, followed each to the letter. "Are you sure you want to go to a shelter? We—"

"Yeah, Daddy. I told you, Olivia's going to be there."

Chris stifled his disappointment. He wanted to take his 1967 Austin Healy on the road and thought it would be fun to drive north and stay in a hotel somewhere. But how could he stand in the way of Melana's relationship with their neighbor Olivia? "Okay, then we'd better—"

The sound of metal twisting against metal exploded through the air, and he broke off.

Melana ran toward the front window. "What was that?"

Whatever it was, it sounded close. "Get away from the window, Mel."

Chris rushed over to the door and threw it open. His eyes immediately swerved toward the driveway where he'd parked his car and he stopped, absolutely still. His mint condition two-seater was squashed between a tan sedan rammed into the back of it and their brick house in front of it. He and Kimmy had spent two years restoring Righteous Red, and in memory of her love for that car, he'd finished the project alone.

Now it was destroyed.

Out of the corner of his eye, he saw the passenger door of the tan car burst open. A black-haired woman tumbled out and, grabbing the door, pulled herself to her feet. He heard Melana gasp but barely registered it as he pushed the door handle. "Mel, come hold—"

The wind yanked the door out of his hand and into the brick wall. Seeing Melana behind him, he ran out to meet the woman. The cold, biting rain drenched him from every side, but he didn't slow down. The woman stumbled into him and when she looked up, her fierce ebony eyes caught him in their tumultuous depths. Suddenly, he couldn't feel the rain or the wind. Good Lord, she was ravishing.

She said something but the words were carried away on the wind before they could reach him. He saw blood pouring from a wound in her left arm and realized she was hurt. Shaking her head, she pushed away from him and staggered toward the door where Melana was standing. When she reached the porch, she fell to her knees and then onto her hands. "Ashanti," she moaned.

Then she collapsed.

Ashanti? Who—? Chris' head whipped around toward the car. Was someone else inside? He'd have to check but first he'd get her inside the house.

He hurried to her side, braced himself against the wind and easily lifted her tall, skinny body into his arms.

"She's bleeding, Daddy!"

"I know." Brushing his face against the woman's wet shirt to clear his vision, Chris carried her inside. "Grab the first aid kit from the closet."

He carried the woman to his bedroom and laid her on the king-sized bed, careful not to further injure her arm. Damn. Two minutes ago, all he had to worry about was getting two people out of here and now he had to worry about three, maybe four.

He raced back down the hallway and almost ran Melana over as she rounded the corner. He caught her by the arms to steady both of them. "I'm going to see if anyone else is in the car."

"Okay, I'll see if the lady is awake."

Nodding, Chris ran outside. Already soaked and numb from his first foray into the rain, he could barely feel the blasts of water and cold on his second trip.

Jerking on the door handle, he stuck his head

inside the car and did a quick sweep of the front and back seats. No sign of anyone. So who had she been referring to?

He forced the door shut and ran back to the house. Once inside, he stripped out of his wet shirt and jogged the few steps down the hallway to the bathroom. Melana had stacked a pile of towels somewhere . . .

He saw the thick mound on the counter, grabbed them and shot off toward the bedroom. Melana was standing at the foot of the bed staring at the woman. Thank God, he could count on her not to panic.

Chris dropped to his knees beside the bed, determined not to lose this round with fate. "Call 911, honey."

He wasn't sure an ambulance could get through, but that was probably their only hope of getting out.

He carefully peeled off the woman's short leather jacket, and then rolled up the sleeve of her black T-shirt. The blood was coming from a straight two-inch cut across the length of her arm.

Melana set the phone back in its cradle. "No dial tone. See, I told you we should've gotten those cell phones."

They'd gone round and round on the issue, he believing she was too young for her own cell phone, she believing otherwise. Right now, he wished he'd given in to her as he usually did. "After I finish this, I'll pull the cars apart and see if hers is drivable. Ours is totaled."

He pressed the towel against the woman's wound to stop the flow of blood and gently pushed her hair away from her face with his other hand. His fingers brushed against a bump just behind her right ear and he jerked away, not wanting to hurt her.

No, fate wasn't getting her, too, he vowed. He hadn't been able to save Kimmy from the drunk driver who had so carelessly gotten behind the wheel of a car, but he wouldn't let this woman die, too. "What were you doing out there with a hurricane approaching? You should've been driving *away* from the storm, not into it."

He spoke softly, not wanting to frighten her. He'd read somewhere that patients had reported hearing voices while unconscious.

Offering a wide-eyed Melana a quick smile, Chris dragged the first aid kit toward him, and then grabbed a roll of white gauze from inside. The knot on the woman's head appeared to be the only other obvious injury.

The lights flickered and he glanced at the light fixture in the ceiling. It was only a matter of time before they went out. He checked the woman's face for any signs of life. As an engineer, he was more familiar with the wires that brought a building to life, not a human. The air force required annual first aid classes, so he could bandage her up okay, but he had no idea how long it was safe for her to be unconscious.

She needed to wake up. They had to get out of here before the road flooded.

Melana watched him closely as he taped a final strip around her arm. "She's pretty, isn't she?"

He was trying hard not to think about that. "Very." He pushed himself to his feet. "Stay with her in case she wakes up, okay?"

He grabbed a shirt from the dresser and tugged the warm material over his head. Hurrying over to the closet, he snatched a jacket off of a hanger and ran down the hallway and out the door. Apparently piqued by his nerve to risk coming outside again, the wind blasted him, pushing him backward. He stopped to brace himself before marching forward.

He opened the car door, and, refusing to give in gracefully, Mother Nature yanked it from him. He decided against wrestling with it and left it open.

Noticing that the keys were still in the ignition, he climbed into the passenger side—the driver's door was crushed—reached across the arm rest, and turned the key. The engine sputtered and died. Damn.

He put the gear in neutral, got out, and ran to the front of the car. He braced himself with his hands on the hood and pushed. The whine of separating metal ranked right up there with nails on a chalkboard, but he kept the pressure on until the cars were apart. He surveyed the damage with a pained expression. The front of her car looked like vacuum-packed tuna. He might be able to force the hood open with a crowbar to see if there were any loose wires, but how would he keep it closed afterward?

Turning to Righteous Red for his salvation, he could only confirm what he already knew. His two-seater was crushed in the front *and* back. Even if he could get it started, the three of them could never get into it. He should have picked up his Audi from the repair shop yesterday, but he'd decided to leave it due to the evacuation.

They were going to have to wait the storm out here. Damn.

Chris reached into the car to push the gear into park and noticed a logo for a rental car agency on the key ring. Then she'd probably have a receipt. The question was, where?

He flipped the visor down and back up with a flick of his index finger. Nothing.

Stretching across the car for the visor above the driver seat, he saw smeared blood on the door. *Blood?* He rubbed his finger against a red splotch, expecting it to be wet. It wasn't. How could it have dried so fast? And what could have cut her? None of the ⌐lows were broken.

He thought about the bump on the back of her head. That wasn't consistent with the crash either. Could she have been hurt *before* she smashed her car into his?

He glanced through the rear window for clues. There weren't any cars parked on the street, so that ruled out an attempt to avoid hitting one. Now that he thought about it, he never heard the squeal of skidding tires, only the impact. How did she end up in his driveway, a driveway on a hill? Was she coming here? Who was she?

He turned to the glove compartment for answers, pushing in the latch and lowering the door until his knees blocked its descent. A perfectly folded pink car rental receipt was inside. He snatched it up and quickly scanned the information typed in the little boxes. Amber Night. The name didn't ring any bells, but she did look vaguely familiar. She'd picked up the car in New Orleans earlier that day.

Chris tucked the paper in his jacket pocket and turned to search for her purse. Renting a car required identification, so she must have a picture ID around here somewhere.

He searched the front and back seats and was reaching to pop the trunk when he saw Melana signaling from the door. Hesitating, he drummed his nails on the dash. The road was probably impassable by now. After he saw what Melana wanted, he'd push the car in the garage and cover it. He had a feeling Amber Night was in trouble.

Melana opened the door at his approach. "What's up?" he asked, shrugging out of his jacket. "Is she awake?"

"No, but she's probably cold with those wet clothes on. Maybe we should take them off."

Chris was chilled to the bone so he figured she'd have to be. God help him. "Okay, I'll meet you there in a sec."

"*Ja Herr.*" Yes, sir, in German. She playfully saluted him, did an about-face, and headed back down the hallway. Having spent her formative years in Germany, Melana was fluent in the language. And she loved it when noncommissioned officers saluted her dad.

Chuckling, he stripped out of his wet shirt, kicked off his muddy Nikes, and tugged his socks off his clammy feet. He'd change his pants later.

He began the short trek down the hallway, his footsteps slowing as he approached his bedroom. In theory, removing Amber's clothes was the practical decision. She would catch cold if they left her as she was, right?

His gaze flickered over Amber's prone body as he entered the room. She hadn't moved at all. Her jeans were plastered to her body, so he would have to cut those off. Her shirt, too, since he didn't want to move her arm or head unnecessarily. The bandage was soaked red, so he'd have to change that as well. "Will you hand me a pair of scissors, honey?"

Melana disappeared into the adjoining bathroom and returned with the scissors. "Be careful so you don't cut yourself," she said, mimicking him perfectly.

He pretended to snap her with a towel before tossing it to her. She giggled and he rolled his eyes playfully. "Dry her hair, would you? And be careful around the bump on her head."

His humor faded as he rubbed the back of his neck. Where to begin? The top? That would make sense. Start at the top and work down.

His gaze lingered over her impossibly long lashes, high cheekbones, and full sensuous lips. On the other hand, the jeans would take longer to cut with the thicker material. He wiped the back of his hand across his forehead.

"What's wrong, Daddy?"

"Nothing," he blurted out.

Melana stared at him as if he'd grown another head before turning back to Amber's hair.

Okay, the top. He gripped her shirt with one hand as he cut along the seam. As each snip teasingly revealed more of her light brown skin, his fingers brushed her cool, firm body. Her muscles were well-formed and solid. She obviously worked out.

His hands shook a little as he started to pull the material away from her body.

Melana grabbed a second towel and quickly covered Amber's chest. "Daddy! Don't look at her. That's private."

He was trying not to look, trying not to see the sexy lace lining the cups of her white bra. "I didn't see anything." Much of anything, he qualified.

Melana was at that stage where every little thing embarrassed her. Of course, her age didn't explain *his* increasing embarrassment as he cut the seams of Amber's jeans and eased her off the wet spot her clothes had left. To keep himself focused, he didn't push the material away but let it rest on top of her.

Moving to the window, Chris pretended an interest in the swirling skies while Melana removed Amber's tennis shoes and underclothes. His reaction to the sight of a beautiful woman was perfectly natural, he told himself. He'd had a tough year adjusting to Kimmy's death and could already tell it was going to be one of those nights when his dreams would be too vivid to allow him any rest, when he'd reach for his wife and not find her there.

From a long way away, he heard Melana gasp. "Look, Daddy. Isn't that pretty?"

He turned to see what Melana was talking about. She'd covered Amber's body with a dry towel, leaving him to view the top of Amber's left thigh. Looking closely, he saw a tiny heart-shaped birthmark.

Melana chewed her bottom lip for several seconds before shaking her head. "Doesn't she look . . . ?"

"Familiar? I was thinking the same thing."

"Maybe we met her at our other base?"

Ramstein? They'd spent the last seven years in Germany on a COT—consecutive overseas tour. Kimmy had fallen in love with the country and vowed never to return to the States. Her wish had come true but probably never the way she'd imagined. It was possible that they'd met this woman there, or during one of their many trips to England or France, but he didn't think he could ever forget meeting such a striking woman. "Maybe. We'll have to see when she wakes up."

The lights flickered again, and Chris sighed. Better get the flashlights out of the bag. No need to stumble around in the dark if they didn't need to.

Leaving Melana to her nursing duties, he strolled toward the living room where he'd left his bags. Unzipping the black duffle bag, he removed three flashlights from inside. He had already moved the computer and sound system off the floor and purchased enough food and water to get them through several days. Even with their unexpected visitor, they should have enough.

The electricity flickered one last time, then went out completely. Light filtered through the windows, casting a comfortable glow inside. It would probably be hours before they'd need to turn on the lanterns or light candles.

Chris switched on the flashlight in his hand to ensure it worked before setting it on the table. "Enjoy the storm, Kimmy."

It was getting darker. Chris set up a couple battery-operated lanterns in the living room and carried a third one into his bedroom where Amber lay so still. Melana was reading a book, but paused to look up from her prone position beside Amber. She'd volunteered to sit with their patient when he'd told her he was going to push the rental car into the carport. He hadn't told her why and she hadn't asked, thank God. She didn't need to be burdened with what he hoped was only a potential threat.

After an impromptu workout rolling both cars downhill, then back up in reverse order, he'd remembered his intention to check the trunk. He'd searched the small confines until, frustrated, he'd flipped the top to the tire compartment where he found a small purse tucked in the corner. Rushing inside, his teeth clenched against the cold, he'd probably used the last of the hot water trying to bring his numb fingers and toes back to life. Afterward, he'd changed into a dry pair of jeans and a black T-shirt.

Melana stretched and laid her book on the table. "Are you hungry, Daddy? I'm going to grab a snack."

"No, I'm okay. I guess it's my turn to sit with our patient."

Melana beamed at his use of the word *our*, before strolling from the room. She loved doing things with her dad, especially playing checkers, which he was teaching her how to play.

Chris settled into a chair in a corner of the room, disappointed. He thought for sure Amber would be awake by now. What was her story? he wondered. Where'd she come from?

Her ring finger was bare, he noticed. Funny, he hadn't thought to check while cutting her clothes away. He felt a sense of relief, which he quickly squashed. What did it matter? Even if she wasn't married, in his heart he was.

The only child of older parents, Chris had met his perfect match in Kimmy. Unlike his parents, who had treasured their relationship and died within days of each other, he and Kimmy had only been blessed with seven perfect years of marriage, not nearly forty-five.

Like his parents, he had only one child, but his had come through adopting Kimmy's two-year-old daughter, Melana. They had hoped for more, but after several years of trying to conceive, he'd concluded that his parents' difficulty in conceiving had passed to him. Even though his parents had sought specialists for their problem, Kimmy never wanted to, explaining that he and Melana were all she needed. Plus, she'd said, referring to her experience with two sisters and a brother who had disowned her for some obscure reason, big families weren't all that. Even though Kimmy never admitted that their rejection had hurt, every now and then a look of sadness would creep into her eyes, especially when she was staring at Melana, and his heart would ache for her loss.

Feeling his throat constrict, he took a deep breath and slid down in the chair to rest his head on its back. Just like that, he was swamped with memories, memories he'd hoped to escape by moving back to the States.

He and Melana had arrived in Biloxi in May, just after the end of the school year, and the long hot summer days had dragged endlessly. He'd thrown himself into buying new furniture and unpacking the few items he hadn't been able to leave behind. Kimmy wasn't a big spender. More Saturdays than he cared to admit had been spent at one flea market or another, and their hodgepodge of furniture and knickknacks, eclectic, to say the least, had been everywhere. But new furniture hadn't brought him any peace.

Indulging in long hours at work hadn't been an option either because he didn't like leaving Melana. As a captain in the air force, he oversaw construction on the base—Saber projects, as they were called. While awarding bids to local construction companies, hammering out contracts, and overseeing sites with weekly inspections was rewarding, he lived in dread of getting a temporary duty assignment.

To stave off using children as an excuse to avoid TDYs, the military required single parents to complete a dependent-care plan, something he'd never had to do before. If push-came-to-shove, he'd leave Melana with their neighbor Jasmine and her daughter Olivia, but he prayed it never would.

Chris heard soft foot steps and opened his eyes.

Melana leaned over the bed to look at Amber. "She's *still* asleep?"

"'Fraid so."

Sighing, she padded over to his chair and eased onto the armrest. "You look tired. Want me to sit with her?"

"Nah, I'm okay."

A sly grin spread across her face. "I could set up the checkerboard in here."

Chris chuckled. "Maybe later. What are you reading?" he asked, noticing the book in her hand.

She folded her arms across her chest, hiding the cover in the process—"*Stargirl.*"

He studied her bent head for a moment, not liking the change in her demeanor. Melana usually shared everything with him. "What's it's about?"

"This girl. She's different than the other kids." Melana's right shoulder went up and down in a shrug. "At first they like her because she's different, then they start to *dislike* her because she's different."

Chris shook his head in confusion. "I don't remember buying that . . . ?"

"I borrowed it from Olivia."

But why? Melana had never been a Dr. Seuss fan, but did she have to jump straight to preteen drama? "Is it . . . something you can relate to?" he asked, dreading the answer.

School had started less than a month ago. Melana had gotten to know some of the kids in the neighborhood over the summer, but starting over in a new school could be tough.

She shrugged again and Chris felt something squeeze his heart. "What is it?"

Sighing, she slid off the armrest. "I'm taller than almost everybody, even the boys. How come I'm so tall?" she asked with more than a little irritation in her voice. "Kimmy was short."

Over the years, Chris had gotten used to Melana calling her mother by her first name—something Kimmy wanted so they'd be more like "friends." He would've argued Melana needed a mother, but, truth be told, the child had been the adult in their relationship.

Kimmy was the quintessential absentminded professor. When it came to work as an interior decorator, she was "on." Away from work, she was often distracted, forgetting to cook or forgetting that she was cooking.

She'd miss appointments, overlook birthdays and holidays, so he and then Melana began to pick up the slack. They'd worked like a well-oiled machine until the day Kimmy forgot to get glue for Melana's project. Apologizing profusely, she'd dashed out the door to go to the store and never returned.

Chris captured her hand and pulled her onto his lap. "Do kids tease you?"

She leaned into him and sighed, a big sigh, as if she'd released a heavy weight. "Some, I guess. But I can handle it," she quickly assured him, straightening.

"Are you sure? Because I can talk to your teacher—"

Melana's eyes widened. "No. Daddy, *no*."

"Okay. Okay." But he'd do something. He wasn't going to have his little girl teased.

"*Dad* . . ."

She gave him the no-nonsense look she'd adopted with Kimmy, and Chris chuckled. He knew he could be a little intense when it came to Melana. She was a special girl and she'd been through enough with the abandonment of her birth father and Kimmy's death. "Let me know if I can help."

She relaxed at that and even smiled a little before standing and walking out of the room.

Chris leaned back and closed his eyes again. During times like these, he wished Melana had a mother. His friends, especially Ron, a guy he'd known since officer training school, were always encouraging him to find a woman to love and mother his child. He'd never even considered it.

Melana didn't seem to mind. Well, not too much. Every now and then she'd talk about the special things Olivia did with her mother and he'd see a look of longing in her eyes. He could do the dad stuff— teach her how to dribble a basketball, sink a three-point shot and when she was older, he'd tell her what lines to expect from boys. Fingernail polish and makeup and the hundred and one things a girl should learn from her mom, he couldn't do. So, there were days when he wondered if having a dad was enough.

"Daddy, wake up."

Chris jerked upright and then groaned as the kinks in his neck made him aware of their presence. What time was it? He must have dozed off.

He automatically glanced at the clock on the night-stand. Dead, the power was still out. Rain was slashing at the window behind him but it was still relatively bright outside and in.

"How long do you think the electricity will be out? I'm bored."

"Days. If we're lucky. What time is it?" From the level of light, he'd say late afternoon.

"Almost four o'clock."

He glanced toward the bed and noticed that Amber had moved a bit, her skin now a warm honey color. Even as he watched, her eyelashes fluttered up.

Melana's gaze flew to his and back to their patient's. "Finally! Look, Daddy!"

Chris was out the chair and bedside in seconds. "You're awake!" His gaze roamed her face, taking in her slightly flushed cheeks, the richness of her eyes. He hadn't imagined the color or their power to draw him. "How are you?" he asked softly.

Before she could respond, Melana wedged herself between him and the bed, her head twisted at an angle so she could glare up at him. "Daddy, you can't be asking her a lot of questions." Shaking her head, she turned to Amber. "I thought you were never

gonna wake up! Are you hungry? Do you want something to eat?"

Chuckling, Chris tapped Melana's shoulder with a
finger. "I thought we weren't supposed to ask her a
lot of questions?"

Melana gave him a sheepish grin. "*I* can ask. I don't
have a deep, scary voice."

"Ah, female logic," he said with a playful grin.

Drawn back to Amber, he saw her watching him and
Melana with a curious expression, then gaze the
length of the room. He couldn't imagine what she was
feeling, though it didn't seem to be fear. Why was that?

CHAPTER 2

Her gaze returned to the two sets of eyes watching her so intently. The colors were different but the expressions were the same. Who were they?

"Where am I?" She glanced around, surprised by the husky sound of her own voice.

"You're safe, Amber. You—"

"Amber? Is that my name?" Oh, God, her head hurt.

"You don't know your name?" the pretty little girl asked.

"Isn't it?" the man said. "I found a receipt in your rental car for an Amber Night."

"You found . . . ? Does that mean you don't know me?"

He looked at her with a strange expression. "No. You crashed into my car six hours ago, and we've been taking care of you." He looked like he wanted to say something else but with a quick glance at the little girl stopped himself.

Amber closed her eyes for a moment. *Amber*. It didn't sound familiar.

"Does your head hurt, Miss Amber? I can get you some medicine."

Amber reached up to feel the tender bump on the back of her head. Her head felt like the bass section of a drum line was practicing for an upcoming competition. If she could just get the noise to stop, she could think. "Please," she whispered.

She waited until the patter of feet against the floor faded to open her eyes. "What did you want to say but stopped because of the little girl?"

His brows shot up. "I'm concerned that your bruises aren't consistent with the crash. I think you're in some sort of trouble."

"Then I should go. I can't put you two in danger." She swung her legs out from beneath the blanket to stand but the man stopped her with a hand against her shoulder.

"Hold on, there."

Only then did she realize she was undressed. "Where are my clothes?" she asked as the heat of his hand spread across her bare shoulder.

"I had to cut them off. They were soaked."

She noticed a slight tinge in his light-skinned cheeks. What did that mean? Oh, her head hurt.

"Let me get my robe."

He dashed through a nearby door and returned with a navy blue robe. She was about to stand and put it on when the little girl barreled back into the room and cried out, "Daddy!"

The man spun around so his back was to Amber and the little girl set a bottle of water and pills on the nightstand before hurrying over to help with the robe.

"Thanks," Amber told her. What was all the fuss about?

"You can't let men see you with your clothes off, Miss Amber."

"You can't? Why?"

"Because it's bad."

Amber wondered at that, but, too tired to ask any more questions, lay back down and closed her eyes.

She was about to doze off when a small hand on her shoulder gently shook her. "Did you want to take some medicine?"

"Later," she mumbled.

Chris gaped at Amber. If indeed her name was Amber. How could she sleep at a time like this? They needed to figure out who she was, where she'd come from. Instead, she was knocked out.

Melana looked at him curiously. "How come she doesn't know her own name?"

"She's probably disoriented from the bump on her head," Chris explained. *And please let it be temporary.*

"I guess I'll keep reading," Melana said on a long sigh.

He watched her lope across the room and out the door. Now what? Wait? He fell back into his chair to do just that, his gaze locked on the beautiful woman in his bed.

She obviously wasn't ashamed of her body. If Melana had returned just a few seconds later, Amber would've stood right up in front of him. Knowing he would have enjoyed the view had had his cheeks flushing beneath his skin when Melana caught him.

Chris pressed his fingers to his temples. Right now, he had a greater concern. If Amber didn't know who she was, how in the world could he help her? How would they know where the threat was coming from?

He turned to the purse on the dresser for the information he'd hoped she could provide. Several pieces of plastic were tucked together inside and he grabbed them.

"What the—?" he broke off as he spread five driver's licenses, all from different states, like a deck of cards. Besides Amber Night, there was Ashley Newton, Abby Naveen, Adrienne Nervelli and Alisha Neal. Stunned, he stared at the woman in his bed. Even though she had different hairstyles in each picture—they had to be wigs—the photos were definitely of her.

What if *she* was the threat?

All the names had the same initials, which had to be significant. Curious, he returned to his exploration. He removed a wad of cash and a couple of credit cards. He felt something cold and hard touch his fingers and pulled out an engraved antique locket. He popped the tiny hook and a small piece of paper tumbled free. He caught the paper midflight as he gazed at a picture of a baby wrapped in a pink blanket. Her hair was black and her eyes were closed so he couldn't see their color, but he'd bet they were the same color as their patient.

He turned the paper over and saw Ashanti Naja written in the same pretty cursive as the signature on the receipt he'd found earlier. There was the significance. Was she Amber's baby? If so, there was probably a husband or significant other out there somewhere as well.

After what seemed like forever but could've only been an hour, Amber's eyelids fluttered open a second time. Blinking, she glanced around the room, appearing to be more curious than fearful. Chris approached the bed slowly. "Hello, again."

Her gaze fastened on his. "Hi."

Her eyes were a little more focused than the last time. Good. This time he intended to get answers. "Feeling better?"

"Than what?"

"Than before. Earlier you mentioned that your head hurt."

Her eyes narrowed for a moment. "Yes, my head still hurts. Who are you?"

She asked so casually, as if waking up in a stranger's home were the norm. "I didn't have a chance to tell you earlier. My name—"

Melana rushed into the room, interrupting the introduction. Her eyes widened and she slowed as she approached the bed. "Are you going to stay awake this time?"

Amber smiled uncertainly. "I guess so—do I know you?"

Hadn't they already done this? Chris scratched the back of his neck. Oh, no—

"Yeah, remember when you woke up the last time, Miss Amber? I helped you put the robe on. Daddy—"

"Miss Amber . . . ?" she asked, glancing around.

"That would be you." Chris jumped in to speed up the process and received a sharp frown of disapproval from his daughter for the effort. Could he stand to be a little more patient? Probably, but he had no idea how long she'd be awake this time. "I'm Chris, her dad. *Melana's* dad," he emphasized, pointing to the little girl.

Amber's brows twisted in confusion. "My name is Amber?"

"Or so I thought. I found a receipt in your rental car for an Amber Night." She closed her eyes before he could continue. "No!" he said more sharply than he'd intended, causing her eyes to pop open. "Don't go back to sleep yet," he finished on a somewhat softer note.

She spoke around a yawn so her words were not immediately clear. ". . . receipt. Does that mean you don't know who I am?"

Chris let his head fall back. They'd definitely done this. "If you will recall—" he began, somewhat impatient at having to explain again.

"My head hurts," she told them, reaching for the medicine and water Melana had set on the nightstand earlier. She twisted off the childproof bottle cap and shook two pain relievers into her hand.

Melana had meant well offering the pills, but he wasn't sure Amber should take them. What if she had some type of allergic reaction?

She tossed the pills into her mouth and quickly chased them down with what had to be warm water by now. Before he could stop her, she slid back down and closed her eyes.

Chris threw his hands up as he blew out a frustrated sigh. "Great," he muttered. He saw a glimmer of amusement in Melana's eyes and stopped to glare at her. "What's so funny?"

Laughing, she said, "You are, Daddy."

He clenched his teeth. "Just sit with her, would you? And if she wakes up again, don't let her go back to sleep!"

Chris stalked out of the room and through the house, double checking the locks. Stopping in the kitchen, he scanned the area outside the back window, seeing nothing but rain so thick it looked like a curtain. He hoped the flooded road imprisoning them would keep trouble at bay.

* * *

She felt someone watching her and opened her eyes. A pretty little girl was perched on the bed, her tawny eyes snapping. "Are you done sleeping now?"

Her gaze slid beyond the child to the man by the window with one jean-clad hip propped on the sill. She looked at the little girl again. "Where's the bathroom?"

"I'll show you, Miss Amber. You might need a flashlight. The electricity is out."

Amber? Her head began to hurt and she paused. She closed her eyes trying to recall . . . something, anything. Who were these people? And why were they watching her so closely?

"Why is the electricity out?" she asked the little girl, ignoring the big man altogether.

"Hurricane. It's our first one. What about you?"

Amber thought about it, or at least tried to until the throbbing ache between her temples intensified. "I don't know."

She gingerly eased her legs over the side of the bed. Her arm hurt, too. She glanced at the bandage on her left arm. How had she gotten hurt?

Her legs wobbled as she stood and the girl slipped an arm around her waist, as if she could really support Amber. She was tall, but skinny.

"I'll help you," she said with an earnestness Amber couldn't doubt.

Out of the corner of her, she saw the man relax. He must've moved to catch her. Amber moved slowly, concentrating on each step, and Melana didn't rush her. "Thanks—what's your name?"

"Melana. Remember?"

"And my name is Amber?"

"Yeah. How come you don't know?"

"I don't know."

Melana opened the door and then handed Amber

the flashlight. Amber continued into the room alone, closing the door behind her. It wasn't too dark, so she left the flashlight off.

She saw a movement and jumped. Then she realized it was her reflection. The black-haired, dark-eyed woman staring at her didn't look familiar. Amber. *Amber*, she repeated in her mind, trying to jog her memory.

Why couldn't she remember?

Using her left hand, she turned on the faucet. Her hand began to tremble and she cupped it with her right one until the quivering stopped.

She could hear the man's deep cadence mingling with Melana's higher one. Who was she to them? Not the little girl's mother because she'd called her Miss Amber. No wedding band, she noted with a glance at her left hand.

Concentrating, she reached for the faucet again and adjusted the temperature to conserve hot water. If the electricity was out, the hot water would soon follow.

Bending over, she splashed the water onto her face, enjoying the coolness on her skin. Before she went back out there, she needed to get her bearings. What did she know? Not much of anything, she realized.

She turned off the water and dried her face and hands on a towel hanging on the rack. The rich purple color scheme reminded her of the man on the other side of the door, dark and mysterious. The contrasting yellow indicated either a whimsical side or a wife. Where was his wife?

Amber opened the door expecting to see the little girl. She was gone, but the large bed was right where she'd left it and it was beckoning her. She wanted to go back to sleep.

"Uh-huh," the man said, intercepting dreamy thoughts of burying her face in the pillow and burrowing beneath the thick blanket. "Why don't you sit here? You can go back to sleep after we talk."

He guided her to the chair with a hand on her arm. "Where's Mel . . . Melana?"

"I asked her to fix you a snack. We need to talk privately, and we don't have a lot of time. Do you remember my name?"

"No," she said, practically falling into the chair.

"So you don't remember our last conversation."

She shrugged her shoulders. "I guess not."

He released a heavy sigh. "My name is Chris. I thought your name was Amber until I found these."

He handed her some ID cards and she glanced through them, recognizing the face she'd seen in the mirror but none of the names. "They're me?"

"All of them, apparently. Like I told you before, I think you're in some kind of trouble. The problem is— at least one problem is—with you having amnesia, we don't know where the threat, if any, will come from."

She handed him the licenses and sat back. "Why do you think I'm in trouble?"

"You crashed into my car earlier today. You have a bump on the back of your head and a cut on your arm. Neither injury is consistent with the crash."

"Are you a cop?" He sounded so professional and he was big.

"No, though that would've been helpful right about now," he muttered especially when a hurricane was coming. "Melana said a hurricane's coming? Shouldn't we be leaving the area?"

"We're supposed to evacuate but both cars are busted and everyone else is gone."

"Which means—"

"We'll be here awhile," he said, sighing. "Which name do you prefer?"

"Huh?" He nodded at the cards in his hands. "Oh. Melana called me Amber, so that's fine."

"Well, then," he murmured with the sexiest smile she was sure she'd ever seen. "It's nice to meet you, Amber."

He offered her his hand and she stared for a moment. Please don't let her hand shake, she prayed. She placed her hand in his and when his fingers closed over hers, he pulled her to her feet.

She looked a long way up from his chest to his eyes. They reminded her of dark chocolate, the melt-in-your-mouth variety. His toffee skin and chiseled jaw weren't hard on the eyes either.

His gaze lowered to her mouth and she felt a funny sensation in her belly.

"Do you want to lie back down?"

Images of Chris joining her in the bed popped in her mind and she watched the display with some interest. Why did that happen? Words formed in her head, tumbling together, running amok, and she knew she'd never get them right in her mouth. So she nodded.

"We should tighten the robe a bit." Amber watched, wide-eyed, as he nudged the edges closer and tightened the belt. "There you go."

"Where's your wife?" she blurted out, then jumped, startled by her own question. It only made sense that he'd be married. He had a daughter after all, so where was she?

Chris' expression changed, darkened as if a shadow had passed overhead. "She died."

His whisper, as if he didn't want to say the words aloud, still managed to fill the room. The sound made her heart hurt, but she didn't know why.

* * *

Amber's eyes didn't leave his and Chris didn't back away, despite his sudden discomfort. On his best day, he couldn't talk about Kimmy, and this day hardly qualified as such.

Amber studied him with those dark eyes of hers. "Your face looks different."

They were so close he could feel her confusion, or was it his own? There was no explanation for his and Melana's loss, and time had not done what anyone had told him it would do. Time did not heal wounds. If anything, time made the wounds worse. "Different? How?"

"Closed. You don't want to talk about your wife."

How did she know? How could she read him so well, this stranger? "Talking about her makes me feel sad."

Amber blinked several times, as if she were trying to process the information. She looked puzzled.

He guided her toward the bed by her arm. "You should lie down. I don't think you're a hundred percent yet." And he wasn't ready for this conversation.

She didn't do quite as directed but sat down and leaned back against the headboard. Once she was settled, he pulled the blanket over her. "My heart feels heavy."

"Your heart? Are you having chest pains?" God help them if she were.

"No, just my heart. I made you feel sad."

A gentle smile tugged at Chris's lips. "It's okay. You didn't mean any harm."

Melana strolled in, carefully balancing a tray in her arms. "Are you hungry, Miss Amber? We have crackers with cheese or peanut butter and jelly."

"Let me take that, honey," Chris said to Melana as he met her at the end of the bed.

There was no measuring the relief he felt at this

interruption. Something about Amber drew him in a way he'd never felt before. It could be the way she looked at him as if she could see into his soul, maybe it was the way she'd so innocently tapped into and soothed his pain. Whatever it was, he needed to focus on their predicament, not his reaction to a woman he didn't even know.

He set the tray over Amber's lap.

"Thank you." She reached for a peanut butter and jelly cracker with her left hand before yanking back and cradling her left hand in her right.

Melana crawled onto the bed beside her. "I'll help you." She picked up the cracker Amber had started to reach for and handed it to her. "I'm a leftie, too."

To date, Melana had always hated being the only leftie in the family, and now she seemed proud. How curious.

Amber finished the first cracker under Melana's watchful gaze. "This is good. You put just the right amount of peanut butter and jelly so it's not too thick or too sweet."

Melana grinned at the compliment. She was in her element taking care of someone else. She'd done it so long she didn't know any different, but he really wanted her to be a kid, to do kid stuff.

Amber ate a few more crackers before taking a sip of water. When she leaned back and closed her eyes, he put his hand on Melana's head and tipped her head back. "We should let Amber rest."

He didn't know if he'd regret that statement or not. Either her mind emptied while she slept or her short-term memory only spanned an hour or so, but he'd prefer not having to explain everything again, especially the part about Kimmy. He never talked about her death, so even saying those two words had taken tremendous effort.

Amber's eyes remained closed even as she muttered "I'm not sleepy," and dozed off.

Melana covered her mouth to hide her giggles but they escaped anyway, making Chris chuckle. "She's just like you, eh, kiddo? Can't admit she needs a nap!"

Brushing a strand of hair off Amber's cheek, Melana said, "I like her, Daddy. She's funny."

"Your turn, Daddy," Melana told him, drawing his attention back to the checkerboard.

He and Melana had set up the game on the cocktail table in the living room, took their positions opposite each other on the floor, and were just beginning to play when he heard a sound. It had gotten dark enough to turn on the lanterns and two were bright enough to light the room. He'd left a flashlight in the bedroom for Amber.

He maneuvered a piece out of Melana's path, his mind on Amber. A light in the hallway signaled her approach and his breath tangled in his throat with anticipation. He'd almost given into the temptation to touch her earlier as the opening in her robe teasingly offered him glimpses of her smooth flesh. He'd closed the material, claiming that victory, and he planned to be just as strong this time.

She stopped in the entryway and he noticed she was wearing one of his shirts beneath his robe. The intimacy of the sight left him feeling unsettled. Kimmy used to lounge around in his shirts.

Chris closed his eyes trying to block images of Kimmy and the inevitable comparisons. Physically, the two women were worlds apart. Kimmy short and plump; Amber tall and thin.

He opened his eyes to see Melana's gaze glance off the clock on the wall. It was almost nine o'clock and she'd been waiting—not so patiently—for their patient to wake up. "I was wondering if you were going to sleep all night! Are you hungry? We already ate dinner, but I can fix you something."

Amber sat down on the couch behind Melana, her back ramrod straight, her feet planted perfectly together. Her hair had dried in wavy curls across her shoulders, like crinkled black satin.

"No, thanks. My stomach's kind of upset."

Melana jumped to her feet, eager to please. "I think we're all out of stomach medicine. I can get you some crackers."

Amber's smile seemed genuine and a little uncertain. "Thank you—"

"Melana," Chris interrupted, deliberately using her name to help Amber. "Will you grab me a soda?"

In her last two excursions back to reality, she'd forgotten their previous conversations, so he didn't know what to expect. Melana rushed off to the kitchen, leaving them alone.

"Thanks. I . . . remembered but I couldn't—" Breaking off, she gestured toward her mouth.

"Get your mouth to cooperate?" he offered. "We all have moments like that." Though he had to wonder if her momentary lapse was injury-related.

She looked at him with narrowed eyes before turning toward the window. "It's quiet out. Do you think the storm's passed?"

"Hurricane," he corrected automatically as he glanced beyond her to the dark starless night. "We're

in the eye. She'll be gone by morning, but it'll probably be days before we have electricity."

Melana returned with the promised crackers and a
bottle of water. Instead of handing him the requested
soda, she set a coaster on the table and then placed
the can on top.

"Thanks." He popped the metal tab, took a swig
and deliberately set the can on the table. Melana
had surpassed neat freak by the time she turned six,
but she wasn't anal about it and she loved it when he
teased her every now and then.

"Daddy!"

Laughing, he set the can on the coaster and flicked
the little bit of the water that had pooled under the
can into the air.

"What am I going to do with you?" she asked him
the way Kimmy used to.

His heart dipped at the reminder. A year later and
thoughts of her still caught him unaware. Today, the
anniversary of her death, didn't help.

"You look . . ." Amber paused as if she were searching for the word. "Sad again."

"Nah, I'm okay." And even if he weren't, he had no
intention of delving into his pain a second time, especially in Melana's presence. The little girl rarely
mentioned Kimmy anymore, and all the information
he'd read about grief suggested not pushing her, so
he wouldn't.

Melana crossed her legs Indian-style and rubbed
her hands together with her usual exuberance. She
was very competitive and hated losing. One time, in
his desperation to end a game any other way than with
her in tears of frustration, he let her win. She had
been furious. She would plead with him to play every
evening no matter how many times she lost.

He saw Amber reach across the couch for Melana's book. Squinting at the back blurb, she took small precise bites of her crackers.

When Melana realized he was about to take one of her pieces, she gritted her teeth and balled her hands into fists.

"Honey—"

"I know, I know. I won't make that mistake again."

He saw Amber's curious gaze settle on Melana. She tilted her head to the right before looking away. "Have you remembered anything?" he asked her.

She shook her head. "No."

"Does your head still hurt?" Melana chimed in.

Amber's eyes were as dark and stormy as the weather outside, so he had a feeling it did.

"A little." She touched an area near her bandage. "My arm, too."

Melana slid her piece into place and turned toward Amber. "Do you know how to play?"

Amber shifted and the robe spread enough to reveal the smooth shape of her left leg. "I don't know," she admitted.

Melana turned back to the game and Amber continued reading, though he could sense her attentiveness to their surroundings.

Chris pushed a piece inevitably closer to the other side of the board. His eyes strayed to Amber's legs against his will. They seemed unending, despite the length of his robe.

He shifted sideways, hoping to block his view. He had to give Melana credit. Her game improved nightly. If she didn't allow herself to get flustered or frustrated, she might be able to challenge him in another few weeks.

He took her last king and braced himself for the

fall out. She jumped up and stomped her foot, her face twisted in a frown. "I'm never going to win! I hate this game!"

Amber's forehead crinkled. "Then why do you play?"

"Because I wanna win!" Melana said with just enough annoyance in her voice to make it sound like she felt she was stating the obvious.

Amber tilted her head to the right and he realized that was something she did when she was considering something. If she could come up with a way to prevent this nightly demonstration, he was all ears.

Finally, she nodded. "You're trying too hard. It's a game, so it should be fun."

Melana paused as if she were considering Amber's words. Could it really be that simple? He'd been on the verge of calling a child-advice hotline.

Just when he thought she was going to ignore Amber's advice in favor of a temper tantrum, her face broke out in a huge grin. "I'll remember that." She yawned. "I guess I'll hit the sack. Goodnight, Daddy. Goodnight, Miss Amber."

Chris braced his hands on the floor and pushed himself to his feet so he could kiss Melana goodnight as he normally did. "Night, honey."

She sauntered out of the room and he and Amber were alone for the night. His gaze roamed over her legs, and he sighed. Sleep. That sounded real good right now. "I feel kind of tired myself. You can have the bed. I have a sleeping bag around here, somewhere."

He was trying to figure out where when she reached forward to put away the game pieces. Normally Melana would have been all over that, proclaiming cleanliness was next to godliness.

"How old is Melana?"

"Nine. Why?"

She set the box on the corner of the table. "I can't decide if she's a little girl or a little adult. She's tall."

He spotted the sleeping bag beneath the table and stooped down to get it. "I'm figuring she'll be around five-eight, maybe taller. She wants to play for the WNBA after college."

"She already knows what she wants to be when she grows up? Wow. Do kids tease her because she's so tall?"

Chris studied Amber. She was about as tall as he expected Melana to be, so she would know what Melana was going through, but he didn't want to have this conversation with Amber, who, after all, was a stranger. He'd rather have this conversation with his wife, Melana's mother.

"Never mind. I shouldn't have asked."

Her head turned to the left and he could've sworn . . . did she just roll her eyes? "Why?"

"Because you have that look on your face again, and I don't particularly like looking at it," she said with a bit of fire in her words.

Not so docile after all, hmm? "She told me earlier that kids at school have been teasing her," he admitted grudgingly. "Do you remember what it was like for you?"

"No, but I was reading *Stargirl*. Why are people so cruel to each other?"

"That's fiction where every plight is magnified. I prefer to believe in the goodness of humanity."

Amber's lips twisted. "Is that what you told Melana? I don't think platitudes are the answer. They minimize the situation, not to mention her feelings. Who are these children?" she demanded.

Oh yeah, she had some serious fire in her. "Why are you angry?"

"Angry? I'm angry?" she asked, sounding confused.

"You're asking me? You sound upset and you're frowning. That usually indicates anger."

Maybe he was confused.

A tear hovered on her lashes before dropping onto her cheek and she gasped. "I don't think I like arguing. Is that what happens when someone is angry?"

"Sometimes, I guess." He peered at her closely. "Amber, have you noticed . . ."

"What?"

"Nothing. Come on, let's get you to bed," he suggested, gently pulling her to her feet. "I'm really concerned about the hit you took to your head."

He wasn't a shrink, but it didn't take one to notice the glitch in Amber's brain related to emotions. Frankly, he couldn't afford to get involved with her issues. He had enough dealing with his grief and trying to raise a child alone.

She looked up at him, her eyes dark and wide. Up close, he could see copper sparkles in her eyes. "I'm not sleepy. Why don't you go to bed? I'll stay out here."

He combed his fingers through the silky strands of her black hair, releasing the scent of rain and wild flowers. "I—I—" He broke off to clear his throat.

"Are you going to kiss me goodnight? Like you did with Melana?" she added.

His hand tangled in her hair and it took a sheer act of willpower to keep from pulling her close. It had been so long since he'd held a woman in his arms, felt her softness, her curves. He wanted to kiss her. But not the way he'd kissed his daughter.

CHAPTER 3

Amber's heart was beating so fast she could barely catch her breath. Chris' head lowered toward her, initiating a shower of hot and cold prickles beneath her skin.

He released her and practically hurled his body away from her, leaving her dizzy by his defection. "Chris—"

"I'll see you in the morning."

Slack-jawed, she stared at his departing back until it disappeared into the darkness. Clutching a throw pillow in her arm, she tucked her feet beneath her in the corner of the sofa. She sighed and allowed her chin to drop onto the pillow.

What were these sensations Chris evoked in her? Why did he leave so quickly? He didn't look sad, like before, but he'd looked different.

Her head began to hurt and, grabbing a flashlight, she went in search of a pain reliever in the kitchen. She'd looked for the small bottle on the dresser when she first woke up, but it hadn't been there.

Her stomach grumbled. The crackers Melana had offered had helped to settle Amber's stomach, but she couldn't say they'd been filling. The living room was connected to a dining room/office that led to the kitchen. There were two distinct piles of food on the counter. One had packages of chips, cookies, and other junk food scattered everywhere, and the other offered a neat arrangement of crackers, fruit, and granola bars. The first was definitely for Chris. His and Melana's differences really complimented each other. Her heart had flip-flopped in her chest when she'd seen him teasing Melana with the can of soda. They were so close.

Grabbing a stem of grapes and a granola bar, she decided to eat first and see if that would ease the ache in her head.

Restless, she went in search of Melana's room to check on the little girl. It was too dark to see her and Amber didn't want to shine the light in her room, but she listened closely for the little girl's even breathing. She thought about Melana being teased and felt anger in her heart again. Not liking the feeling, she shied away from it.

Closing the door, she went back to the living room.

Several hours later, she was trying to read *Stargirl* by candlelight when she heard footsteps coming down the hallway. Unable to sleep, she'd turned off the lanterns so the brightness wouldn't disturb Chris or Melana.

Chris stopped just inside the room. "Why are you still up?" he asked in a sleepy voice as he rubbed his eyes with his fists.

He'd changed into a pair of gray shorts and a white tank top, and she had to admit he looked downright sexy. "I'm not tired." He glanced at the clock and her eyes followed his direction. It was one a.m. "Why are you awake?"

"I thought I'd check on you. You do have a nasty bump on your head. How's your arm?"

Her right hand immediately covered the spot under discussion. "It's probably time to change the bandage. I don't know if I faint at the sight of blood or not, so I didn't want to do it myself."

"All right. Let me get the first aid kit."

She watched Chris walk toward the closet, his white socks cushioning his feet. He pulled a case from the shelf with his large hands.

"You might want to close your eyes," he said with a soft chuckle as he joined her on the sofa.

She liked the sound of his laughter. As he gently loosened the bandage, his fingers brushed against her skin, and she trembled a little. His head was bent over his task, so she couldn't tell if he'd noticed or not. She took the opportunity to study the cut of his temple fade and the waves on the top of his head.

He pulled the bandage away and she glanced at the cut across the length of her arm. "It's a knife wound."

He paused to look up at her. "How do you know?"

"I don't . . . know," she said slowly. "But I recognize it."

"Then you are in trouble as I suspected." He sighed. "With your amnesia, we're at a disadvantage. They know who you are, but we don't know who they are."

"Do you think they know I'm here?"

"It's a possibility."

He finished bandaging her arm, his movements quick and efficient, gentle. He had probably been a good husband. In fact, if his relationship with Melana was any indication, he had been a great husband. "What was your wife like?"

"Kimmy?" His gaze met hers before quickly lowering to his task. "Friendly. Spontaneous. Fun. The first time

I saw her, she was twirling Melana around in the rain, laughing. She'd probably be out there right now trying to catch the hurricane if I let her."

And he'd be right out there with his Kimmy, she'd bet.

But if Melana was already born when Chris met her, that would mean he wasn't the little girl's birth father. "So Melana's—"

"Adopted."

Amber would have never guessed. They were so close, such a team. "Does she know?"

"We told her, asked if she had any questions, and that was that. I'm her dad, and according to Kimmy, the best thing that ever happened to them. I never believed in love at first sight until I saw her."

Had she ever been loved so intensely? she wondered.

"On our third date," he continued in a far away voice, "I told Kimmy I would be leaving for Germany, and she asked me to take her with me. We got married at a justice of the peace and in seven years of marriage we never disagreed, never argued, really."

They sounded like the perfect family and now a part of them was missing. Were there people out there somewhere who felt lost without her? "Do you think I have a family?"

A gentle, knowing look crept into his chocolate eyes. "I'm sure you do. In fact, you might have a little girl. Let me show you. I'll be right back."

She watched him grab a flashlight and hurry down the hallway. A little girl? Like Melana? Someone who wanted to play checkers with her, to laugh with her, to love her?

Chris returned carrying a small black bag with leather straps tied into a knot. "I found this in the spare tire compartment of your rental car."

Amber stared at the object before slowly reaching out to take it. The spare tire compartment? She studied the bag from different angles, hoping something about it, the texture, the weight, anything would jog her memory.

She felt Chris watching her as she dumped the contents onto the table. Her life lay before her in the form of five photo IDs—which she'd seen already—a wad of cash, and an engraved antique locket.

"The picture's in the locket?" she asked.

"You remember the locket?"

"No, it just makes sense."

He made a face and she felt a tickling sensation in her chest. She popped the tiny hook on the side and slowly separated the pieces, unsure of what she'd find. Inside was a picture of a light-skinned baby with black hair.

"I have black hair, right?" She grabbed a handful of hair to double-check. "She's lighter than me but it looks like one of those newborn hospital pictures. Her skin could've darkened. I wonder what her name is."

"Ashanti Naja."

He showed her a tiny scrap of paper she had to squint to see. Picking up one of the driver's licenses, Amber compared the handwriting. "I wrote this. It's my handwriting."

She leapt to her feet, then, rocked by a dizzy spell, froze until it passed.

By the time she opened her eyes, Chris was standing in front of her. "Are you okay?"

"I have to remember," she sobbed.

"You will." He captured her hands in his and held them against his chest. She could feel the strong steady beat of his heart. "As soon as conditions allow, we'll contact the police. We'll get you home."

The steadiness of his heartbeat began to calm her. "Home?"

Chris ran the tip of finger down her cheek. "I wouldn't wish the loss of a loved one on anybody."

"You look sad again. Tell me why."

His lids lowered, hiding his eyes from her. "A drunk driver broadsided Kim's car. Killed her instantly, the coroner said. He took her life and walked away without a scratch." Amber watched Chris's Adam's apple bob with his struggle to speak. He started to turn away but she held him tighter. "I was helping Melana with a school project. We always said I love you when one of us was leaving the house . . . but . . . she was supposed to come right back . . . only, she didn't. She died a year ago."

Amber tugged her left hand free, leaving the right one snuggled in his. She touched his cheek and the heat of his skin penetrated her fingertips. His jaw was firm, unshaven. The hairs bristled against her sensitive flesh.

She rubbed her thumb along his bottom lip and when his lips parted, slid the tip of her finger inside. He started to pull away, stopped, and then twisting his hands in her hair, held her still as he closed the short distance between them.

They touched, their slightly parted lips layered his–hers–his–hers. Chris didn't move to deepen the kiss, and yet she felt his touch in every part of her body.

Suddenly, he yanked away from her, thrusting her backward. He stared at her with expressions she didn't understand, his breathing ragged, harsh in the stillness of the night. "What am I doing?" he groaned. "I'm in love with my wife, Amber."

The jarring release shook her head, shooting pain

from one side to the other and all around. She pressed the heels of her hands to her temples. "You're *married*?"

Chris threw his hands up and spun around.

She lowered her hands, staring at him. "What's all that about?"

Chuckling, he shook his head. Then he cupped her cheek with a gentle hand. "Go lay down, Amber. I'll make an icepack for your head."

Dizzy, she felt her way down the dark hallway with a hand on the wall. Once she reached the bedroom, she slid beneath the blanket and closed her eyes, remembering the way Chris' lips had felt against hers. Why did he stop?

She felt the bed dip and opened her eyes to see him propping a pillow against the headboard on her right. He placed a cool, wet cloth against her scalp and she shivered.

"Too cold?"

His voice rumbled in his chest, deep and seductive. "It feels good." She closed her eyes with a long sigh. "I like the way you kiss."

"You won't even remember come morning."

She smiled. "I guess we'll see, won't we?"

She didn't remember.

Chris opened a bottle of water and dropped the cap on the dining room table. It bounced around with a tinkling sound before finally settling down.

Amber's pain had been so intense it had left her weak and confused. Surely after a night's rest, total recall would be impossible. Of course, sleep hadn't offered him that sweet release. As brief as the kiss had been, he could still taste her and inhale her sweet scent.

He heard a door open, then the sound of running

water. Melana was a heavy sleeper and took every
opportunity to sleep in, so it could only be Amber. He
always kept extra toothbrushes, a carryover from
TDYs, and he'd left one on the counter for her. The
water was too cold for anything more than a quick
wash-off at the sink.

He still couldn't figure out why he'd had her stretch
out in the bed instead of the relative safety of the
couch. Knowing she lay beneath that blanket half-
dressed had kept him up half the night. He'd awakened in the front room to a steady, heavy rain, but it
was bright outside, so they probably wouldn't need
flashlights until this evening.

Out of the corner of his eye, he saw Amber stop
just inside the living room dressed in another of his
T-shirts that left her long legs and bare feet exposed.
As she approached, he could see the faint outline of
her nipples straining against the material.

"Good morning, Chris."

He forced his gaze to meet her copper—copper?—
eyes. He blinked to make sure he was seeing right.

"G-good morning," he sputtered, as enchanted
with her light eyes as he had been mesmerized by their
darker version. He'd never seen such a drastic change
in eye color before.

She combed her fingers through her hair, looking
uncertain for the first time since they'd met. He closed
his eyes, took a deep breath, and slowly released it
through his nostrils. "We should talk. About last night,"
he added.

"Okay." She slid onto the chair beside his and he
instinctively shifted away from her. Her questioning
eyes met his, and he immediately regretted his action.

Even though he'd said they needed to talk, he
didn't know what to say.

"It's still raining?" she asked, glancing over his shoulder. "I don't think this storm is ever going to pass."

Storm? Twice he'd told her it was a hurricane. If she couldn't remember that, she definitely wouldn't remember last night. "Have you remembered anything?"

"No, not really. Just . . ."

"What?"

"You kissed me last night, didn't you? Or was I dreaming?"

He opened his mouth to say something, anything, but his mind wasn't cooperating. He could let Amber believe it had been a dream but his conscience wouldn't let him lie. Melana, his godsend, slid her arms around his neck from behind him and kissed his cheek before he could answer.

"Good morning, Daddy. Hi, Miss Amber. Are you feeling better today?"

"As long as I don't think too hard, I feel pretty good."

"That's great! Do you want to help me study my spelling words later?"

Study her spelling words? Melana rarely needed help with her school work.

"Sure. Why not?"

"I'm going to grab some breakfast. I'll be back."

Melana left before he could stop her, so to avoid Amber's question, he slid the first aid kit toward him. "I'd better check your arm."

She didn't argue or resist but laid her arm on the table. Trying hard to avoid any skin-to-skin contact— a hands-off policy would be best, he decided—he carefully removed the bandage. The blood had stopped and a small scab had begun to form over the red gash. "Does it still hurt?"

"A little. Are you going to ignore my question?"

"I shouldn't have kissed you. It was wrong."

Her brows rose. "Why?"

"My wife, remember? No, you wouldn't," he said impatiently. "I don't want to talk about this."

Melana strolled back into the room eating a breakfast bar and carrying a glass of orange juice. "Are you ready?"

Chris closed the lid with a snap. "She's ready."

He pushed himself away from the table and stalked over to the front door. When *would* the storm end? He could hear Ron now. Move on. Find love again, a mother for Melana. But Chris had never looked at another woman, touched another woman, until last night. Commitment meant a lot to him, and he'd committed himself to Kimmy.

Frustrated, he spun around to leave. He saw Amber and Melana bent over the notebook with their heads tilted at the same angle, Melana's black hair loose around her shoulders and Amber's in a ponytail, and frowned.

He had to get out of here. Unfortunately, he had nowhere to go. No escape. He went to the bathroom to wash his hands and saw Amber's bra and panties hanging on the rack. His gaze froze on the flimsy material. Surely she wasn't *completely* naked beneath his shirt. He swallowed hard at the image, his heart pounding in his chest. Blinking to break the trance he seemed to be in, he thrust his wrist beneath the cold water to cool his flesh. They had to be dry by now, hot as it was. He'd ask Melana to talk to her. If he were going to hold onto his, admittedly, old-fashioned views, Amber had to wear her underclothes!

* * *

Amber closed the spiral notebook with a soft thud. "One hundred percent correct, Melana. I don't think you have anything to worry about."

Melana swallowed the last of her orange juice. "I have to be smart, just in case I don't make it to the WNBA, or if I get hurt."

The probability of getting into the WNBA had to be astronomical, and although she didn't doubt Melana's ability—after all, Amber had never seen her play—there had to be more to childhood than worrying about adulthood. "A good education is important, but what do you do for fun?"

"Layups."

Of course. "Do you have any friends?"

"Olivia's my best friend. She lives across the street. She likes to play with dolls, but that's silly."

Amber couldn't put a name to her tone but she didn't think it was positive. "What's silly about dolls?"

Melana shrugged. "They aren't real."

No, they weren't. They were for playing make-believe and Amber had a feeling this half-child, half-adult wouldn't know anything about that. "Do you have any dolls?"

"In my bedroom. I'll show you."

Amber followed Melana down the hallway. Listening closely for any sound, she tried to figure out where Chris was. Something wasn't right, the way he'd left like that. He wasn't angry or she would have seen a frown on his face. His bedroom door was closed, so he had to be in there, but she wouldn't disturb him. Maybe he was just tired from being up with her last night.

Melana pulled a trunk from the closet and dragged it over to the white twin-size captain's bed. It boasted six drawers beneath the bed—a practical decision if

Amber had ever seen one—and an unadorned chest and desk completed the set. "I like your room. It's very . . . functional. And clean."

Melana offered her a wide grin. "I picked it out all by myself. Daddy wanted to get some girlie-girlie stuff, but that's silly."

Amber suppressed a grin. No nine year old should be this stoic.

Melana pulled three black dolls from inside. "My mom bought me these two and Daddy bought me this one last Christmas."

"They look awfully sad being locked away in a trunk. Why don't we name them?"

"That's silly, Miss Amber."

"I don't think so." Amber picked up the doll dressed in a pink one-piece sleeper. "What do you think? Isabelle?"

Melana crinkled her nose and shook her head.

"How about Raine?"

"R–a–i–n?"

"R–a–i–n–e."

"That's pretty. What about that one," Melana said, pointing to the doll in a white cloth diaper and a light green bib.

"Why don't you name her?"

Melana tapped her finger against her lips. "How about Kasie?"

"She looks just like a Kasie to me, and you see her little smile? That means she's sad. I mean . . . happy. Right?"

"Miss Amber . . ." she began in a clearly-you're-out-of-your-mind tone.

"Shhh. Don't make her feel sad."

Melana giggled into her hands. "You're silly." She stared at the doll dressed in a yellow shorts set for a long time before gently placing her across Amber's legs. "Okay, let's give her a name she'll like."

Amber felt her heart expand and placed her hand on her chest. What was that? She smiled, enjoying the feeling. "Do you like Brianna?"

"Yeah, that's pretty." Melana gasped as if she'd just come up with something. "Do you want to comb each other's hair? Olivia and her mom do that."

Melana got that same look Amber had seen on Chris' face. Sadness. "Did you and your mom do that?"

"No." Melana touched Amber's hair. "I have black hair just like you."

Amber glanced in the mirror to double-check. "Yep. How do you wear yours?"

"In a ponytail. I'm trying to learn how to French braid, but I can't do one yet. It's hard."

"A French braid? I think I can teach you."

Melana looked like she was about to jump up and down with joy, but a millisecond later she nodded and turned to pull out a tray of organized hair accessories from a drawer in the desk. Amber stared at the perfectly aligned hairballs and barrettes before looking at the child again. No nine year old should be this structured.

Melana fingered Amber's hair. "I like your bangs. Do you think I would be pretty if I had some, too?"

"You're already pretty."

"But I'd be prettier *with* bangs."

Amber realized where Melana was going with this and shook her head. "I'm not cutting your hair, Melana."

Her bottom lip popped out. "Please?"

She'd bet Melana had gotten her way plenty of times with that look. Boy, she was cute. "You're going to be a heartbreaker one day, but not today. Got it, kid?"

Melana's little shoulders slumped and Amber almost broke down despite her bravado. What would it hurt to give her hair a little style, with Chris's permission, of course?

With a grudging smile, Melana said, "Will you at least braid it?"

"Of course." She set the dolls aside and motioned Melana to sit on the floor between her legs. Melana settled down with her back to Amber but she could see the little girl's face in the mirror. Amber released the ponytail and her hair shimmered in thick waves across her shoulders. "What grade are you in?"

"Third."

Amber combed Melana's hair and watched the teeth snake through the black strands. "Do you like school?"

"It's my first year in the States. It's different. I don't know anybody except Olivia, and nobody knows what to say because of my mom. She died."

Amber began to braid her hair. "Does it make you feel sad to talk about her?"

"Sometimes. I'm the tallest girl in my class, probably the school," she admitted.

"Do kids tease you?"

She nodded and Amber felt something squeeze her heart, or at least that was how it felt. Without really knowing why, she found herself trying to say something that would take that sad look off Melana's face.

"They call me 'beanpole.'"

"Well, I'm *way* taller than you so what does that make me?"

"You're not *way* taller."

"Uh, huh. Look." Amber straightened her back and lifted her chin high in the air.

Melana laughed. "That's because you're sitting on the bed!"

"Oh, yeah. I'm still taller, though," she said, pretending to grumble.

"You're funny, Miss Amber. Did kids tease you?"

"Probably. But who cares what people say? You'll have the last laugh when you're out there on the court doing your thing, making that bling."

"What's bling?"

"Money, lots of money."

Melana nodded. "Yeah, I'll be rich!"

"And beautiful. Take a look."

Melana stood up in front of the mirror and Amber glanced down at her trembling left hand. She'd finished, but just barely. She heard Melana's breath catch and before she could look up, Melana spun around and threw her arms around Amber's neck. "I love it!"

Caught off guard by Melana's spontaneous show of affection, Amber slowly closed her arms around Melana's waist. She smelled like the cinnamon granola bar and orange juice she'd eaten earlier.

"Will you fix your hair the same way? That way we'll look like twins."

"I can't, honey. My hand . . ."

Melana sat down on the bed beside Amber. "Did you tell Daddy?"

"Why? Is he a doctor?"

Now that she thought about it, she didn't know what kind of work he did. How weird when she felt so close to him.

"No, but he always knows what to do to make me feel better when I'm hurt. Do you want me to comb your hair?"

Melana's expression had changed from happy but Amber wasn't sure what this new face was all about. She looked kind of sad, but not exactly. "Sure."

Melana picked up the comb. "I used to brush my mom's hair. She always forgot."

"Did she have black hair like yours?"

"Brown, light like blond but darker. I was taller than her, too. She's in heaven with the angels, so she's finally happy."

The comb swept across the bruise on the back of Amber's head and she winced. "What do you mean?"

"She didn't want to come back to the States. She said if anything happened to her to make sure Daddy's happy."

"Happy?"

"When you feel . . . um . . . like laughing," Melana explained, gesturing with her hands. "When you smile."

So Melana's mother had put the outcome of Chris' happiness on her shoulders? Why would an adult put such a stressful burden on a child?

"Do you have a daughter?"

Amber tucked her hair behind her ears. "I don't know."

Melana set the comb on the dresser and sat on the bed beside Amber. "Are you going to leave?" she asked in a small voice.

Amber rubbed the back of her neck as the pain in her head began to spread downward. "Why would I leave?"

Melana piped up. "Then you'll stay forever?"

"I don't know, Melana," she said absently as she tried to catch a nagging thought in her head.

Melana looked at Amber through the mirror with

a solemn expression. She didn't say a word, so stoic, so strong.

Picking up one of her dolls, she cradled her in her arms. "Maybe dolls *are* better. They don't leave."

"Mel—"

She ran out of the room and Amber slumped forward.

CHAPTER 4

By the time Amber reached the front room, Melana and Chris were speaking quietly to each other. He looked up at Amber with a frown marring his face as she stopped in the doorway. His gaze flickered between her and Melana, and she could tell he was angry. She spun on her heel and went into his bedroom, closing the door behind her.

Yesterday, she'd gotten around Melana's near-tantrum, but Amber didn't like anger. It made people argue, and she didn't like arguing either.

She spotted a pair of scissors on the dresser. If she could find a pair of jogging pants she could cut them into shorts and leave. All the sadness in this house made it hard to breathe.

Using her right hand, she tugged the bottom drawer open and saw a pair of navy blue jogging pants inside.

The door opened and Amber straightened. Chris walked inside carrying a tray. "I thought you might want something to eat. You haven't had anything this morning."

The sight of the granola bar and grapes made her stomach growl a little, and she coughed to cover the sound, though she didn't know why she'd done that. Hungry, she reached for the granola bar but caught herself. "I'm still stuffed from a snack I had after you went to bed last night." That wasn't true but she knew Chris would see her hand shaking, and she didn't want him to see. "Is Melana okay?"

"Your hand's trembling. Here." He set the tray on the nightstand and placed his hand between them palm up.

When she didn't move, he captured and carried her hand toward him. "How long has this been going on?"

"I don't know. Since I woke up, I guess. Off and on."

"Why would Melana be upset?" he asked as he continued to observe her hand.

"We were talking about her mother and you were frowning just now. I should leave. I can cut a pair of your jogging pants into shorts. I'll pay you, if I have any money."

Her head began to pound and she squeezed her eyes shut against the pain.

"I like what you did with Melana's hair."

"She's a beautiful girl," Amber said, confused by the turn in the conversation. Chris's eyes were too intense. She looked away but felt drawn back. His touch was so gentle. "Are you going to kiss me again?"

His eyes crinkled as he smiled and she glanced away before getting impatient with herself. Why couldn't she look at him directly?

"I thought you'd forgotten."

She met his gaze directly. "No."

"Mel says you're leaving?" he asked quietly.

For some reason, the way he asked the question made her feel sad inside. "The storm's passed."

Her hand stopped shaking under his careful

ministrations, and he released her to grab the granola bar and peel the wrapper back. "Try now."

She reluctantly reached for the food. Her hand didn't shake, thank goodness, and she took a bite, but it wasn't food she wanted to taste right now.

"There's probably debris and flooded roads, not to mention your car's totaled. What's the plan, to head off on foot? Where would you go?"

She stared at his mouth, suddenly fascinated by the way it moved. "North," she said offhandedly.

"North? You're just going to head north? You're hurt."

She started to set the granola bar down, but Chris stopped her and she took another bite.

"Have you forgotten you're in some kind of trouble?"

"All the more reason to leave." That was as close as she'd get to admitting that she had indeed forgotten.

She had a bump on her head and she'd heard of amnesia, but she couldn't seem to remember things from one hour to the next, except Chris, Melana and last night when Chris kissed her.

"I can't let you leave, Amber."

"You can't tell me what to do!" she flared back. He was winning this battle of wills, and she couldn't figure out how.

He took a deep breath and slowly released it. "You're right. Forgive me?"

She blinked, taken back by his reversal.

He picked up the bottle of pain relievers from the nightstand and tapped two into his hand. He handed them to her. "Your head hurts."

"It does? I mean, it does, but how do you know?"

"Your eyes are copper, but turn ebony when you're in pain."

"They do?" She glanced at the mirror on the dresser. Why hadn't she ever noticed that?

He handed her the carton of orange juice and kept his hand near, probably to make sure she didn't drop it. It was wet but still cold, which meant the ice in the cooler had probably melted.

She swallowed the pills and handed him the bottle. "Why don't you rest awhile . . . before you leave?"

She was tired all of a sudden. She eyed him suspiciously. Was he making her tired?

"You should be feeling better in no time," he promised, gently pushing her onto the bed.

She laid her head on the pillow and closed her eyes. "I'll just rest for a few minutes."

"Okay. Sweet dreams, Amber."

Unable to stop himself, Chris brushed his thumb across Amber's cheek. He listened to her even breathing, relieved that he'd gotten her to lie down. Her memory was so sporadic, she probably wouldn't remember wanting to leave when she woke up. Of course, if she did, she'd have a fight on her hands. He'd never let an injured person walk off to parts unknown in an amnesiac state. Not to mention, he could no longer deny the similarity between Amber and Melana.

From the beginning, he'd felt something was familiar about her. Melana was tall and lanky and their hair was black, but there was something else, something he couldn't quite put his finger on.

He'd known this day would come. Kimmy had such a screwed up family. He'd never met them, but from what she'd told him, the closeness she'd shared with her family had ended with them disowning her. Kimmy had two sisters and a brother, and Chris had a feeling Amber was one of her sisters. Had she come for Melana? He'd adopted the little girl, but would a legal bond outweigh a familial bond in court? Because he'd fight for her. Unless . . . Melana preferred to be with them.

Chris picked up the tray and closed the door behind him. He strode through the living room, bypassing Melana who was curled up on the sofa looking at her hair in a small mirror.

She lowered the mirror and perked up. "Is she still leaving?"

"No." *Not if I can help it.* Even if she were here to take Melana, he couldn't let her leave. In her state, whoever had hurt her would have too great an advantage.

He continued toward the kitchen and began to straighten up. They still had plenty of fruit and snacks, but he could use a burger about now. His neighbors wouldn't return until the commander cleared them, which would probably be in a couple of days. The power and phone companies would follow, but it could be several days, maybe even a week, before full power was restored.

Assuming Amber had a family, locating them would be his first priority, but if she didn't know them, would she feel safe with them? He could contact the police and hope they'd use discretion as they searched. He had a least a day or two to worry about that. Right now he had to figure out how to keep Amber here.

Even though he was sitting in the living room watching Melana with his own eyes, Chris couldn't believe what he was seeing. She was playing with dolls. The impact Amber had had on his little girl in such a short time was amazing.

Melana looked down the hallway for the tenth time. "Maybe I should go sit with Miss Amber. She might be scared waking up alone."

She'd been asleep for a few hours now and Melana had already peeked in on her twice. He'd let her sit with Amber, but he knew Melana wasn't above "accidentally" waking her. "I think she'll be okay."

"Do you think she'll forget us again? That's scary. I don't want her to forget. She might leave."

Chris ran his hand over her hair. "She's going to leave eventually, Mel. I'm sure she has family somewhere."

Melana let her head fall to the right and he withdrew his hand. "She might not."

He heard the bedroom door open and couldn't prevent a sigh of relief. Until he confirmed his suspicions about Amber and Melana's relationship, he wouldn't share his thoughts. Melana was obviously getting attached to Amber and would be hurt if he turned out to be wrong.

Amber peeked into the room before walking in, still wearing his shirt and apparently abandoning his robe altogether. "Hi."

She spoke with a tentativeness that made his heart sink. *Please don't have forgotten us again, especially Melana.*

Melana jumped up, ran over to Amber, and threw her arms around Amber's waist, hiking the shirt to midthigh. "I thought you were never going to wake up!"

Chris forced his gaze from her luscious legs to the world outside. The heavy rain had yet to let up, leaving a crisp dampness in the house. She really could use a robe, he thought.

He'd asked Melana to show Amber where her underclothes were and she'd agreed, but the reprieve didn't seem to be anywhere at hand. Trying to appear relaxed from his position on the floor by the table, he said, "How'd you sleep?"

"Pretty good, I guess."

Melana hugged her. "Do you remember me?"

He tried to catch Amber's eyes, so he could mouth Melana's name but she was too busy smiling at her. "Tadpole, right?"

Melana shook her head.

"Shrimp?"

She giggled. "No, I'm Melana."

"Oh, yeah," she said, nodding her head. "Hi, Melana."

He didn't know what that was all about, but Melana seemed happy enough. "Dr. St. Clair made you a fruit salad," he said, referring to Melana. "Are you hungry?"

He'd seen Amber's embarrassment when her hand began to shake earlier and with only the slightest bit of encouragement on his part, Melana had happily removed the peeling from the orange, separated the slices, and taken the grapes off the stems.

Grabbing the bowl of fruit from the cooler by the door, Melana led Amber to the sofa and gently guided her onto the cushion closest to him.

"Thanks, Melana. This looks delicious."

Melana crowded into the space between Amber and the arm of the sofa, forcing them all to the left. Noticing that Amber's legs were at eye level, Chris scooted even farther away.

Amber reached for an orange slice. Her hand wasn't shaking, but it wasn't cooperating either as she tried to close her fingers. She gave up. "Forget it. I'm not hungry."

Chris placed his hand on hers. "You're frustrated."

"Frustrated?"

"Discouraged," he explained.

"I don't like not being able to do what I want."

"No one does."

"I feel like a baby," she said through her teeth, her gaze trained on her lap.

He put the fruit to her lips and she pressed her lips together, refusing the nourishment. Patiently, he rubbed the fruit across her bottom lip and a drop of juice slid between her lips, tempting her. Thirsty, she closed her lips around the fruit and sucked the juice into her dry mouth.

Chris reached for a second slice. "We don't know how your head was injured. You could have a concussion or something."

He offered her the fruit and when he placed it in her mouth, her tongue brushed against his finger. His gaze shot to hers and she recognized the look in his eyes from last night. He wrenched away from her and, standing, strode off toward the kitchen.

Melana's little lips turned down as her wide-eyed gaze followed Chris's receding back until he disappeared around the corner. Amber felt that heaviness in her heart again.

What was wrong now? she wondered, pushing herself onto her unsteady legs.

Melana looked up at her with the same expression. "Where are you going?"

"To talk to your dad. Stay here, okay?" Concentrating on each step, she forced one foot in front of the other until she reached the kitchen. Chris was leaning against the counter gulping down a bottle of water when she hobbled in. "What's wrong?" she huffed, exhausted.

His head lower and he choked. "Nothing!" he sputtered. "I—I mean, go back in the living room, Amber."

"Why?" She stepped up to him and noticed that his cheeks were flushed, and he couldn't meet her eyes. "Are you . . . angry . . . with me?"

"Of course not." His voice sounded labored, uneven.

"I didn't forget," she said, remembering their conversation last night.

His laugh held no humor. "I wish you had."

She put her arms around his waist and pressed her face to his chest. "Do you? Really?"

She felt his lips against her forehead and tipped her head back a little. He pressed his lips to her temple, then across her jaw. His arms encircled her, bringing her closer with only the slightest pressure.

She slid her hands over his strong back as her lips parted beneath his. His kiss was slow, gentle. He worked his way across her bottom lip, giving her time to savor the taste of orange-flavored soda, to know intimately the length of his mouth.

Moaning, she deepened the kiss. There was something to be said for slow, but as her pulse drummed beneath her skin and her heart pounded, she surrendered to Chris utterly, floating with, not against, the sensations swimming through her. She leaned into him, straining toward pleasure, seeking, yearning, sighing as the kiss lingered.

He pulled back, and, not wanting to lose contact, she leaned forward.

"Amber," he whispered against her mouth. "Amber, we can't do this."

She looked at him for a long moment trying to find the words, frustrated at her inability to do so. She forced herself to take several deep breaths and try again instead of giving up. "I like it when you kiss me, Chris."

"You probably won't remember by tonight."

"I didn't forget last night."

"What's my wife's name?"

Amber grimaced. "I don't *want* to remember that. She died, right? So she's not your wife anyway."

He pushed her away from him, putting a wide berth between them. "Do you feel compelled to say whatever you think?"

She frowned. "Sure. Why not?"

"Because something you say might be hurtful."

She had to be careful here. Her goal wasn't to hurt Chris, but she didn't want him to think that what she'd said was wrong. "If what I said hurt you, then I apologize. But if it didn't and you're just trying to me feel bad, I don't." She strode out of the kitchen and back into the front room. Melana hadn't moved from her place on the sofa and her face lit up when she saw Amber approaching her. "Melana? Do you have a notebook and pen I can borrow?"

She jumped up. "I'll be right back."

Amber would admit her memory wasn't the best. Her brain wasn't working right, sending wrong signals to her hand, refusing to release the correct words to her mouth, but there was no way she could forget her and Chris's kiss.

But just in case . . .

Melana returned and handed her a green notebook and matching pen. Amber sat down on the sofa and wrote the reminder on a sheet of paper. Just in case she was wrong, she'd have the paper to remind her.

Melana tucked her feet beneath her and curled up in the corner of the sofa. "What did you write?"

"Something special. I have something for you, too. Amber wrote *Melana is a very special girl,* and carefully tore the sheet in half.

Melana read it and her sweet little lips broke out into a wide grin. "I hope you stay here forever!" Her smile turned wicked all of a sudden. Cupping her hand around her mouth, she said, "You know what we should do?"

Amber couldn't help smiling, not having seen this side of Melana. She really liked this little girl. "What?"

"Ready to play, Daddy?"

Any distraction would do at this point, Chris thought from the doorway. It was hot and muggy and even though Melana had done as he'd requested and Amber was wearing her underclothes, he still couldn't keep his eyes off her.

They'd had dinner—if ready-made tuna on crackers with chips and more fruit could be called dinner—a couple of hours ago so he'd figured Melana would be ready for a game of checkers.

Grinning at Amber, Melana set the checker box on the table. They'd been huddled together in Melana's room doing a lot of giggling, which Melana never did. If he didn't know better, Chris would swear they were up to something.

He sat down by the cocktail table and leaned back against the couch, trying hard to ignore the sight of Amber's legs. Now that he thought about it, cutting a pair of his jogging pants might work. They'd be big around the waist, but maybe she could pin them somehow.

Melana glanced at Amber who moved over to the loveseat and stretched her *long* legs as far as she could. She leaned forward to place a piece of paper on the end table and her loose-fitting shirt dipped, exposing more flesh.

Concentrate, Chris, he told himself. It wasn't like he'd never seen a woman's legs before. Kimmy had beautiful legs, too. Not as long or shapely, but beautiful nonetheless.

Melana started to move a piece, paused, and pulled back.

He still couldn't believe he'd kissed Amber again. They were strangers for heaven's sake. He moved another piece and Melana countered quickly, but he didn't think too much about it.

Not when he had Amber to think about. Her parting shot about Kimmy not being his wife still rankled. Amber wasn't embarrassed about whatever she felt or thought. She liked kissing and he liked kissing her, but he hadn't said so out loud.

He watched Melana move a piece, his mind only half on the game.

"King me, king me!" she shouted triumphantly, bouncing up and down in excitement.

"What?" He stared at the board trying to figure out how she'd maneuvered that coup.

He set a black piece on top of hers and made his next move.

As they continued to play, he noticed Melana's furtive glances in Amber's direction, but overall he was impressed by her moves.

"King me again, Daddy!"

Chris jerked out of his thoughts and looked at the board. Melana was about to win her first game. "How . . . ?"

He saw Melana's quick thumbs up at Amber and realized she'd been helping her. He turned toward Amber, who was trying to suppress her laughter with both hands over her mouth.

"Are you helping her?" he asked, pretending to be indignant.

She burst into laughter and it sounded like . . .

music. "You should see your face," she said breath-
lessly. "It's priceless."

But Chris could barely register her words as the
melodic sound of her laughter washed over him. It
was the first time he'd heard her laugh.

"I beat you, Daddy. There's no way you can come
back."

Melana was right. She had all his men covered.

Melana jumped up and ran over to Amber who
opened her arms for a hug. "We got him *good*, Miss
Amber."

Laughing, Amber pulled Melana into her arms.
"You've got some serious skills, girl. Why did you
need my help?"

He'd seen Melana play and even have fun, but never
anything like the kind of happiness he was seeing
right now. She was like a kid instead of a miniature
adult trying to raise her parents.

"I needed you to help make it fun."

Amber placed her hand over her heart. "I'm glad
I helped make it fun."

"I'll be right back," Melana said as she grabbed a
flashlight and ran off, not even bothering to put the
game away.

Chris jumped up, not wanting to be alone with
Amber, not right now.

Her smile faded. "Going to bed?"

"No, you can have the bed, if you're ready. You are
ready, right?" Okay, that sounded a little more desperate than he liked. But he was desperate.

"Melana and I are going to finish reading *Stargirl,*
so I thought I'd let you have the bed tonight. Or you
can sleep out here with me. It's hotter back there."

Visions of the two of them sleeping together flooded
his mind. Did she know what she was suggesting?

"No, I'll take the bedroom."

"Suit yourself."

She didn't seem disappointed. In her innocent mind she had probably been thinking comfort, not sex.

She grabbed the paper she'd set on the end table and walked over to him and gave him a hug. "Sleep well. Will you kiss me goodbye. I mean goodnight? See I didn't forget."

"What's that?" he asked, nodding toward the paper.

"Just a little reminder, in case I forget. See?"

She showed him the paper and he groaned inwardly. There went any hope of her forgetting after all, he guessed.

He ran the back of his hand along her jaw line. Actually, he liked her honesty and openness. "Goodnight, Amber."

He brushed his lips against her mouth and her lips opened like a flower beneath the sun. He delved inside for a brief taste of her sweetness, drinking in her innocence. Keeping his eyes open, he watched a wondrous expression spread across her face. Every time they kissed, it was like her first time. He wanted to teach her about these new sensations, but she didn't belong to him. And he couldn't forget that, couldn't afford to.

He broke the kiss but couldn't get his arms to release her.

"I think I could kiss you all night," she admitted. Thunder boomed in the distance and she jumped. "What was that?"

He could feel her heart thumping against his chest. "Thunder. Don't be afraid. It won't hurt you."

"Why do you think I'm afraid?"

He placed his fingers over her heart and felt the furious beat. "Your heart is pounding."

He would've never thought anything could scare
Amber. She relaxed at his words, though, making
him aware of how much she trusted him. And that act
of faith demanded he keep his head where she was
concerned, starting with throwing that piece of paper
away. Better if she'd just forget. Better if he forgot, too.
Kissing her all night was not an option.

CHAPTER 5

Chris flopped onto his back and untangled the sheet from around his legs. Amber's feminine scent was all over this bed and the heat wasn't helping. The storm had kicked up a notch with heavy rain and tree limbs lashing the windows. He heard another loud boom and winced. The thunder was getting louder. Amber was probably scared, and he was torn between going to see about her and staying the hell away from her.

The door creaked opened and he almost cussed. Why hadn't he locked it?

Amber rushed in as he sat up. "Did you hear that? It sounds so . . . near." Her eyes lowered to his bare chest and widened. "Are you naked?"

He'd taken off his shirt to cool off. "No, I have on shorts. I told you not to be afraid, remember?"

"I remember in my head, but my heart is afraid. It's pounding hard. Is it okay if I stay here with you?"

His mouth opened but nothing came out. "Amber . . ."

"I like it when you say my name like that. It makes me feel funny inside. A good funny."

Right. Okay. They could sit in the front room, all night if necessary. She was not getting into this bed.

The thunder clapped again and she jumped onto the bed. "All that noise makes my head hurt."

His shoulders slumped with resignation. There had to be irony in this somewhere. "Did you want me to get you some medicine?"

"Will you rub my head?"

He pushed the sheet off his legs and started to get up. "Let's go in the front room."

Amber didn't budge. "Why?"

"Because, because . . ."

She stretched out on her back, facing him, and suddenly his hand was massaging her head. Bemused, he stared at the circular motions of his fingers on her temple. He hadn't told his hand to do that!

"Mmm . . . that feels good." She groaned.

She couldn't groan, for heaven's sake! "Go to sleep."

Amber closed her eyes and he took the opportunity to look at her as he combed his fingers through her silky tresses. For all his grumbling, something about this felt so right.

"You're staring at me," she said with her eyes still closed. "Do you want to kiss me again?"

His eyes lowered to her mouth and his tongue snaked out to taste her mouth. "Yes, I do," he admitted, falling completely under her spell.

A quick rap on the door robbed him of the pleasure he was about to take and he groaned.

Melana rushed into the room. "Miss Amber I couldn't find you!"

Amber sat up. "Were you worried about me?"

Melana shivered. "The storm's getting worse. I thought you might be scared."

"I don't think anybody wants to be alone in a storm like this. Come on, you can sleep with us."

Melana crawled onto the bed and Amber scooted up against Chris, her back to his front, and he jerked back. Her arms closed around Melana and the little girl snuggled closer.

"Do you want a goodnight kiss?" she asked Melana. "Sure."

Amber kissed her cheek and that was pretty much that. She'd forgotten all about him. He started to get up one more time. The thought of sleeping with Amber held no appeal and he couldn't do what he wanted to do with his daughter in the bed.

Amber grabbed his arm. "Don't leave, Chris."

Her plea had barely left her lips and he was settling back against the headboard. Resisting her wasn't going to work if he couldn't deny her the simplest requests.

He watched the rain pooling on the window sill and sighed. Dawn was a long way off.

Amber washed her panties in the cold water, squeezed out the excess liquid and laid them on the rack behind her to dry. Opening two large safety pins, she set them on the bathroom sink and pulled on the boxers she'd confiscated from Chris' dresser. She'd tried cutting a pair of jogging pants, but even with the drawstrings they were big and the material was too thick to pin. The scissors worked on the boxers, though, and smiling at her ingenuity, she quietly slipped out of the bathroom. She and Melana had awakened earlier, but Chris was still asleep. The rain had stopped, and with it the terrible thunder that had made her head hurt.

Amber entered the living room to find Melana

munching on an apple from their quickly dwindling assortment of fruit. She saw the book they'd finished last night on the end table and that reminded her to get her paper from Chris's bedroom.

Retracing her steps, Amber headed back down the hallway and into the bedroom. She stopped beside the bed to look at him. The sight of his bare chest last night—

Amber broke off as she realized she remembered last night, coming into Chris's room, even reading the book.

She thought hard, wondering what else she remembered. The kiss in the kitchen! But she couldn't remember why she'd been in the kitchen, or what they'd talked about.

Picking up the paper, she smiled, knowing she hadn't forgotten that either. Chris could say what he wanted, her memory was getting better and she would never forget their kisses.

Melana looked up when Amber came back into the room. Giggling, she said, "You look funny in Daddy's underwear, Miss Amber."

"I had to wear something and your puny little underwear didn't work."

She stood up as Amber approached and rose onto her toes. "I'm almost as tall as you. See?"

Amber couldn't resist a quick hug. "Almost. But *I'm* still growing."

Melana laughed. "Uh-uh."

Amber noticed three dolls sitting on the sofa behind Melana. "What are your dolls names?"

"We named them a few days ago. Don't you remember?"

"I'm still having trouble remembering, especially

when my head hurts." She saw Melana's concerned expression. "But it doesn't hurt right now."

Pointing to each doll, she said, "Her name is Raine, that's Kasie, and this is Brianna. Do you still think it's okay for me to play with dolls?"

"Definitely."

Amber picked Raine up and sat down on the sofa. Melana sat close beside her, her lips turned down in a sad frown.

"What's wrong, sweetie?"

"Do you think you'll forget me, if your head is hurting?"

"Never."

"Will you write my name on your paper just in case?"

"If it'll help you feel better, but I won't forget you." Melana handed her the pen on the end table and Amber wrote the requested reminder. *Melana is the best little girl in the whole wide world.*

Melana looked at the note and giggled.

"What's so funny?"

"Daddy kissed you? That's gross."

Amber laughed. "I have trouble saying the right words at times, but I don't think gross is the word I'd use."

But, would Chris?

Chris woke suddenly and automatically glanced at the clock on the nightstand. Then he remembered. The electricity was out.

When had he fallen asleep, he wondered, glancing at the empty space beside him. He'd almost shouted when dawn broke and that was about all he could recall. For a while he'd thought the rain would never stop. Amber and Melana had slept on peacefully while he lay beside them cursing the fates for putting a woman he couldn't have in his pathway.

His head whipped back around to the table. Amber's note was gone. He'd meant to take it after she fell asleep.

He heard Amber and Melana talking as he got up to go to the bathroom. If they were planning to beat him at checkers again, they could forget it. He'd be prepared tonight.

Chris chuckled, thinking about their little ruse.

He brushed his teeth and washed off quickly, shivering from the cold water. Through the mirror he saw Amber's panties hanging on the rack behind him again. So what was she wearing, another shirt and nothing else? Surely, they wouldn't be holed up in this house much longer.

Going back into his bedroom, he pulled on a pair of black jogging pants from the dresser and, noticing the blue pair gone, took hope that Amber had borrowed them.

He strode toward the front room, confident that the less than sexy big-pants-look would help keep him on the straight and narrow, and stopped in the entryway. Amber was lying on her stomach on the sofa with her behind encased in a pair of his black boxers.

Chris spun right back around and bolted into the bedroom, locking the door behind him. He'd stay right there, all day if need be.

Amber began to worry about Chris when lunchtime came and went and he hadn't shown himself. Of course, the one time he hadn't been around, she'd fed herself with steady hands.

He finally emerged around two, according to the clock on the wall. Melana ran to greet him with a hug.

"Hey, Amber," he greeted, his eyes skimming her body before jerking away. "I'm starved," he mumbled as he dashed off toward the kitchen.

Amber stared after him. He was acting funny again and, as usual, she was in the dark as to why. Last night he had admitted to wanting to kiss her. Did he regret the admission? Maybe, like Melana, he thought kissing was gross after all.

She pushed herself to her feet and followed him, intending to find out. He was finishing a bottle of lukewarm water when she walked into the kitchen. Without looking at her, he reached for an oatmeal cream pie on the counter.

Stopping directly in front of him, she waited for him to acknowledge her.

He took his time ripping open the plastic wrap. That was okay. She could wait.

"Everything okay?" he finally asked.

"Did we keep you up last night? You've slept half the day away." And he still looked tired, poor thing.

"I didn't get to sleep until around dawn. I thought another hurricane was coming through the way the windows were rattling." He took a bite of his snack.

That was surprising. She'd slept like a baby with him beside her. Anyway, that wasn't why she'd come in there. Leaning against the counter beside him, she said, "Do you think kissing is gross?"

His brows shot up in response. "Where would you get an idea like that?"

"Melana."

His brows knitted into a frown as he took another bite. "You're talking about kissing with a nine-year-old?"

Amber shrugged. "She saw my note."

He raised his hands as if to say that explained it. "Of course."

"So do you?" she asked, folding her arms across her chest.

He polished off the cream pie. "What?"

"Think kissing is gross?" she asked slowly, enunciating each word.

He shook his head. "No."

Amber sighed. If he'd said *yes*, they'd have a starting point for discussion, but now they were back to square one. "Then how come you take so long getting to it?"

He pushed away from the counter, then stopped as if he didn't know which way to turn. "Because, because . . . kissing strangers is bad, Amber."

Amber felt a great pain in her heart and gasped. "We're strangers?"

"We've only know each other three days, not to mention you're suffering from amnesia. Have you considered the idea that you might be married?"

"I'd remember that."

He rolled his eyes. "You can't remember yesterday."

Hot tears welled up in her eyes and her vision blurred. How could he say they were strangers? Refusing to let him see her cry, she spun on her heel and stormed off. When she didn't see Melana, she continued into the bedroom. With them being strangers and everything, he wouldn't care if she left, right?

Amber saw a woman with flushed cheeks and dark eyes in the mirror and realized it was her reflection. Would she ever look familiar to herself?

She saw Chris in the mirror and turned away. "I guess my eyes darken when my heart hurts, too."

"I see you have a temper. Planning on running away again? That seems to be what you do when you're upset. Where're you off to this time? North?"

"South."

"We are South," he snapped. "We're in Mississippi."

She blinked. "Oh."

He rubbed a hand across his forehead and then around to the back of his neck. "You can't leave, Amber. I'd be worried about you."

She lifted her chin a notch. "Why would you worry about a stranger?"

His hand lowered to his side. "You know I didn't mean it like that."

Did she? Why would he assume that? "I know what you said. Why'd you say it if you didn't mean it?"

"Sometimes the meaning doesn't come out with the words." He reached out to touch her but drew back. "I'm sorry I hurt your feelings."

She shrugged. "It's not like you could really kiss. I was just being nice."

Chris laughed and she felt a warm sensation spread through her chest.

He propped himself against he doorjamb. "Is that right?"

"That's right," she fired back to hide her response to him. "*Way* too wet."

He looked like he wanted to put her challenge to the test but with a quick grin backed off. Thank goodness.

"Don't be embarrassed," he told her.

That threw her. "Embarrassed? Is that what I feel? I don't like this feeling."

He moved forward and she stepped back. "I like kissing you, Amber. It's just not right when we don't know . . . anything about you. I don't want to take advantage of you."

How touching, diplomatic even with his use of *we*—

as if they were in this together. "That was probably the nicest rejection I've ever heard. But it's still a rejection."

The bedroom door opened again that night and Chris jerked upright. Amber had been cool toward him since his earlier gaffe. *She probably wouldn't come in here if thunder knocked on the door.*

Melana climbed onto the bed and sat, facing him. "Daddy?"

"What's wrong, honey? Can't sleep."

"I want to keep Miss Amber."

Chris sputtered. "*Keep* her? Honey, Amber's not a stray dog we can just . . . *keep.*"

"Why not?"

Melana had never asked the really difficult questions like, does God really exist? Why is the sky blue? He'd prefer those questions tonight. "She has a family, I'm sure."

"But she doesn't know them. They were probably mean to her, and that's why she can't remember them. We can adopt her and keep her forever." Melana nodded. "Yeah, that'll be cool."

Chris rubbed his eyes, suddenly feeling extremely exhausted. "Adoption doesn't work like that."

"You don't want her to stay forever?"

Melana's small voice made him feel like a heel. "It's not that."

He couldn't believe they were having this conversation, but why not? Melana and Amber were growing closer every day, and even if they didn't know it, there was a bond drawing them together. Still, he didn't feel right getting Melana's hopes up until he could explain everything, and that wouldn't happen until either Amber's memory returned or they found her family.

Melana tapped her finger against her chin for a moment before her lips parted in a wide smile. "We can keep her, and I know just how to do it."

Chris didn't know what to say. He'd seen sides of Melana he'd never seen before Amber. Could she get Amber to stay and did he want her to?

Chris threw another branch into the growing pile of debris the following afternoon. The hurricane had done its damage, yanking limbs from trees, pulling up small bushes. He'd thought working up a sweat would take his mind off Amber, but it wasn't working. She'd been distant since he'd made that stupid stranger statement. Ultimately, he had rejected her, but not because he didn't want her.

He saw a couple of cars coming down the street. One of them belonged to Olivia's parents, Mike and Jasmine. Mission essential people—personnel required to get the base back in working order—had begun returning a couple of hours ago.

Chris went into the house to get a bottle of water and to see if Amber was still angry. She was sitting on the couch, with her eyes slightly closed.

Dressed in a pair of jeans and an air force T-shirt, Melana was perched on her knees beside her, looking out the window. "Daddy, Olivia's home. Can I go say hi?"

"Okay, but don't go anywhere else and don't—"

"Talk to strangers," she chanted. "I know." Spinning sideways, she hugged Amber. "I'll be back, okay?"

She ran outside and Amber gazed after her. "You're

going to let her go by herself? Is the neighborhood safe?"

"It helps that it's a military installation and we watch out for each other, but she knows not to talk to people she doesn't know."

Amber laid her head on the armrest and closed her eyes.

"I could ask Olivia's mother if she has some extra clothes she can loan you. She's not as tall as you, but maybe a pair of shorts or a skirt would fit." Amber didn't respond and he reached out to touch her cheek. Maybe he should ask Jasmine to check Amber. She was a PA and she'd be discreet. "You know, she's a physician's assistant. Maybe she could take a look at you."

Amber's head popped up enough for her to glance at herself. "Why would she want to look at me?"

"Examine you," he clarified.

She shook her head. "My memory's improving. I remember everything from yesterday to today."

"Still having headaches?" He could look in her eyes for the answer to that question, and they both knew it.

"Should we let anyone know I'm here? You said I might be in danger, right?"

"She won't say anything. I trust her." Why was Amber resisting this? Didn't she want to get better?

"Do you like her? I mean, are you . . . do you like her?" she finished impatiently, sitting up.

What had he said to make her think that? "No. I don't."

Amber was dressed in yet another pair of his boxers, which didn't bother him as much as the sight of her dark eyes. Her hands slid down and back up her thighs. "Is she pretty?"

Chris shrugged. "I guess, but she's married, and so am I."

Amber just looked at him before standing and walking away from him. He closed the distance between them with a couple of steps and captured her arm. Touching her probably wasn't his best idea, but he didn't like to see her upset or hurt. "Don't walk away, Amber. Tell me what's wrong."

She tugged her arm free and kept walking. "Tired, I guess. Your friend can examine me."

Ten minutes into the "examination" and Amber was exhausted. She repositioned the pillow against the headboard but still couldn't get comfortable.

"So basically" she told Jasmine. "Other than a lapse or two, I remember everything I did yesterday and today."

She was pretty, Amber admitted to herself, short and spry. She may be Chris's friend, but Amber just didn't like the woman.

He was pacing back and forth near the foot of the bed and her gaze strayed to him. Why did he keep insisting he was married when he'd told her his wife was dead?

"Chris says your hand shakes?"

"Sometimes."

"Those are probably seizures from the brain's swelling and should go away as the swelling goes down."

Amber rubbed her aching temples. "Seizures?"

"Partial seizures," Jasmine explained. "Which basically means different parts of your brain are sending simultaneous, contradictory signals and your hand doesn't know what to do."

"I've seen people having seizures, but never like that," Chris told her, casting a worried glance at Amber.

"Seizures can look like the typical rhythmic jerking

movements of the arms and legs we see on TV, but they can have many different appearances depending on which brain cells are affected."

Well, that was enlightening. Now that they had the medical terminology down, she wanted to know something else. "How long have you known Chris?"

Chris stopped pacing to look at Amber, and she glared back. He was making her feel very angry, but she didn't know why.

Chuckling, Jasmine turned to Chris. "Why don't you give us a few minutes alone? I want to examine Amber."

His gaze jerked back and forth between the women before he stalked out. Good. Good riddance.

"Hmm. Interesting. Let's look in your eyes." Jasmine pulled a small black instrument from a bag. As she peeled back Amber's left eyelid, she said, "I've known Chris and Melana since they moved in at the beginning of summer. About three months now."

She peered into Amber's eye until the penetrating light made her head hurt worse.

"What's going on between you two?" Jasmine asked.

Amber didn't answer and Jasmine lowered the light. "You don't like me, but I can understand that. I knew him first."

Jasmine grinned at her and Amber tried to resist letting the other woman engage her but she did seem to be nice. She chuckled, unable to resist.

"Ah, now that we're friends, will you tell me what's going on between you two?"

Amber leaned back against the bunched pillow with a heavy sigh. "He kissed me, but I think he feels sad that he did."

"He regrets it?"

"Regret, yeah."

Jasmine pushed Amber's right eyelid back and pointed the small beam toward her pupil. "I feel I have to tell you, he's the hottest catch around, but he's devoted to his deceased wife. Apparently, he loved her so much he doesn't want to be with anyone else."

Amber pushed the light away and cupped her chin in her hand. "What does it feel like when you love someone?"

A slow smile spread across Jasmine's lips as a dreamy expression crossed her face. "You have all kinds of intense feelings for the person you love. You feel a desire to please him, to make him happy. You want to spend all your time with him and think about him constantly when you're apart. And you feel a strong physical attraction that means even more because of the emotional connection."

Amber's heart fluttered in recognition of Jasmine's words. She definitely liked being with Chris and she wanted him to be happy, but that was how he felt about Kimmy. "I don't think I like Kimmy very much."

Jasmine chuckled. "Do you know why?"

"Because Chris loves Kimmy, right?"

Chris was waiting for Jasmine on the porch. She was barely through the door when he started talking. "What's the diagnosis, Doc?"

It was beginning to get dark outside, but even in the faint light, he could see her hesitation. "Amnesia is not my specialty and without being able to do a full examination, I can't give you an accurate assessment of the extent of her brain injury."

They strolled down the cemented walkway side by side. "Tell me what you know."

Anything would be better nothing. He'd done his

best by Amber, but had it been enough? What if his inability to get her to the hospital meant she'd be this way forever? Could he have done anything differently?

"Despite being encased in the thick bone of the skull, the human brain is still quite vulnerable, and even minor trauma can injure delicate brain tissue. Since Amber was injured before she arrived at your house we have no idea how the injury was inflicted, but from what you two have said, I suspect she's suffering from both retrograde amnesia and PTA."

"Retrograde, PTA?" Both sounded serious and they were still days from getting her to a medical facility. "What are they?"

"Retrograde amnesia produces a period of memory loss preceding the injury. PTA, or posttraumatic amnesia, is when the patient suffers a period of confusion and can't retain new memories after an injury."

They reached the end of the driveway and Chris turned toward Jasmine. "But the PTA is clearing up, right? She couldn't account for a couple of things today, but she used to forget things within in hours, minutes even."

Jasmine nodded, her head tilted back and to the left so she could meet his gaze. "It sounds that way, and I'm sure that's a good thing. PTA can span several minutes to several weeks or months and if I remember correctly—the severity of the injury parallels the length of the amnesia. Other than the seizures, has she mentioned any additional physical problems?"

"No, why? What other problems could she have?"

"Just checking. Edema, that's when the brain swells, occurs soon after a head injury, and it can affect even the uninjured parts of her brain, causing temporary impairments. They disappear with the swelling, and since it's been several days, we may be past that problem. I'd keep a close eye on her, but once she can give a clear, accurate and ordered account of events and can remember day-to-day, we'll know she's on the road to recovery."

Which could take weeks or months, too? They probably didn't have that kind of time. Besides, he'd promised to help her find her family once power was restored. Restless, Chris walked into the street. "Will she remember everything at once or piecemeal?"

With a glance to the left and right, Jasmine followed him across the street. "Every case is different to some degree, but generally speaking, she should recall older memories first, and then more recent memories, until almost all memory is recovered. And there is a chance she'll never remember the events around the time of the accident."

Chris sighed. So they may never know how she was hurt, or if someone had hurt her and why? "I appreciate your time, Jasmine. I did the best I could, but I didn't know. . . ."

"You kept her safe and you did your best for her. No one could ask more of you."

"Thanks." Her words went a long way in soothing his feelings of inadequacy, but he was still worried about Amber. "Did you notice that she doesn't understand emotions? She feels them, but somehow they aren't connecting somewhere."

"That could indicate she suffered some type of emotional trauma prior to her injury. Unfortunately, it's locked away in some part of her brain."

"Maybe it's so terrible she doesn't want to remember." The thought bothered him but had to be considered.

Jasmine's steps slowed and then stopped altogether. "It's possible." She studied him for a moment.

"Amnesiac's have a childlike trust in people, simply because they don't have the experience to know better. Same thing with self-control, it's a learned process, so she may become agitated over little things, she may exhibit poor social skills and impulsiveness."

That explained a lot, her forthrightness, her quick flare, and extremes of emotion. Did that mean she wouldn't be like that when her memory returned?

Jasmine placed her hand on his arm. "Amber's nursing some serious feelings for you even if she can't fully understand or articulate them."

Chris almost laughed at that last statement. Amber said just what she wanted to say and could get her feelings across very well. "I'll remember that. Where's Mike?"

"At the firehouse. He'll probably be working twelve-hour shifts until things are back to normal. Luckily, he'll have enough time to bring me the car before my shift. Let me get those clothes for Amber."

Chris waited on Jasmine's porch to keep an eye on his house. Through the screen door, he could see Melana and Olivia playing a board game in the front room. Jasmine returned with a few outfits and he headed back across the street. He saw a man wearing a hat low on his head with his jacket's lapel pulled up to his ears.

"Captain?"

Chris tried to hide his surprise. The guy knew his rank. Could be he'd gotten the information from the nameplate on the house, but since Chris was coming from across the street, how'd the man know he lived there? "Yes? May I help you?"

"Just getting back?" he asked conversationally.

Chris noticed a small cut on the guy's bottom lip. "Do I know you?"

"I'm looking for this woman." He showed Chris a picture of Amber. "Have you seen her?"

"'Fraid not. I'm just returning from a mandatory evacuation of the area. Beautiful lady. Runaway wife?"

He tried to phrase it like a joke but the possibility of it being true had the words sticking in his throat.

"Something like that."

"Daddy?" Chris glanced over his shoulder at the sound of Melana's voice. "Can I have a snack with Olivia?"

"Sure, honey." He turned back to the man who staggered back a little. "If she's missing, maybe you should call the police."

"I'll do that. Thanks." The man hurried away and several houses down jumped into a car and sped off.

It looked like trouble had just presented itself.

CHAPTER 6

"I'm jealous. That's what I feel inside."

Chris reared back, surprised at Amber's statement. "But I told you I'm not attracted to Jasmine."

Concerned about Melana being outside alone, Chris had gone back to Jasmine's to see if she'd keep Melana inside until he came for her, then hurried back to his place to find Amber still sitting against the headboard in his bedroom.

"Of your 'wife'," she bit out. Looking up at him with eyes as dark as the night, she said, "Why do you love her?"

He dropped onto the edge of the bed beside her, searching for the right words. "She's my wife. She's a part of me, you know? We shared seven years of our lives together. We share a child together." Chris sighed. He just didn't have time to explain the complexities of love.

Amber's eyes lowered to her lap, then rose back to his. "Then I'm not jealous. I wish she was here and I wasn't. That would make you happy, wouldn't it?"

Chris hesitated, cautious. "I would be happy if she

was here, but I'm not unhappy because you're here. Do you understand?"

Amber shook her head, looking sad and dejected.

Chris groaned, wishing he knew what to say to make her feel better. Right now, he needed to focus on her physical safety. "There was a man asking about you just now. I couldn't get a good look at him, but I saw a cut on his bottom lip. If you had an altercation with him, that would explain your bruises."

Her shoulder's straightened. "What did he say?"

"Not much. He wanted to know if I'd seen you. Thing is, he only asked me so he either knows you're here or thought you were coming here."

She swung her legs over the side of the bed. "I should go."

Again when he expected her to show some fear, she was daring, resolute. Who was this woman? "We've been through this before, Amber. You can't just leave. You have no place to go."

"I can't put you and Melana in danger, Chris." She placed her hand on his arm, distracting him. "I like your . . . desire to help me but it's not right."

There was a list of things that weren't right, like her ability to sidetrack him with one touch, but they'd be all night just discussing that one issue!

"It's not right to let you go off alone," he countered, going with the current topic. "I have a friend in Georgia. Mel's godfather. We can stay with him until we figure out what to do next."

"How will we get there? I saw the car. It looks like somebody crashed into it."

Chris laughed despite himself. And she thought he'd let her go *anywhere* by herself? "I'll ask Jasmine— No, her husband has the car. In the morning, I'll ask

Mike to take us to Mobile since the hurricane wasn't headed that way and we can rent a car from there."

Her ebony eyes lifted to his and he felt the same drowning sensation he'd felt the first time he'd looked into her eyes. "Why are you doing this, Chris?" she asked softly. "Why are you putting yourself out for me?"

"Because you watch out for people you care about."

Amber stared at the map Chris had laid out on the table. He'd gone to bed some time ago. Melana, too. As usual, Amber hadn't been sleepy. Either she'd had too much sleep lately, or she was nocturnal by nature.

Chris had come up with a plan. Jasmine's husband would take them to Mobile in the morning. They'd rent a car and drive to Georgia, with the bad guy right on their heels. That, of course, was dependent upon them surviving the night.

Amber strode over to the window and peeked through the blinds, seeing nothing in the darkness. The stranger had way too many hours to put any plan he may have into action. He could be watching them right now. How would they be any safer if he followed them to Georgia?

It was a plan, but not the best one. Chris could be so . . . what was the word? He wouldn't listen to her, so determined to do things his own way. While basically telling her she was too addled to know anything, he'd put the clothes Jasmine had given her in his suitcase and mapped out a route to Georgia. But she wasn't about to let him and Melana get hurt. Regardless of her medical condition, she wasn't beyond coming up with a plan herself.

Abandoning the window, she went back to the map on the table. What she needed to do was lure the guy away, in another direction. If she went ahead of them—

She shied away from the thought even before she could finish it. Chris would have a fit if she did this.

Then again, he'd be alive to have a fit.

Okay. She rubbed her hands together. If she went ahead of him and Melana, whoever was after her would follow.

Positioning the lantern to see better, Amber found the mark next to Biloxi that Chris had made. Georgia was to the right, via Alabama. She'd go through Mobile and Montgomery and then onto I-85 toward Atlanta. The direct path would take a little over seven hours but she would head off in the opposite direction toward New Orleans until Chris and Melana were safely on the road.

So how would she do this? On foot? She studied the blue line, trying to calculate the distance to New Orleans. What choice did she have? The phone lines were down, the city evacuated. She'd never lose the guy in a cab, but she'd never get a cab in the first place.

Amber shook her head. Chris was going to be so angry, but he and Melana would be out of harm's way, and, like he said, you watch out for people you care about.

She would see them safe on the other side of this present danger. She would.

Amber wrote Ron's address on her paper beneath the two reminders and her name, which still didn't seem familiar. Then she wrote Chris a brief letter. If he and Melana left as scheduled, they'd all be together by one o'clock tomorrow.

Using a flashlight to guide her, she went to Melana's room and kissed the little girl goodbye. "I'll see you in just a few short hours," she whispered.

She walked across the hallway to Chris's room. He was asleep on his stomach, his face partially buried in the pillow. Laying the note on the pillow beside him, she set the flashlight to illuminate the note and not shine directly in his face. She thought about what Jasmine had said about love. Chris made her feel so many emotions, most she didn't understand. She touched his cheek with her fingers but didn't kiss him. His heart belonged to Kimmy.

Following the light of the lantern, she tiptoed back into the dining room, grabbed a hundred dollars from the stack in Chris' wallet, her note, and another flashlight, then slipped out the front door, closing it softly behind her.

Flicking on the flashlight, she followed the path toward the driveway. It was hot and muggy outside, dark like the earth had been colored in with black ink.

She paused at the end of the driveway and listened for the night sounds to guide her. She didn't hear anything. The storm had thrown nature off balance. In the quiet, the distant swishing of running water touched her ears and Amber followed the sound to the left, swinging the flashlight back and forth to draw attention to herself.

The sound of breaking twigs filled the night as she walked, then she heard a car engine start. She waited for the accompanying lights and when none were forthcoming, she smiled. Gotcha.

Stepping around debris, she made her way to the end of the block, guided by the sound of rushing water. The driver hadn't attempted contact so he must be waiting for her to get out of the residential area.

A bright beam of light caught her attention and she rounded the corner and saw four men and two women sitting around a light pole of some kind at the end of a driveway playing cards.

Amber walked in their direction, hoping to get a view of the car in the light. She glanced at her wrist, pretending to look for a watch. Lowering her arm, she said, "Anybody have the time?"

"Almost two," one guy told her without looking at his watch. "Hot night, huh? Taking a walk?"

"Yeah." She glanced behind her to see the car. Midsize and black, or at least it looked black. It could be navy blue. "I'm headed to New Orleans."

"Long walk." A second man lounging back on a plastic recliner smoking a cigarette blew a curl of smoke from his mouth.

"Family emergency," she said.

The headlights of the car flickered on, their faint beam barely penetrating the darkness. She could make out a lone figure behind the wheel but it was too dark to see anything else, even the license plates.

"I haven't seen you around base housing," he continued, taking a puff. "Just moved in?"

The taillights vanished in the darkness beyond the light and she could hear the car idling. If she didn't leave soon, he may turn his attention back to the house, to Chris and Melana. "I'd better go."

A lady in a camouflage uniform and black boots stood up before she could move. "I'm off to work myself. I can take you to the nearest working gas station on I-10, within twenty miles anyway."

Amber smiled at the friendly woman. "That'd be great. Are you sure you won't be late?"

She smiled. "It's a family emergency, right? I'm Deana, by the way."

"Amber." Wow, Chris was right. The people in base housing did look out for each other.

She followed Deana to a car parked on the street and slid into the passenger seat. Deana started the car and drove forward, passing the black car. Two beams reflected off the glass of the side mirror as the car pulled in line behind them and Amber nodded. *That's right. Stay right behind me, fella.*

"Is your family in New Orleans? I hope you weren't planning to rent a car. The hurricane hit there, too, and most of the city is without power."

No power? Amber didn't know if that would work in her favor or not. It would definitely be easier to lose him in the dark but she needed to be a visible, moving target until she was sure Chris and Melana were on the road.

Several turns led them onto a road bordering a body of water, the outline visible in the headlights for only a moment. It was dark. Maybe too dark.

Chris saw light from beneath his eyelids and opened his eyes. Realizing it was a flashlight, he reached out to turn it off. Wait. He didn't remember having a flashlight last night.

A knock on the bedroom door interrupted his thoughts and he rolled onto his side.

Melana walked in, rubbing her eyes. "Miss Amber?"

"She's sleeping on the couch, honey."

"I checked. She's not there."

"What?" Chris began to get up, until he saw the folded sheet of paper on the pillow. His heart sank as he reached for the letter and read the message out loud. "Dear Chris, please don't be angry with me. I care about you and Melana, too, and I want to protect you. I'll meet you in Georgia. Tell Melana I'll see her soon."

"Oh, no! We have to find her, Daddy!" Melana

burst into tears and Chris stared, shocked. "What if her head starts hurting and she forgets where she's going?"

Chris pulled Melana into his arms. "It's all right, honey. We'll find her."

"How?" she cried.

He had no idea. Why would she leave? he wondered. *Because you watch out for people you care about.* He groaned as his words came back to haunt him.

"Honey, go get dressed. I need you to stay with Olivia while I look for Amber."

Melana scurried out of the room and he threw on a pair of jogging pants and his boots. Reclaiming the flashlight, he stomped down the hallway to the dining room to check his suitcase. Amber's borrowed clothes were there which meant she was still wearing the red shorts and his white T-shirt.

He checked his wallet to see if she'd taken any money. She wouldn't have remembered that he'd stuck her purse on the closet shelf in the front room. He was a hundred dollars short, so she had money. That was good.

He met Melana at the front door. She'd stopped crying but the aftermath of her tears made her breath catch every time she breathed. "Amber will be fine, Mel. We have to believe that."

She nodded but he wasn't sure if she was convinced. Hell, he didn't know if he was convinced.

He hustled her across the dark street and practically banged on Jasmine's door until she answered.

"Chris? Mel? What's wrong?"

"Amber's gone. Can you keep Mel while I look for her?"

"Of course," she said, ushering the little girl inside. Melana offered him a small wave while Jasmine looked on sympathetically. "Take your time," she told him.

Holding the lantern up, he anxiously searched the housing area for any signs of Amber. He picked his way over debris, cutting his fingers against broken limbs. It wasn't cold but it was wet and muddy, no place for anyone.

He would've taken care of her. Why hadn't she trusted him to take care of her? Then again, why should she when he was running around making statements like that? With her state of mind, it was hard to determine how she internalized anything he said. He should've been more careful.

He made his way to the river bank outside base housing and searched each pier for her. The mist from the water sprayed his face and dampened his shirt. His heart in his throat, he scanned the water's surface for her, praying—please God—that he would not find her there.

Finally, he trudged back to Jasmine's as he tried to figure out how he'd explain to Melana that Amber would be okay, wherever she was. Before he could even knock, the door flew open.

The look of anticipation on Melana's face dissolved into despair and he knew there'd never be enough words to comfort her. She burst into tears and he thought his heart would break.

"Mel . . ."

She buried her face against him and he could feel her tears soaking his shirt. It was a pretty straight shot from here to Georgia and Amber's letter had been lucid, but he knew how vulnerable she was, especially when her head hurt. Not to mention her trusting nature.

Why hadn't he insisted she take the bed! She

would've never gotten passed him if he'd been on the couch. He thought about her being out there alone, hurt and confused. He thought about how he'd made her heart feel sad as he'd tried to hold onto to thoughts of Kimmy. If anything happened to her, he'd never forgive himself.

Amber dashed into Mabel's Roadside Café later that morning and the clanging overhead bells made her wince. She'd been okay until about an hour ago when they'd driven into a storm, complete with thundering and lightening and her head had begun to pound. Now every little sound felt like a dagger in her temple. The sweet scent of maple syrup and warm pecans was almost enough to drive away the pressure, though.

A gray-haired woman with her tresses in a net gave Amber the once-over, her left brow arched above her eye. Amber automatically ran a hand over her wet hair. She hadn't brought a comb and probably looked a mess.

Amber squinted at the nametag fastened to the woman's uniform. "Hi, Mabel."

"Child, you look like you haven't had a decent meal in days. Sit right down and let me fix you something good to eat. Menu's on the counter."

Amber slid onto a stool. "Okay, thanks."

She'd met several other nice women on the road, too. With the help of one lady who liked to sing along with gospel music on the radio, Amber had lost her tail heading west on I-10. She'd backtracked carefully, changing cars twice before she met up with a woman headed toward Selma, Alabama, about an hour before Montgomery.

The words were blurry and the effort to see them too

great so she chose the first platter on the list. "The daily special, please." Exhausted from the effort, she folded her arms on the counter and laid her head on top, listening to the griddle sizzle and the deep fryer bubble.

"You traveling alone?" she heard Mabel say.

Amber glanced over her shoulder at two men playing cards and another one reading a newspaper. "Yes, ma'am."

"Where to?"

Amber pulled her note out of the back pocket of her shorts. "Warner Robins, Georgia."

Out of the corner of her eye, she saw a man with olive skin and silky black hair come from a back room. He slid onto the stool beside her and grinned at her, revealing a pair of dimples in each cheek. Amber felt her face warm.

Mabel set a large plate of pancakes, eggs, and sausage on the counter. "Here you go, honey."

Amber sniffed appreciatively. Though she had nothing against fruit and granola bars, this was *food*. "Mmm. It smells good."

Mabel clucked her tongue. "You're skinny as a rail. You need the kind of food that sticks to your ribs."

The man looked her over from head to toe. "I would not add one ounce of flesh to this lovely lady."

Amber's cheeks warmed again at the melodic sound of his voice. Their gazes met briefly before she looked away. This was the first man she'd met other than Chris.

"My name is Remy, by the way. Would you care to have breakfast, you and me together?"

Amber closed her hand over the warm bottle of syrup and paused to let the heat sink in. "I like the way you talk. It's different."

"The ladies love my accent. They swoon at my

feet." His eyebrows wiggled and Amber laughed. "So we will have breakfast together, yes?"

Sure. Why not? He seemed nice, like Chris. "Yes."

He grinned and his dimples reappeared. "You are nice lady to share meal with me."

Mabel placed his food in front of him. "I didn't see you pull up in a car. How are you getting to Georgia?"

"Hitchhiking," Amber said as she watched the pancakes soak up the liquid. "But hitchhiking can be dangerous, so I'm only doing this one time."

The lady with the bad back had fussed at her for a long time, extracting a pledge from Amber that she'd never hitch a ride again.

"I should say so," Mabel said in the same tone as the woman with the bad back. "How old are you?"

Amber thought about that for a moment. Chris had never told her and she couldn't remember. "I don't know."

Mabel looked at her funny before stepping closer to the counter. "Are you in some kind of trouble?"

"Yes." The guy who had been following her had been pretty tenacious, too. She hadn't allowed him to get too close, so she had no idea what he looked like, other than what Chris had told her.

"Want me to call the police?"

She ate a forkful of the pancakes and groaned. They practically melted on her tongue. "I have to meet Chris and Melana in Georgia, or else they'll feel sad."

The overhead bells jangled and Amber pressed her fingers to her temples. Would the pain ever cease? The piercing pain subsided with the noise and she lowered her hands. Rain blew in with a pretty teenager and her family. The girl pushed the hood of her slicker off her head and when their gazes met, her hand froze midway.

Amber smiled at her before turning back to her

food. Seeing the girl made her think of Melana. She and Chris definitely had to be on the road by now. It wouldn't be long before she saw them again.

Now she understood what Jasmine meant by wanting to be with someone you loved. She'd kept the guy following her on the run until nine, giving Chris and Melana plenty of time to be on the road and the whole time she'd wanted to go back, to be with them.

"Excuse me." Amber turned toward the teenager standing beside her. Her eyes were bright, her grin engaging. "Are you Honor, the model?"

The model? Why would she think that? "No, I'm Amber."

The teenager showed Amber the fashion magazine in her hand. "You look just like her, except the hair is different."

The woman on the cover was pretty with curly auburn hair and a sassy grin. "She doesn't look familiar, and she can't be me because my name is Amber. See?"

She showed the girl the paper with her name written on it and her face fell. "You must have a twin then."

"Okay, I'll write it down so I'll remind . . . remember . . . to tell Chris."

The girl stared at Amber for a moment before slowly walking away. Amber wrote the model's name on the back of her note and looked up just in time to see Mabel slip through a pair of swinging doors.

Taking one last bite of her pancakes, she slid off the stool, took a ten dollar bill from her back pocket, and placed it on the counter. "I'd better go."

Remy stood as well. "Mabel will call the police, yes? I see the concern on her face."

"That's what I'm thinking, but I have to meet Chris and Melana in Georgia. I promised."

"I have a rig out front. I'll give you a ride." Before she

could respond he said, "You are smart to hesitate, but have I done or said anything to make you feel unsafe?"

No, and she appreciated the offer. She still had a ways to Georgia. "You are kind to offer a stranded lady a ride." She mimicked his accent, drawing a chuckle from him.

He removed his jacket as she followed him to the door. "You are funny, Bellezza."

"Bellezza? What does that mean?"

"I referred to you as beauty because you are beautiful."

He looked at her the way Chris did. They were so different. Chris so intense, Remy playful. She missed Chris.

Holding the jacket above their heads, he guided her outside to a maroon diesel with two silver stripes on the side. She got a little wet climbing into the cab. Glancing around as she settled into a warm leather chair, she was surprised by how nice the truck was. Over her shoulder, she saw a mini-apartment with beige and maroon furnishings that included a bunk bed, refrigerator, swivel chair and a TV and VCR combo.

Remy jumped into the seat beside her and started the truck. "Nice, yes?"

"Very." Amber closed her eyes and released a long sigh. Maybe if the ride was smooth, it would lull her headache away.

"Why don't you stretch out on the bed in back, get some rest, Bellezza?"

"I think I will. Maybe by the time I wake up, I'll see Chris."

"Maybe," Remy murmured. "Maybe."

Amber felt a cool cloth on her forehead and opened her eyes. The truck had stopped moving. Had they reached Georgia already? It didn't seem like she'd been asleep that long.

Remy strolled through a door on her left and she blinked to bring him into focus. "How are you feeling, Bellezza? You were moaning in pain, so I put the cloth on your forehead."

Her head still hurt but not as much. "I'm okay. Are we in Georgia?"

Was she about to see Chris and Melana?

"No, I had to stop to nurse you." He knelt down beside her. "I am concerned for you, too."

"I'll be all right. Let's just go." She could see through the windshield that the rain had stopped. Where were they?

"I'm afraid not, Bellezza."

"What do you mean?" Her heart began to feel very afraid. She knew because the way it was pounding. Maybe she should have only driven with women. But Chris was a man and he was nice, and Remy seemed nice, too.

He touched her hair, which had dried in the warm truck. "You are so beautiful, do you know that? No, you don't and that only enhances your beauty. You are just as lovely as that model, if not more so."

Amber started to stand but her vision doubled and she stopped. Remy placed his hand on her shoulder and gently held her down. "You can't leave, Bellezza. You will stay with me until—"

She tried to push his hand away but his grip tightened. "No. I have to get to Georgia. I told Chris to tell Melana I'd see her—"

He began to knead her shoulder with his hand. "Relax. I will take care of you."

"But—"

"Hush," he whispered, leaning toward her.

* * *

Chris hit I-65 North toward Montgomery with his foot pressed hard on the gas pedal despite the rain. Melana was buckled in the backseat fumbling to open the cell phone he'd just bought.

"We need to charge it," she told him.

He switched the wipers up another notch. "I bought a car charger. We can use it as long as it's plugged in."

Jasmine's husband had driven them to Mobile where Chris had rented a car. The hours since he'd realized Amber was gone had passed like lifetimes, but he'd found a measure of peace minutes ago. He'd stopped at every gas station on the highway, frantically describing her to one cashier after another until a straggly-looking man said he'd seen her with a woman in her mid-fifties with a short, tapered hair style. But who was the woman? Where had Amber met her?

Melana handed him the cell phone. "Is Miss Amber going to be okay?"

"She'll be fine, Mel. We'll find her."

Melana had been withdrawn after her initial distress. She'd sat quietly, holding one of her dolls, refusing to sleep until they found Amber.

Chris searched the road on the left and the right, through the blurry rearview mirror, side mirror and left again in case he'd missed something until he was almost dizzy. He didn't know if he wanted to find Amber walking or in a vehicle with a stranger. Both presented dangers he didn't want to consider.

He plugged the cord into the lighter socket and punched in Ron's number.

"Hello?"

"Ron, I'm on my way to your place and a . . . friend

of mine is coming ahead of me. You haven't heard from a woman named Amber, have you?"

"Nah, man. What's going on?"

"It's a long story. If she calls, tell her I said to stay where she is and not to go with anyone else, even if they say they know me. Then hit me on my cell. It's on your caller ID, right?"

"Yeah, but what's wrong with her? Is she slow or something?"

Chris grimaced. "Vulnerable. I'll explain everything when we get there."

"Tell Uncle Ron I said hi."

"Tell her hi," Ron said before Chris could relay the message.

"Will do. Thanks." Chris pushed the end-call button, then punched in HP for highway patrol. Damn. "Mel, did you grab the address book off the table?"

"No, I thought you did."

Chris sighed. He'd have to call Ron back to get his address.

"Alabama State Police," said a man's voice. "Do you have an emergency?"

"I'd like to report a missing person. Her name is Amber Night. She's five-eight, African American with black hair and copper, no, black eyes." It was raining so her head was probably hurting.

"What's your name, sir?"

"Christopher St. Clair."

"And your location?"

"I-65 North," he said, searching the road.

"Sir, we'll need you to come into the nearest police station and file an official report—"

"I don't have time to find a police station! Look, she's suffering from amnesia. She hit her head in a car accident four days ago."

"Where was she last seen, sir?"

"En route to Warren Robins, Georgia. I have reason to believe she's on highway 65 North heading toward Montgomery.

"Why do you think she's there?"

Does it matter, he wanted to shout? "We were talking about going there last night and she was seen heading in this direction with a woman in her mid-fifties with a short tapered hairstyle about two hours ago. I figure she's maybe fifty, sixty miles from Montgomery."

"Do you have a description of the car?"

"No." He'd asked but it had been too dark for the guy to make out the color.

"What is your relationship to the missing party?"

"She's my fiancée," he lied, afraid the police wouldn't help him if he told him the truth.

Since he wasn't a relative, he didn't know if the police would take Amber into custody or what, and until she knew who the bad guy was, Chris didn't want her going off with anyone.

"Sir, we'll start looking for the victim and make all on-duty officers aware of this situation. The officers go the extra mile in cases like these—helicopters, dogs. They'll find her. We'll contact you at the cell phone number you've provided."

Chris pushed the off button and tossed the phone on the passenger seat. Melana's worried gaze met his in the rearview mirror. "The police are looking for her, too, honey." Noticing a sign for a diner up ahead, he decided to stop. "Do you have to go to the restroom? I'm going to run in and see if Amber's been here."

"I'll go with you."

He parked and they got out. As they crossed the graveled driveway, Melana slipped her hand into his. He opened the door and the clink of bells greeted them.

An older woman standing behind the counter was speaking to a police officer while a couple of men played cards. "She was here when I went into the back. She said something about meeting Chris and somebody."

The sound of his name caught Chris' attention. "Melana? Chris and Melana?"

The woman looked over sharply, as if she hadn't known anyone else was there. "I think so. Yeah. She was talking to a young man, a Latino, when I went into the back. I was concerned about her because she sounded so innocent, you see. She didn't want me to call the police, but I felt duty-bound. One of my customers said he saw her getting into his truck."

"How long have they been gone?" Chris was trying hard not to sound panicked with Melana right beside him, but this didn't sound good. Who was this man, and why would Amber go with him?

"Forty minutes or so."

He saw the cop reach for the black radio on the counter. "What's he driving?"

"A maroon diesel with two silver stripes on the side."

Chris grabbed Melana's hand and ran for the door. He couldn't wait for the police officer to radio the information. He had to get to Amber now. "Come on, Mel."

He heard the static reception of the radio and then the cop's voice. "All units be on the lookout for . . ."

They ran to the car. Why hadn't he left Melana with Jasmine? She would've been upset, perhaps never forgiven him, but she didn't need to be a part of this.

He slid behind the wheel as she scrambled into the backseat. "Is Miss Amber with a stranger?"

Jamming the key in the general vicinity of the

ignition, he started the car, yanked the gear into drive, and shot off. "Yeah, honey."

All the times he'd told Melana not to talk to strangers or go with strangers because they may hurt her or take her far away and he probably never thought it would really happen. And here it was happening to a grown woman.

As Chris sped down the highway, he heard a helicopter in the distance. This guy better hope the police get to him first.

He saw a truck parked on the side of the road and slammed on the brake. The car skidded and swerved, spitting gravel as the tires stopped. He turned in the seat and took hold of Melana's hand to reassure her. "Stay here and lock the door. Don't open it for anyone except me and Amber."

He waited until Melana nodded to open the door and climb out. The diesel's engine wasn't running and as he crept behind the truck and up the passenger side, he listened for voices, screams, any indication of distress.

He tried to scope out the inside of the truck through the rearview mirror, but all he saw was two empty seats. Gripping the handle, he gave a gentle tug to see if the door was locked. It wasn't.

Damn. He didn't know if they were inside, how much room there was, or if the guy was armed.

Hoping to catch him off guard, Chris opened the door slowly. *Please don't let it squeak or in some way alert the guy to his presence.*

Behind the seats was a small apartmentlike area. Chris saw the man sitting beside Amber on the bed, holding her down with a hand on her shoulder. He flew across the seat and snatched the guy up by his shirt as he took in Amber's dark, unfocused gaze.

"No, Chris. He—"

"It's okay, Amber. I'm here now."

Holding the guy with two fistfuls of his shirt, Chris yanked him forward. "I'm going to kill you."

The punk gripped his wrists and tried to pull free. "Hey, guy, it's not like that—"

"Yeah, what's it like?" Chris said through his teeth. "She's injured and vulnerable and you take advantage of her? You—"

"Chris, you don't understand—!"

"Police! Don't move!"

Chris didn't even bother to turn around. "You're going to have to shoot to stop me."

CHAPTER 7

Amber stumbled out of the truck and nearly doubled over as she drank in the pine-scented air. Oh God, her head hurt. Even the sound of chirping birds and cars whizzing by hurt.

Chris was so out of control that the cop had forced her to leave. Why wouldn't he just listen to her? Remy hadn't hurt her.

She heard a door open and suddenly little arms were around her. "Miss Amber! Come on, we have to get in the car."

Melana held Amber as she struggled to put one foot in front of the other until she practically fell into the backseat.

"Are you okay, Miss Amber? Did the bad man hurt you?" Amber heard the car lock, and then Melana's arms were back around her. "That's how come Daddy always tells me not to talk to strangers. Where is Daddy?"

Melana kept firing questions at Amber without giving her a chance to answer. She saw a second squad car park near the truck and a female officer approached the car and knocked on the side window closest to Amber. Neither of them moved to open the door.

"Ma'am," the cop knocked on the window again. "You're safe now. You can open the door."

"Daddy said not to open the door," Melana told Amber.

"Could you check on Chris?" Amber asked the bulky, blond woman through the window. "He's in the truck."

Before the woman could move, Amber saw two cops pushing Chris back as he tried to get around them.

Tears spurted into Melana's eyes and she spun around and threw herself against Amber.

Confused by Melana's reaction, Amber held her close. "It's okay, sweetie," she told her, hoping her words would help her feel happy.

She watched Chris yank his arm free from a police officer and march around the car toward her. He was angry, but the realization didn't frighten her. Chris would never hurt her.

He banged on the window and Melana jumped.

"It's okay, sweetie. Look, it's your dad."

Amber tugged the little girl's arms from around her and unlocked the door.

Yanking the door open, Chris pulled Amber out of the car. "Come here," he growled as his arms closed around her. He was shaking and his heart beat so fast she could feel it thumping against her cheek.

She tried to lean back to look at his face. She knew he was angry but his heart was beating like he was afraid. "Why is your heart pounding so hard?"

"I was so scared for you," he admitted. "I didn't know where you were or if you were all right."

His skin was cold and clammy, his shirt drenched in sweat. He released her enough to tip her head back and look into her eyes. "He didn't hurt me, Chris. He was just trying to take care of me, the same as you."

"He didn't touch you?"

She shook her head.

"Why did you leave without me?" he asked, his voice thick.

"To protect you and Melana. You said that's what you do when you care about someone."

He closed his eyes for a moment. "Well, now I'm saying you're never to leave me again, no matter what. Do you understand?"

His gruff words didn't frighten her, knowing they were coming from his heart. "Okay, but I'll have to write it down so I won't forget."

Chuckling weakly, Chris pressed his forehead against hers. "Yeah, write it down."

Chris stopped the car at the perimeter gate and punched in the entry code Ron had given him seconds ago over the phone. Ron lived in Huntington Crest, a privatized housing area of Warren Robins Air Force Base.

As Chris drove through the open gate, he glanced at Amber through the rearview mirror. Melana had finally dozed off with her head in Amber's lap. She had stared at the little girl for a long while before her gaze had turned to the scenery outside. He didn't know if she'd seen any of it, though.

He turned into Ron's driveway.

They would have been here hours ago, but an ambulance had been dispatched so paramedics could examine Amber. They'd taken her to the hospital where they'd run all kinds of tests that basically confirmed what Jasmine had already told them.

Chris opened the car door for Amber and Melana just as Ron bounded down the stairs. Melana climbed out first and sprinted across the yard. "Uncle Ron!"

Chris captured Amber's hand as Ron approached them, his hand extended toward Chris. "You look good, man. Who's this lovely lady?"

Chris shook his hand. "This lovely lady is Amber. We caught up with her near Selma."

"It's nice to meet you, Amber. Come on inside. I have the grill fired up, thought I'd cook some steaks, give you guys time to rest, take showers, etcetera."

"I could use a hot shower," Chris admitted. He turned to Amber. "Do you want to eat, lay down for a while?"

"A shower sounds good."

"Nell took Kevin back to college after a long week-end, so I'm all by myself. I didn't know if you two were sharing a room or not . . . ?"

"Not," Chris said firmly.

Amber's sharp glance seared him, but she didn't say anything.

From the quirk of Ron's lips, Chris knew he hadn't missed Amber's look. "Then she and Mel can have my room and you can take Kevin's. I'll take the sofa bed."

"We can't put you out altogether. I'll take the sofa bed." That way, he'd make sure Amber didn't slip away again. Despite her promise, there was no guar-antee he wouldn't inadvertently say something to send her off again.

Ron nodded. "All right. You know where everything is." He captured Melana's hand. "Ready chef?"

"Yeah!"

Ron and Melana walked around the side of the house toward the backyard. Chris led Amber inside the house. The front door opened into a large living room furnished in burnt orange and yellow. The master bedroom was in the back of the house.

Amber was quiet as they walked through the living and dining rooms and down the hall.

Chris opened the door and stepped aside so she could go inside first. Unlike his bedroom, this room had a feminine touch. A queen size bed with a champagne colored comforter dominated the room and in a sitting area two wicker chairs were separated by a small table with a stack of magazines resting on the top.

"The bathroom's through there," Chris said, pointing to the door. "I'll get you a towel and washcloth from the hallway closet. You okay?"

She nodded, and after a moment's hesitation, he left her.

He heard the water running in the bathroom and thought he'd slip inside the bedroom to leave the items. Amber was unbuttoning her shirt when he walked in and they both stopped.

"I, uh. Here you go." He offered her the bath items. "I'm going to take a shower. I'll come back once you're dressed."

She nodded and then slipped into the bathroom.

Chris showered and changed into a pair of jeans and a T-shirt in Kevin's room. This was definitely the room of an eighteen year old, with posters of half-dressed women plastered on the wall.

The aroma of grilled steak lured him to kitchen, where he spotted a large salad on the counter. He picked out a cherry tomato and popped it into his mouth. He'd gotten a hamburger on the road and eventually tossed it into the garbage, too tense to eat.

Melana was standing in front of the microwave

watching a mug turn in a circle. "I'm fixing Miss Amber some hot chocolate."

"I need the corn, Mel!" Ron yelled from the patio.

Melana turned toward a plate of foiled corn-on-the-cob. "Can you take the milk to her?"

He fingered another tomato from the salad bowl. "Sure."

The microwave beeped and Chris carefully removed the hot mug. If Amber wasn't too tired after lunch, he'd suggest they go to the Base Exchange and buy her some clothes that fit a little better.

He carried the drink to the bedroom and knocked on the door. It felt a little weird knocking when they'd had no barriers between them in Biloxi, but after her shyness moments ago, he didn't know how to behave.

She opened the door wearing a long shirt Jasmine had given her. It fell midthigh on Amber.

"Melana made you some hot chocolate."

"Oh, I'll have to thank her." Her teeth sank into her bottom lip for a moment. "I really scared her, didn't I? I didn't mean to."

"I know." He handed her the cup. "Maybe you should talk to her."

"I will." She raised the cup in a salute. "Here's hoping I'm not lactose intolerant. Wouldn't want to add stomach cramps to the mix."

Despite her humor, he saw her lips tremble. "What's wrong?"

She curled up on the bed and took a sip of her milk. "I was scared, too. Sometimes."

A tear escaped from her eye and Chris captured it with his thumb. Taking the cup, he set it on the nightstand and pulled her into his arms.

She rubbed her face against his chest. "I like how I feel when I'm with you."

Chris placed his lips against her cheek. "Me, too, my . . ."

He almost said *my love*. Was that what he felt, love?

Her eyes were closed and his gaze followed the curve of her thick lashes. He touched his lips to hers. They were soft and puffy, salty from tears.

He lingered, kissing her softly, slowly until her mouth relaxed beneath his and she began to kiss him back. She was like a delicate flower spreading its petals for the first time. He could clearly see what he'd known in his heart. He loved her.

He traced her bottom lip with his tongue and felt her breath escape in short spurts.

Drawing her closer, he eased his hand beneath her shirt and traced a circular pattern against her soft skin. She trembled.

He kissed her, delving in and out of her mouth with his tongue, and she moaned. Reaching her breast, he flicked his thumb across her tight nipple through her bra. She moaned again.

Chris knew from seeing her bra hanging in the bathroom that it had a front closure. He captured the clasp between his thumb and forefinger, then paused. "I'm going to unfasten your bra. Is that okay?"

She nodded, her eyes downcast.

"Look at me, Amber."

She met his gaze, but he'd never seen her look so vulnerable, not even during the worst of her physical pain.

He unfastened the clasp and her breasts spilled into his hands.

He wanted to linger over her breasts, to kiss and suckle each one until he drove her to the brink of ecstasy and beyond. But his fingers were just too greedy and he slid his hand down her belly to the edge of her panties.

His fingers were trembling as he allowed them to brush across her moist center. She tensed the length of a heartbeat before her legs opened for him.

His train of thought quickly derailed as her hips arched toward his fingers. Before he instinctively buried his finger in her hot, hollow cavern, he yanked his hand away.

He couldn't do this! Nothing had changed. Amber was still an amnesiac, still vulnerable.

Her eyes flew open and she clutched at his arm. "Don't stop, Chris. I—I . . . like it when you touch me."

His body flexed at her words, driven by a desire to share the ultimate intimacy with her. In his mind, though, he knew he couldn't. "We can't go any farther, Amber."

She looked close to tears of frustration now. "Why?"

"Because you're vul—"

"I love you, Chris. I know I have trouble with my words sometimes, but I know what I'm saying."

No. Jasmine said patients with PTA were impulsive and trusting. Amber trusted him simply because he'd been the one to find her and care for her. Besides, how could she suddenly understand love when she'd struggled with every other emotion? No, he couldn't trust whatever she thought she felt. It couldn't last.

Amber eased onto the dining room chair Chris had pulled out for her. Melana smiled at her before leaning over to give her a hug. Realizing she felt that same sensation in her heart that she'd felt with Chris a few moments ago, she knew she loved Melana, too. It was such a weird feeling, both pleasure and pain as she thought of how much she'd hurt them and how she never wanted to again.

She gazed at Chris. Yes, she loved him. She hadn't been sure when Jasmine first described the emotion, and it was a vague depiction in her memory right now, but Amber knew the way any woman would know.

Ron carried the steaks into the dining room and set them on the table with the corn on the cob, mashed potatoes and salad.

Amber stared at her hand in her lap, hoping it wouldn't betray her. She hadn't had any seizures today that she could remember, and she definitely didn't want to have one in front of Chris's friend.

"Everybody dig in," Ron suggested. "I haven't had much opportunity to cook since Nell and Kevin left."

Melana fixed her plate and then Chris reached for it. "Do you want me to cut your steak?" he asked her. "I'll cut the corn off the cob, too."

Melana looked insulted, then with a quick glance at Chris grinned and handed him her plate. "Okay. Do you want me to fix your plate, Miss Amber?"

Amber looked at Chris who was paying way too much attention to cutting Melana's steak. "Thanks," she said to Melana.

Ron looked at Amber and she shrugged.

Chris and Melana exchanged plates. He cut Amber's meat and corn as well, then placed the plate in front of her.

"Do I get the VIP treatment, too?" Ron quipped.

Chris winked at Amber. "That's only for the ladies."

She smiled, touched by Chris' thoughtfulness. He had to be the sweetest man ever.

Using her right hand, she pierced a piece of steak with a fork and carried it to her mouth. It was tender and juicy, good enough to rival Mabel's home cooking any day. "This is delicious, Ron."

"Thanks."

Ron caught Chris up on the lives of mutual friends as they ate, and Amber's mind wandered to the few precious minutes she and Chris had just shared. Her body was still sensitive to his touch, quivering whenever his arm brushed hers or their eyes met.

Chris combed his fingers through her hair. "Your head's beginning to hurt, isn't it? Why don't you lie down? I'll get some medicine."

She was beginning to get tired and feel the tinge of a headache. It seemed like it would be disconcerting having someone know what she felt almost before she did, but it wasn't. Instead, she felt . . . safe, protected. And she liked that. "Okay, thanks."

Before Chris could turn around, Amber slid her pants down her legs and crawled onto the bed, allowing him a good look at her sweet derriere.

He buried his fingers in his temples, massaging his own headache. Her faith in him had obviously not been shaken and he wasn't sure a healthy dose of caution wasn't warranted on her part. Even though he hadn't considered making love to another woman since Kimmy's death, his mind had been in two places during lunch—catching up with Ron and lying in the bed next to Amber.

His body tightened at the thought even now.

He pulled the blanket over her legs and sat down with a small space between them. Handing her the glass of water from the nightstand and then the pills, he watched her swallow them.

"Okay, beautiful lady, you rest and I'll see that Melana doesn't wake you."

"She's such a sweet little girl, I don't mind. I miss her when we're apart. Besides, she likes taking care of people, just like you do."

"Is that right?"

Amber scooted down on the bed. "Yep. What kind of work do you do?"

"I'm an engineer."

"Mmm . . . I would've never thought that. Did you want to be a social worker or a therapist when you were growing up?"

"Not really. My dad had a stroke just before I started college. I immediately made plans to stay home and help my mom take care of him but she insisted I go. Every time I could get home, I took over his care to give her a break."

"So you're used to taking care of people, Melana included. What's the plan once she's grown? Who will you take care of then?"

"I guess I could keep you around. Melana says your family must have been mean to you and that's why you can't remember them."

Amber chuckled and closed her eyes. "Do you think that, too?"

"I don't know, but if they did, they won't get another opportunity."

Amber's eyes opened and a smile lurked in their depths. "I may have to hold you to that."

Chris sat with Amber until she dozed off. He hadn't thought about his dad's stroke in a long time. His recovery period had been long, more than a year, and Chris had just done what he was supposed to. Same with Amber, at first. Somewhere along the line, however, taking care of her had become personal.

No one else was going to hurt her.

He kissed her forehead and she turned toward him, as if she could sense his presence even in her sleep. Trying not to make any noise, he closed the door behind him and almost walked into Melana who was hovering in the hallway.

"Isn't it great that we found her?" she asked.

"Yeah, it is."

"She didn't forget us either."

He started down the hallway and Melana fell into step with him. "I don't think she'd ever forget you, Melana. I'm going to the Base Exchange to get her some clothes. Will you stay with her in case she wakes up? I don't want her to be frightened."

"Okay." She brightened. "If she didn't forget us, that must mean she wants to stay with us."

How had she come to that conclusion? "Listen, honey. When I get back from the store, I'm going to start looking for Amber's family—"

Melana spun toward him but quickly controlled her surprised reaction. "You are? How?"

"Searching the Internet, for starters. It's a bit involved," he added, especially when he'd never done a people search. Not to mention he didn't know Kimmy's maiden name. She'd kept her first husband's name after the divorce and had rarely talked about her family.

"Can you get me and Miss Amber matching outfits?"

Chris hesitated a moment. He couldn't keep the bond between the two women from growing if he wanted to—which he didn't—so why deny her? "Okay. Don't wake Miss Amber after I leave, okay? She needs to rest."

Smiling, she looked as sweet as an angel. "I won't, Daddy."

* * *

Amber stretched and rolled over, right into Melana.

Her frown was ferocious. "It's about time! I thought you were never gonna wake up." She sounded grieved.

"We're you missing me?"

"Yeah." Melana crawled into the bed beside Amber. "You know what? I never saw Daddy so scared before. I was scared, too."

Amber put her arms around Melana. "I didn't mean to frighten you."

"Why did you leave?"

"I don't know. I thought . . . I thought . . ."

It all seemed so clear at the time but right now she couldn't think of one reason to have put them through so much distress.

"It's okay. You were on a great adventure, right? And you had lots of fun, but you probably don't want to go on anymore without me and Daddy."

"That's what Chris said, not to leave him again. Or was that a dream?" Amber sighed. One downside to amnesia was never knowing what was real. Sometimes she couldn't recall exactly what Chris said or did but she always remembered his kindness.

"I heard him say it, when he hugged you. You should do what Daddy says because he's always right. Except about getting cell phones. But he bought me one. See."

Melana pulled a small silver phone from the pocket of her dress and Amber dutifully admired it before noticing the dress. It was pink and she didn't remember seeing it in Melana's suitcase. "You look pretty. Did Chris buy you a new outfit, too?"

"He went to the BX and got both of us lots of stuff."

Amber noticed the bags near the door. How long had she been asleep? "What's a BX?"

"Base Exchange. It's like Walmart, but it's on the base. Daddy was going to wash my hair, but I thought you might want to, if your hand doesn't shake."

Her hand had remained steady through lunch, so she thought it might be okay. "I'd love to."

"Daddy bought you a pink sundress, too."

"He did? Well, why I don't wear it so we'll look alike. People will think we're twins."

Melana giggled. "Do you think you'll stay with us forever?"

"I guess so, since Chris said he never wants me to leave."

"All right! I told Daddy we should adopt you. I was adopted, too," she whispered in a confiding tone. "But Daddy loves me more than anybody in the world, and now he loves you, too."

Did Chris love her? She'd have to ask him. Or not. What if he said *no*? She realized she was afraid and wondered why.

Amber and Melana were sitting together on the couch. Amber had washed and dried Melana's hair, and though they had both seemed to enjoy it, around six o'clock, Amber began to look flushed. Side by side with their heads close together, it was hard to miss the resemblance between them, and Chris had seen Ron's curious gaze resting on them.

Amber had kept close to Chris, though they hadn't had a chance to talk with Ron and Melana hovering. Every time he even attempted to get near Ron's computer, Melana would go into a near panic. For her sake, he'd decided to put off the search until tomorrow, but he wouldn't give in again.

From some of Amber's statements, he could tell she wasn't sure if today's events were reality or a dream. It was probably best that way, he decided.

He saw her lay her head back and close her eyes as Melana chattered, so happy to have Amber back. "Why don't you go to bed, Amber?" he suggested. "It's been a long day."

"I think I will," she said, standing. "Did you want to come with me?"

Chris' gaze flew to Melana and Ron, both of whom were looking at him curiously. "No. I'll, uh, I'll come check on you in a little while."

Melana jumped up. "I'll go with you."

Amber smiled at the little girl before taking her hand, and they left together.

Ron shook his head. "Man, until today I thought you were one of the smartest guys I knew."

"She didn't mean it like that. She's innocent."

Ron laughed. "You always were one to take the high road—"

"Don't start—"

Ron had been a playa up until the day he proposed to Nell and probably still had a wandering eye.

Ron put his hands up in an innocent gesture. "I'm just saying, if I had a honey looking at me the way she looks at you . . ."

Chris let his head drop back on the couch. "She's just too vulnerable. I already made one mistake, and I won't make another. One statement sent her off alone and defenseless. She could've been raped or killed or . . . just gone."

"You can't blame yourself, and she's fine. Don't beat yourself up."

"She told me she loves me, but I don't think she remembers that. Or at least I hope I don't. I don't think."

What the hell? Was *he* suddenly having brain trouble?

"Chris, no offense, man, but you sound like a blubbering idiot. What's the problem? In English."

"She doesn't even know her own name. She has no memory of anything before five days ago and even that's spotty. Should I continue?"

"Where did she come from?"

"Beats me. She showed up at my house, hurt. She had five IDs with names all with the initials AN, and that's all I know."

"She and Mel . . . have you noticed the resemblance? It's subtle . . ."

"But it's there. I think she's one of Kimmy's sisters, and she's come for Mel. They are her blood relatives."

"But you're the only father she's ever known."

"I'm going to have to contact Kimmy's family. I know she has a brother in Florida. Jace, I think. I can probably get his last name from Kimmy's ex-husband. Amber should be with her family, if they're good to her. Don't you think?"

Ron gave him an odd look. "Whatever you say, man."

CHAPTER 8

Chris saw Melana's reflection on the computer screen the next morning. "Hey, sweetie."

"Hi, Daddy."

He glanced at the clock on the bottom right hand side of the screen to see what time it was. Nine o'clock. He thought Melana would be upset when she saw him using the computer, but she only smiled. A little too brightly, he decided. "Where's Amber?"

"Still asleep. I tried to wake her up, but I guess she's tired."

"Are you hungry? I can fix you something."

"Nah. I just want some cereal and fruit. Where's Uncle Ron?"

"Work."

Melana strode into the kitchen and he went back to his search for Kimmy's ex-husband. It was going to take longer than he first thought. He'd already checked in with the base through an assigned eight-hundred number. There was no projected return date, so he didn't have that worry. He'd also searched several Web sites for more information about amnesia, but learned little more than what Jasmine had told him.

"I'm going to check on Amber. I'll be right back."

She was curled up on her left side, her note firmly clasped in her hand. He carefully removed it and saw with some surprise her latest entries. *Never leave Chris again* and *I love Chris.*

He pocketed the note—it was for the best really—then reached in to remove the troublesome thing and tossed it back onto the nightstand. He couldn't take her memories away. "Amber?" Her eyes opened, instantly alert. "How are you feeling?" he asked, somewhat disconcerted.

Amber stretched and rolled onto her side facing him, and she never looked more stunning. "I feel like I want to make love with you."

He leapt back and almost tripped on the rug. *"What?"*

"I read this great and very informative magazine last night." She pointed to a *Cosmopolitan* with "The Multiple Orgasm" printed in bold letters across the cover on the nightstand.

Well, it was his fault for asking. "Listen, Amber." How did he even begin to explain? "You can't just tell people everything you think and feel."

She appeared to ponder his statement and then looked at him with a frown. "But you asked me how I was feeling."

He did, didn't he? "Okay. If anyone else asks you how you're feeling, just say *fine.*"

"The article described how a woman's body feels when she's making love. Will you touch me there and make me feel that way?"

"No!" Dammit. He'd seen the magazines. Why hadn't he gone through the stack to see what they were? "That's private. Your private area and nobody can touch you there, not even me."

He knew he was doing a full one-eighty from yesterday but she could barely remember, and he wasn't going to touch her again until her memory returned. It just wasn't right.

Her hands balled into fists. "No."

The firmness in her voice threw him off guard, but he rallied. "Yes! Now write it down. On your note," he said, gesturing wildly.

"No!"

Melana burst into the room. "What's all the yelling about?"

Amber spun toward Melana, her dark eyes fiery and tempestuous. "Chris—"

"Nothing," he interrupted before Amber could share the unnecessary details. "Go finish your breakfast, Melana. I need to talk to Amber."

Amber threw her legs over the side of the bed. "I want some breakfast."

"Stay right there," he warned.

Both Amber and Melana looked at him with wide eyes. His daughter scampered out of the room as Amber turned toward him.

"Don't use that tone of voice with me."

"What tone of voice?" he asked, crossing his arms.

He knew by the way her eyes narrowed that she understood the challenge in his question. Of course, if she could put a name to his tone, the point would go to her. Even though he and Kimmy had never argued, he didn't mind arguing with Amber, but her penchant for running away whenever they disagreed wasn't working for him.

"You're trying to boss me around, but nobody bosses me. You got that?"

She poked him in the chest with that last statement and he chuckled, totally disarmed by her temper.

"You think I don't remember things," she continued, thrusting her hands onto her hips. "But that doesn't mean—"

Her night shirt rode up, exposing her thighs. As he stared, riveted, he knew he was about to lose this argument.

"What are you looking at?" she demanded.

"You—" He forced his gaze to meet her. "You need some clothes on."

That was another thing they were going to straighten out today.

"Well, generally I bathe undressed, and I'm about to get in the shower."

She stripped off her shirt—he never saw that coming!—and strode toward the bathroom in her bra and panties. Unable to stop himself, he started laughing.

Amber turned around. "What's so funny?"

"Come here. Please," he added when she didn't move.

She retraced her steps back to the bed, her hair swaying side-to-side as she moved. Her fire diminished to the level of a burning ember—which could be more troublesome—as she slid onto the mattress.

"I don't like being angry or arguing. I don't even know why we were angry or arguing."

At this point, he didn't know either.

"You treat me like a kid, that's what it is. And that makes me very angry."

But he didn't see her as a kid. She was very much a woman, and that was most of his problem!

"I can't always remember what's real and that's . . . what's the word?"

"Frustrating." An emotion he could relate to very well at this moment.

"Yeah, so . . . sorry," she almost spat, as if even the idea of apologizing was distasteful.

Chris suppressed a grin. "I'm sorry, too."

"So, we're friends again?" she asked pensively.

"I guess I can put up with your temperamental behind." She plopped her fists on her hips, and laughing, he pulled Amber to her feet and hugged her. "I was just teasing. Nothing can rock our six-day friendship."

"Is that how long it's been? Seems like it's at least . . . eight."

Her eyes crinkled with her smile and little lines fanned out from the edges. She was so gorgeous.

Before he could stop himself, his lips lowered to hers.

"I don't hear any yelling!" Melana hollered through the door. "What are you guys doing?"

Amber felt better after her shower. She dressed in a turquoise capri set Chris had bought and then found him and Melana in the living room.

He offered her an appreciative gaze from his seat in front of the computer as Melana scooted over to give her room on the sofa.

The news was on and Amber glanced at the little girl curiously. "Why are you watching the news, kiddo?"

Melana stared straight ahead, her lips set in a mutinous line. "I'm not."

"I'm watching for any reports that you're missing," Chris told her.

"Oh." She looked at Melana. That would explain the face she was making.

"I'm also—" he began.

"Do you want to sit on the patio with me?" Melana interrupted almost desperately.

Willing to do almost anything to get that anxious look out of Melana's eyes, Amber agreed. "Sure."

Chris's eyes narrowed on Melana before he turned back to the computer, and Amber followed her outside into the cool air. "It's fall, right?"

Melana looked stricken. "Are you remembering?"

"No, the leaves are falling off the tree so I just figured. What month is it?"

"This is the first day of October."

"So what is your dad doing that you don't want me to know about?"

Her bottom lip popped out. "Looking for someone who knows you."

"My family?"

Melana's right shoulder rose and fell.

"There's bound to be someone, don't you think?" Amber asked softly. In response, huge tears spilled onto Melana's cheeks. Feeling all mushy inside, Amber pulled the child onto her lap and held her. "No matter what happens, Melana, I won't leave you, okay? I promise."

Melana laid her head on Amber's shoulder.

"You know what we should do?" she asked to cheer the little girl. "We should have a girls' night. We can pop some popcorn and watch movies until we fall asleep."

Melana straightened. "We can ask Uncle Ron to get us some movies on his way home. What about the *Princess Diaries*? I'll call him to see when he's coming home."

They went inside together. Chris set the phone down and scratched a line across a piece of paper on the desk. He looked at Melana and she turned her head. His left brow shot up but he didn't say anything.

His gaze switched to Amber. "Do you want to know what I'm doing?"

Cupping Melana's cheek, she shook her head. Whether it was normal or not was probably up for debate, but she didn't feel a burning desire to discover her identity. It wasn't a fear of finding anything negative. She'd just grown fond of Chris and Melana and didn't want to leave them.

"We're going to have to talk about it eventually," he warned.

Amber glanced around the dark bedroom, wondering what had awakened her. A loud boom made her wince and she closed her eyes against the noise. It was raining. Listening closely, she could hear the rain falling.

She peeked out from one eye to confirm what she'd heard and saw water streaming down the window.

Melana was asleep beside her and rolled over as Amber watched. Distracted, she smiled at the little girl. Melana had stayed right by her side to make sure Chris didn't mention her family, but he never said a word. She could tell he was torn, but resolute. And, of course, they couldn't go on like this indefinitely.

As requested, Ron had come home with the *Princess Diaries* as well as *Ella Enchanted*. Amber hadn't been sure Melana could sit through two movies, but she'd munched popcorn and a caramel apple while sipping orange soda late into the night.

She glanced at the clock. Almost five a.m.

Yawning, she eased out of the bed and slipped into the robe Chris brought her. As she padded barefoot down the hallway, the rain began to fall harder, the thunder to boom a little louder. Her head began to hurt, but she hoped the pain would pass.

Chris was asleep on the sofa bed, and she watched him. He'd looked a little lost by Melana's cold-shoulder treatment, but she'd buckled first, giving him a big hug just before dinner.

His feelings for his daughter were quite clear. It was how he felt about Amber that confused her. She didn't have to have her memory intact to know Chris liked kissing her. She knew that the way all women knew.

She just couldn't figure out why he kept holding back.

A loud clap of thunder had her simultaneously reaching for the remote and diving under the covers beside Chris. She pressed her palms to her temples. If the pain didn't stop in a few minutes, she'd take some medicine.

He must have fallen asleep watching the news. She watched for a few minutes before pushing the channel button. When she got to Lifetime, she stopped to see how long the movie had been on. It was about to go off and there was another one coming on.

Closing her eyes to block the light, she snuggled beside Chris to wait. His arm curled around her and she lay there enjoying the feel of his body pressed against her.

She listened to his heartbeat and counted each one. They were strong and steady—like Chris, and like her relationship with him, there was a barrier blocking direct contact. This physical wall protecting his heart, she couldn't break through. What about the emotional one?

"Chris?" She touched his mouth with her fingertip, and his lips parted slightly. "Chris?"

His only response was to squeeze her closer to him.

She relished the sensation, wanting to be nowhere else but in this man's arms. She wouldn't wake him, she decided. They could talk in the morning.

The movie's introduction began to play, and she started to turn over to watch. Before she could pull away, Chris rolled partially on top of her, lodging one knee between her thighs. He pressed into her with a light rhythmic pressure and her eyes rolled back in her head. Held captive by the weakness invading her body, she didn't move. She didn't breathe.

His hand tangled in her hair as his lips found hers. She tried to resist at first, afraid he would awaken and pull away from her. He dragged his hand across her sensitive body to her breasts, leaving a trail of heat despite the clothes blocking flesh-to-flesh contact.

He squeezed her nipple—not painfully—but hard enough to make her gasp as desire rippled through her in an outward arc. With her mouth open, he took the opportunity to slip his tongue into her mouth, and groaning, she found herself twisting her tongue with his as all resistance faded.

She wasn't wearing a bra and the soft cotton shirt provided little barrier, but, as if he weren't satisfied, he yanked the material down and cupped one breast and then the other. Her head spun and she felt as if she were falling and soaring at the same time.

Long past any pretense of trying to hold back, she drew his hand to the spot between her thighs, remembering the pleasure she'd felt before. "Touch me, here, Chris. *Please.*"

Her body jumped and twisted with desire as he stopped at the edge of her panties. His hand rested on her lower belly and, quivering, she waited anxiously. Finally, his fingers slipped beneath the edge of her panties, and her breath froze in anticipation. He traced a circle around the bead of her sex, pressed and circled again. She opened her mouth, but the plea never left her lips as his finger plunged deep inside her. Shuddering, she closed her eyes as sensations coursed through her. Her thighs trembled open, welcoming, demanding. He continued kissing her as she rotated her hips, rising to meet each thrust.

He pushed a second finger into her softness and she toppled right over the edge. She clenched, resisting the fall and soared. He ravaged her mouth as she lay spent, sucking, nibbling. He drew her to his hardness, clamped her hand around him, and she automatically slid her hand up and down his hot, silky length.

"Kimmy . . ." he moaned.

Amber froze. Kimmy?

Stunned, Amber's hand froze as she tried to remember who Kimmy was. He began to stir so she quickly disengaged herself and jumped up, hitting the remote with her knee in the process. He had only touched her like that because he thought she was another woman?

Not wanting him to see her, she fled from the room before he could fully awaken. Before she could reach the safety of the bedroom, Ron barreled around a corner—already dressed in his military uniform—and they ran into each other.

"Hey! Where are you going in such a hurry?" His humor faded as he looked at her closely. "Amber? What's wrong?"

Shivering, she rubbed her arms with her hands. "Nothing."

"You're upset." He glanced at his wrist before offering her a wry grin. "Forgot my watch. Come with me so you can tell me what's wrong."

"Where?"

"My room. I need to get my watch—"

She didn't follow as he started toward his bedroom but leaned back against the wall. Ron had been nice to her and she knew he was a good guy, but she didn't think she should go in his bedroom.

When he realized she wasn't following him, he stopped and turned around. He leaned against the opposite wall. "Okay, what happened? Did you and Chris get into an argument?"

"No. Who's Kimmy?"

"She is—or was—Chris' wife. She died in a car accident."

That sounded vaguely familiar, though neither Chris nor Melana had mentioned her since they'd been here. "And he liked to kiss her, right?"

Yeah, it was coming back now, the conversation she'd had after Chris's friend . . . Jasmine examined her.

"I would think so," Ron said dryly.

"They were a part of each other." She let her head drop back against the wall as total recall hit her like a fist to the jaw. "He *loves* her."

"Yeah," Ron said with a sour expression Amber could relate to. "But he . . ."

Ron trailed off, looking miserable, and Amber touched his shoulder. "Don't feel bad. We can't help who we love, right?"

Because if she could, she'd stop loving Chris right now!

Chris reached for Amber and instead got a handful of pillow. He buried his face in the thick material and sighed as her scent filled his senses. She was everywhere, even in his dreams. He'd known if he opened his eyes, she'd disappear. It had seemed so real, though. Amber had come to him, asking him to touch her. She had been free in her response to him, open.

The thought that Kimmy had never responded to him like that had made him guiltily try to conjure her image into his mind, but the attempt had left him feeling empty and alone.

He heard someone moaning and looked up to see a couple having sex in a hot tub. Squinting, he noticed a small bunny in the right hand corner. He didn't remember leaving the TV on last night, especially not on the Playboy channel.

Hearing footsteps, Chris groped the blanket for the remote. This wasn't anything Amber or Melana needed to see as it could lead to two different discussions, depending on the female. Neither of which he wanted to have.

Ron strolled into the room wearing his BDUs—a green camouflaged military uniform—and glanced at the TV with amusement. "Taking care of that early morning hard-on yourself?"

Stretching, Chris spotted the remote at the foot of the bed, grabbed it, and changed the channel to the news. He'd stayed glued to the tube, watching for any reports of a missing woman fitting Amber's description but nothing so far. "Is that why you shell out a monthly fee for the premium channel?" he shot back.

Ron laughed. "No, I have a woman for that. Speaking of which, our girl's hurting. She ran into me in the hallway. I invited her to my bedroom for a little chat, but she wouldn't go. I tell you what, though, if she looked at me the way she looks at you, she wouldn't have to ask me to come to bed."

Chris rubbed his eyes, blinded by Ron's gleaming smile. "Did she say why she was upset?"

"Yeah. She has to be the most honest woman I've ever met. No pretence about her."

"That's because she doesn't know to be embarrassed or ashamed, to lie. She has the innocence of a child."

It was too damned early to have this conversation.

"Well, she's encased in a roughly twenty-five-year-old body. Your love life is your own and if you don't get it together, you'll be in it alone."

A part of Chris knew Ron was right. A year ago, he'd closed off his heart to all women. In essence, he'd died with Kimmy, but Amber was showing him how much more living he had to do.

"I can appreciate this almost angelic spin you've woven about Kimmy and your marriage, but it's time to face facts."

"Yeah, yeah, yeah. It's time to move on, find a mother for Melana. You've said that before."

"I did, didn't I? But the facts I'm talking about relate to the aforementioned spin you've woven. Your marriage wasn't all that and, deep inside, you know it."

"What?"

"You never argued, right? How realistic is that? Love is messy. Sometimes you say hurtful things, you do hurtful things. It's like you two were so afraid of losing each other, you couldn't be natural. I'm not a shrink but it seemed a little too co-dependent to me."

"Why would we be afraid to lose each other?"

"Well, you were caught up in having the perfect marriage like your folks, if there's any such thing, and who in hell knows Kim's motivations. I never really cared for her anyway."

Chris stared at his friend, dumbfounded. Where had

all this come from? Ron had never said anything like this before.

"Anything on Kimmy's ex yet? It'd be interesting to get his take on her. He had to run off for some reason."

Chris just didn't get it. What in the world did Amber say to set all this off? "I've narrowed the list to three and left messages. Hopefully, I'll get a response today."

"All right. I'm off to work, then. Kiss the kids for me."

Chris grimaced at Ron's offhanded remark. Kissing Melana that first night was what had set everything with Amber into motion. He should've shaken her hand. That he could handle with Amber. Maybe.

Well, he could always count on Ron to say it how it was, but how it was wasn't always what it was. Wait—What?

Chris sighed. Better deal with Amber, he decided.

First, he folded the blanket and secured the bed inside the couch, his mind scrambling for comebacks he'd wished he'd had during Ron's unflattering assessment of his marriage and still coming up short. True, he and Kimmy had never argued, but that just wasn't their nature.

He stopped outside the bedroom door, knocked, and waited for Amber to answer. Had she gone back to sleep? Testing the knob to see if it was locked, he flicked it to the right and entered. She and Melana were both curled up on their sides, facing the wall.

He saw Amber's note on the bedside table and looked closer. Beneath her confession of love for him was *Chris loves Kimmy.* Why would she write that?

Kimmy. The ache of losing his wife touched him again, but only briefly and with less pain than usual. Was he finally ready to let go?

He sat down beside Amber and laid his hand on her arm.

She glanced over her shoulder, and then sat up quickly. "Chris? What's wrong?"

"Ron said you were upset?"

Her gaze skittered away from his, something he'd never seen her do before.

"I'm fine."

"Are you saying that because I told you to, or because it's true?"

"I just don't want to talk about it, Chris."

She looked so dejected, and he felt really bad about that, but knowing she could talk to Ron and not him grated on his nerves. "Since when did you start confiding in Ron? Usually you tell me everything."

"I didn't tell him everything."

When her eyes met his with their usual boldness, he knew she was telling him the truth, and he felt a little better. "You don't want to tell me what's bothering you?"

She shook her head.

"Amber? Never mind," he said impatiently. He couldn't force her to share something she wasn't ready to tell him. "I'll see you later."

CHAPTER 9

Amber pretended to be asleep until Melana left the bedroom. She knew she couldn't hide out in bed all day but she wasn't ready to face Chris. Seeing him earlier had been bad enough when she didn't know if he'd figured out she had been in the bed with him.

Having already showered, she slipped into a pair of jeans and blue T-shirt and straightened the bedroom. She gathered the soda cans, apple cores, and the bowl with the unpopped kernels and carried them out of the room.

She saw Chris leaning against the wall in the breakfast nook and staring out onto the patio. His head swung around in her direction as she entered the kitchen. It took everything in her to meet his gaze, but she did it.

Without saying a word, he turned back to the patio. So now he was giving her the cold shoulder, huh? Well, fine.

She set the items on the counter and stormed into the living room. She stopped when she saw Melana looking at a calendar on the desk. "Guess what? Tomorrow's Daddy's birthday. Do you want to have a party?"

Amber almost laughed. Instead she buried her forehead in her hands. Here she was mad at Chris—again—and why? He couldn't help who he loved anymore than she could. "That sounds wonderful, honey."

"He'll be very surprised. We haven't celebrated birthdays since . . . forever. We can get a cake, a card, and decorations!"

"Why haven't you celebrated birthdays?"

"Because Daddy didn't want Kimmy to feel bad when she forgot."

Kimmy? Why did Melana call her mother by her first name? Did she already explain that? "She forgot a lot?"

"Birthdays and stuff. Remember I told you?"

No, she didn't remember. What irony. Why hadn't Chris mentioned his birthday?

"I'll call Uncle Ron to see if he'll help us since we don't have any money."

"I have money. I think," she added. Where did she put the money she found in the pocket of her red shorts? "Why don't we get Uncle Ron to take Chris to work tomorrow, then we can walk to the . . . BX, did you call it? And have everything set up when they get back.

Jumping up and down, Melana hugged Amber. "You have the best ideas! I'll call him on my cell phone," she added with an impish grin.

Melana loved that phone and took every opportunity to use it.

An hour later, Amber was in the kitchen, torn between getting something to eat and making peace with Chris when he strolled in and opened the refrigerator.

She caught herself staring at him and turned toward the counter. He might have dreamed last night with Kimmy, but Amber knew it was real and her body clenched remembering.

He reached around her to open the cupboard, his body directly behind her. She leaned back so he could open the door and stepped into him.

Her mind shot off in several directions as she contemplated running, staying, apologizing, explaining. Unable to grasp any of the alternatives, she waited.

She felt his breath on her neck and her belly quivered.

"You all right?"

The tenderness in his voice made her eyes roll back in her head. "Yeah, I—I"

He pulled the glass from the cupboard and stepped back, giving her room to think. Without his support, her legs trembled and she gripped the counter.

"Want something to drink?" he asked.

It was hot all of a sudden. "No, thanks. What—have you found out anything about me?" she asked before she realized what she was saying.

He glanced toward the door. To make sure Melana wasn't nearby, Amber guessed. "I think you're related to Kimmy."

"*What?*" Her nemesis?

"She has this crazy mixed up family—no offense. The short story is her family disowned her and you and Mel have physical similarities that can't be ignored."

"We do have the same color hair and we're both tall, but that could be coincidence." There was no way she was related to that woman.

"It could be, but it's worth checking out. Kimmy has a brother named Jace. I don't know his last name, so I've been trying to find her ex-husband. I zeroed in on three men, and I'm waiting to hear back."

Amber stared at Chris, her words lost to her again,

but not due to amnesia. Chris could be her brother-in-law.

Ron smirked at Chris from his position next to Amber on the couch. His friend was smitten with her and not bothering to hide it. Ron was also trying to make Chris jealous and the hell if it wasn't working.

Chris couldn't deny he was attracted to Amber. She was open and honest and maybe he'd stifled that by telling her not to share everything she thought or felt, but he'd done that to protect her. She had to learn self-restraint, for her own safety.

Chris turned back to the computer screen but didn't see anything. Ever since Ron had come home, he and Amber had been inseparable, talking in the kitchen as he cooked lasagna for dinner, then in the living room as Chris cleaned the kitchen after they'd eaten.

Ron had about five more minutes to end this farce before Chris did it for him.

"Hey, man, I told some of the fellas you were in town. I thought we could drive over to the compound together in the morning."

Chris shook his head. "I don't think I should leave Mel and Amber . . ."

"I'll have you back by lunch time."

"We'll be fine, Chris," Amber said.

"I guess it'll be okay," he admitted reluctantly. It would be cool to see some of his old buddies.

He heard a musical sound and glanced around curiously until he realized it was his cell phone. Everyone froze, then Chris looked at Melana whose lips turned down as if she were about to cry. To prepare her for this moment, he'd explained that he was waiting for a call about Amber.

He pushed the talk button and put the phone to his ear. "Hello?"

"Hi. Is this Chris?" A woman's voice came through the phone, soft and uncertain.

"Yes."

"You left a message for Tyrone Anderson? It sounded important so I wanted to let you know he passed away six months ago."

"I'm sorry to hear that," Chris said.

"Thanks. He was my husband, and I'm sure he was never married to the woman you mentioned."

"Well, I appreciate you calling to let me know."

"You're welcome and good luck with your search."

"Thanks." Sighing, Chris clicked the off button and set the phone on the desk. "Wrong guy," he told the others.

"Good!" Melana snapped.

Amber put her hand on Melana's head and twisted her head until they were face to face. *I love you,* she mouthed, and Melana jumped onto her lap for a hug.

Ron put his arms around both of them and Chris ground his teeth. "Amber, may I speak to you in the kitchen?"

Ron's silly grin set Chris' teeth on edge.

"I'm really tired, Chris," she said, standing. "Is it okay if we talk in the morning?"

Unable to force her to talk to him, he stifled his disappointment. "Sure. Okay."

Melana jumped up and grabbed Amber's hand. "I'm going to bed, too. Good night, Daddy."

Chris watched them walk away and slumped back in his chair.

"Blew that, huh?" Ron quipped. "It's probably all that glaring you're doing. You're scaring the girl."

"This is just a frustrating situation. I can't believe it's taken this long to track someone down."

"You sure that's it? Because I'm seeing green."

Ron sauntered into the kitchen, whistling, and Chris followed Amber and Melana. "Amber?" They both stopped and turned toward him. "Mel, go on to bed. I just need a minute with Amber."

Mel trotted off and when Chris stepped closer to Amber, she backed away.

He sighed. "Are you ready to tell me what's bothering you?"

He knew the idea of her being related to Kimmy had thrown her for a loop. In fact, she'd seemed downright disgusted by the thought. But she'd become upset before then.

"Nothing's wrong, Chris. I felt frustrated again because I forgot something, but I won't forget again."

That last phrase sounded almost angry. "What did you forget?"

"Do you think you'll always be in love with Kimmy?"

Chris rolled his eyes toward the ceiling. "Just because someone dies doesn't mean you stop loving them, Amber."

"I guess, but you should at least bury her."

Sharp laughter erupted from his mouth before he could stop it. He saw Amber's consternation and laughed even more.

"I didn't mean to say that. I mean, I meant it, but I didn't mean to say it out loud."

She looked further dismayed by her explanation before burying her face in her hands.

Clearing his throat to stop the last of the chuckles, he pulled her hands away. "I'm sorry I told you not to share your thoughts and feelings with people. I think that's what I like most about you, your directness."

"And I like it when you laugh. You should do it more often."

He carried her hands to his chest and held them between his. "I haven't had much to laugh about, but I think that's changing."

Amber and Melana were up early the next morning. Chris would be leaving with Ron and Melana wanted to be the first person to wish him a happy birthday.

He was in the living room when they walked in and Melana flung herself into his arms. "Happy birthday, Daddy!"

Amber saw his stunned expression and realized he hadn't thought twice about today being his birthday.

"Thank you, honey. I'm surprised you remembered."

"I always remember."

Ron was standing by the door and Melana rushed over to him. Amber put her arms around Chris' neck and kissed him lightly on the cheek. "Happy birthday, my friend."

"Is that all I get?"

"For now," she said with a playful grin. She heard Melana muttering something about kissing being gross and chuckled. "That's a good attitude for her to have, huh?"

"For at least the next fifty years."

"We'd better go, Chris. Can't be late."

"You two will be okay? I left my cell phone number on the desk. Call if you need anything."

"Okay, don't worry," Amber told him.

Chris was barely out the door before Melana squealed and started pulling out the decorations Ron had slipped into the closet last night. Turned out the

An Important Message From The ARABESQUE Publisher

Dear Arabesque Reader,

I invite you to join the club! The Arabesque book club delivers four novels each month right to your front door! It's easy, and you will never miss a romance by one of our award-winning authors!

With upcoming novels featuring strong, sexy women, and African-American heroes that are charming, loving and true… you won't want to miss a single release. Our authors fill each page with exceptional dialogue, exciting plot twists, and enough sizzling romance to keep you riveted until the satisfying end! To receive novels by bestselling authors such as Gwynne Forster, Janice Sims, Angela Winters and others, I encourage you to join now!

Read about the men we love… in the pages of Arabesque!

Linda Gill
PUBLISHER, ARABESQUE ROMANCE NOVELS

P.S. Watch out for the next Summer Series "Ports Of Call" that will take you to the exotic locales of Venice, Fiji, the Caribbean and Ghana! You won't need a passport to travel, just collect all four novels to enjoy romance around the world! For more details, visit us at www.BET.com.

A SPECIAL "THANK YOU" FROM ARABESQUE JUST FOR YOU!

Send this card back and you'll receive 4 FREE Arabesque Novels—a $25.96 value—absolutely FREE!

The introductory 4 Arabesque Romance books are yours FREE (plus $1.99 shipping & handling). If you wish to continue to receive 4 books every month, do nothing. Each month, we will send you 4 New Arabesque Romance Novels for your free examination. If you wish to keep them, pay just $18* (plus, $1.99 shipping & handling). If you decide not to continue, you owe nothing!

- Send no money now.
- Never an obligation.
- Books delivered to your door!

We hope that after receiving your FREE books you'll want to remain an Arabesque subscriber, but the choice is yours! So why not take advantage of this Arabesque offer, with no risk of any kind. You'll be glad you did!

In fact, we're so sure you will love your Arabesque novels, that we will send you an Arabesque Tote Bag FREE with your first paid shipment.

* PRICES SUBJECT TO CHANGE.

YOU'LL GET 4 SELECT ROMANCES PLUS THIS FABULOUS TOTE BAG!

Visit us at:
www.BET.com

BX wasn't in walking distance and Amber couldn't get in without a military ID, so Ron had done all the shopping yesterday.

"Can I help you decorate the cake?" Melana asked.

"You sure can. Are you sure your dad likes butter pecan?"

"He likes pecans, so he must like pecan cake, right?"

"I guess so."

She and Melana spent the morning decorating the living room and cooking barbecue ribs, baked beans, and coleslaw for lunch. Amber hadn't been sure she could cook until she realized she could recall the recipes.

She pulled her note from the pocket of her denim skirt and laid it on the counter. Smiling, she read each sentence, recalling when she'd written each one. She figured she must be out of the posttraumatic stage of her amnesia because she could remember everything since they'd been at Ron's house.

"They'll be here any minute now," Melana shouted from beneath a mound of balloons she'd blown up herself.

Chris was going to be so surprised. She'd seen his suspicious glances whenever she talked to Ron, but he couldn't have figured out they were throwing him a party.

Some of his military friends would be here, too. Chris would think they're coming to meet her and say hi to Melana. They would only be able to stay for about an hour, then she and Melana would have him to themselves for the rest of the afternoon.

She opened the oven and the heat made her step back. Pulling the pan from inside, she lifted the foil and took a whiff of the honey barbecue sauce. The ribs smelled delicious.

"They're here, they're here." Melana ran into the kitchen and grabbed Amber's hand. "Let's stand by the door and say *surprise* when he comes in."

Amber gave Melana a quick hug before following her. She loved her daddy so much. What type of relationship did Amber have with her father, she wondered?

The door opened and Chris walked in first, with Ron and five or six other men behind them.

"Surprise!" Everyone yelled as Melana threw her arms around his waist. "Are you surprised, Daddy?"

"I sure am!" he said, hugging her. His gaze met Amber's and she saw something she'd never seen in his eyes before, a softness, an openness. He leaned over Melana and kissed her.

"Thank you," he whispered into her mouth. Then he closed his lips over hers, sealing his breath inside her body. She closed her eyes and allowed him to fill her.

"Will you two cut it out?" Melana shouldered them apart. "We're trying to have a party here!"

Amber heard the men laughing and opened her eyes. Chris wasn't laughing. He just looked at her with that something in his eyes.

"Wasn't that a cool party, Daddy?" Melana asked, picking up a couple of dirty plates.

Chris stacked the used paper cups before carrying them into the kitchen. "The best one ever."

"We should have a party every year!"

Amber listened to their conversation with a smile. From the way everybody ate, she'd say the party was a success. Chris had looked impressed with the cake, then embarrassed when they sang the birthday song.

Her gaze swept across the paper she'd left on the counter and she reached for it.

"Writing something else down?" Chris asked as he grabbed more dirty dishes.

"Actually," she said, following him into the kitchen. "I'm ready to throw it away. I don't need it anymore."

Melana was carrying a couple of plates into the kitchen when Amber pitched the note. It floated and twisted in the air until it landed on top of the garbage can face down.

She noticed something written on the back and looked closer just as Chris stepped toward it.

"Honor, the model?" he asked. "What does that mean?"

Amber squeezed her eyes shut, trying to remember. "The girl . . . at the diner. She . . . thought—She showed me a picture of a woman on a magazine and she thought I was her." The picture faded from her mind and Amber groaned in frustration. "I thought . . . that wasn't a dream?"

Amber heard a crashing sound behind her and spun around to see several broken plates on the floor at Melana's feet. The little girl went into a frenzy picking up the broken pieces and pushing them down into the trash bag on top of the paper. "It was a dream, wasn't it, Daddy?"

"Mel—" he began.

"Somebody told you during your adventure, right?" Melana interrupted. "You wrote it down and now you believe it."

Amber put her hands on the little girl's shoulders to stop her before she cut herself. "It's okay, Melana. Go wash your hands. I'll clean up this mess."

"You won't leave?" she asked, her voice high-pitched, desperate.

"No, honey." She spoke calmly, hoping to soothe the little girl's fear.

Taking a shuddering breath, Melana ran off and Amber stooped down to pick up the rest of the pieces.

Chris knelt beside her. "You remember, don't you? What's your name?"

Their eyes met. "Cai. Cai McIntyre."

Cai pulled a chair next to Chris as he sat down in front of the computer. He typed her name into the search engine with no results, and then Honor and model. A picture of a tall, light-skinned woman with curly, auburn hair showed up on the screen.

"That's my sister," Cai said, her voice cracking. "But I don't understand. The last time I saw her she was fourteen and chubby. She looks like a grown woman, and she's skinny."

"What else do you remember?"

A subdued Melana crept back into the room and stopped beside Cai's chair. Cai pulled the little girl onto her lap. "I have another sister, Mia."

Just the two, so that ruled out any chance of Kimmy being related. Amber would have had herself adopted out at this late age to avoid the relation, so this saved her having to break legal ground.

"You're leaving, aren't you?" Melana asked in a small voice.

Cai hesitated, torn and not wanting to hurt the little girl any more than she was already. In a rash moment, she'd promised the little girl she wouldn't leave her, but ultimately it was up to Chris how much of a relationship they had. "I have a family who loves me. I don't want them to worry."

"What's your real name?"

"Cai."

"Where do you live? Far away?"

Cai thought for a moment. "Ohio. Columbus, I think. That's not too far."

She could live in Timbuktu and that wouldn't be too far to come see this little girl.

Chris turned toward them. "It doesn't look as though anyone's reported you missing. Have any idea what type of job you have?"

Cai shook her head. "The last I remember is working the concession stand at a movie theatre when I was sixteen. But I can't be sixteen, right?"

"You can't be. If you were a minor, your parents would definitely be looking for you. Besides, your IDs put you between twenty-five and thirty."

IDs? "What IDs?"

Melana slid off her lap and scampered out of the room with her shoulders bowed. Cai's heart softened at the sight, distracting her from her question. Before she could go after Melana, Chris stalked off in another direction, leaving Cai alone.

Chris plopped back into the chair in front of the computer and closed his eyes. Of course he'd known, had hoped for Am—Cai's sake, that this moment would come. The moment when she would remember her name, her life. In that regard, he was happy, but with her memory came the reason she'd come. For Melana. Seeing Melana right now, Chris knew a court battle to keep his daughter would be futile. Melana loved him, but she loved Cai, too.

Cai. A beautiful name for a lovely woman. Opening his eyes, he pulled up a search engine on the Internet to find the definition of her name. Rejoice. Now, what did Cai have to rejoice about? he wondered.

She trudged into the room, her dark eyes telling their own story. "Mel all right?"

"Scared I'll leave her more like it. I told her I wouldn't . . ." She trailed off, looking about as miserable as he felt.

He was fully grown and couldn't comprehend the thought of Cai leaving, how would a nine year old? "I'm assuming being related to Kimmy, you were coming for Melana, so you always intended to have a relationship with her anyway. Right?" he questioned.

"I'm not related to Kimmy. I only have two sisters."

"A cousin?"

"I don't think so, but all I remember are my parents and sisters."

"Do you know your phone number?"

Her eyes narrowed as if she were thinking. "No. I don't have total recall. I remember . . ."

She broke off and shook her head.

"Don't try to force it," he told her. "It'll come."

Neither spoke for a while. Chris didn't know what to do from here. Now that they knew Cai's name and where she'd come from, he really had no reason not to involve the police. He just didn't want to. Not yet. Cai didn't say anything about calling the police. He just didn't know if she didn't want to or if it hadn't occurred to her.

"Did you want to read about your sister?" he asked. "Maybe she mentions you in an article or something."

"I'd like that," she said softly.

He typed in Honor's name again. Before he could move to give Cai room, she eased onto his lap and took control of the mouse.

She smiled at him over her shoulder, and he pulled her back into him and rested his chin on her shoulder. She must have bathed with some type of floral bath wash because she smelled like lilacs. Her ponytail brushed across his cheek and he pushed her hair aside, exposing her ear. He'd never noticed their delicate shape.

Cai chuckled softly. "She told the interviewer I call her 'brat.' I remember that."

"What else does it say?" he asked absently as he traced the shell of her ear with his fingertip. He felt her tremble and saw her eyes close for a moment.

"She's twenty-six and I'm two years older, so I'm probably going on twenty-eight."

"So you're missing roughly eleven years of your memory."

"I guess so. Do you think that's normal?"

"Every case is unique but from what I read, amnesiacs usually remember earlier memories first."

She clicked on several links. "Apparently, Honor lives in Virginia. For her own protection, she wouldn't have her address or phone number available to the public."

"So I guess you're stuck with us."

"That doesn't sound bad at all," Cai admitted with a second smile over her shoulder.

Her hand flew to her throat. "My locket? Where—? My mom gave me her pretty locket when I was a little girl. I . . . I didn't want to go to kindergarten. I was scared. So she gave me a picture of the two of us to keep near my heart."

"It's in Biloxi, but now there's a picture of a baby named Ashanti Naja inside."

"Ashanti Naja?"

"We were thinking she might be your daughter."

He'd planned to bring it with him but in his rush, he'd forgotten it. "The phone lines are probably still down back home, but I have Jasmine's cell number. I'll call her, ask her to send it overnight. Maybe the picture will help you remember."

He reached around Cai for his phone and dialed Jasmine's number. While he was at it, he'd get an update on the base, see when Mel's school would reopen.

"Hello?"

"Jasmine. This is Chris. I was wondering if you could do me a favor? There's a black bag, kind of like a purse, on the closet shelf just inside the front door. Could you overnight it to me? I left the address with Mike and there's an extra key beneath the rock in the garden."

"Let me make sure it's there before you hang up. How's Amber?"

"Actually, her name is Cai. Her memory returned today, but she's missing the last eleven years or so."

"That sounds right. Don't let her push herself, the rest will come if it's meant to. Is she still having headaches and seizures?"

"Not in the last few days. Her short-term memory is good, too."

"That's great. How's Mel?"

"She's fine, misses you guys. School open yet?"

"Not yet. The latest rumor—uh, oh. Your garage door's been broken into."

Chris bolted forward, almost knocking Cai to the floor. He slipped an arm around her waist, catching her. "What? Is the purse still there?"

"I see it." He heard a noise, like the sound of a heavy object being moved. "The place is wrecked. There's an address book on the table, looks like the

M page is missing. Still want me to mail the purse, or are you coming back?"

After all they'd gone through someone had trashed his house and still knew where they were? At least here, they were inside a gated community. "Cai's safer here. Can you get Mike to seal the door some kind of way? I don't want the police involved yet."

"You bet. You three be safe, okay?"

Chris set the phone on the desk as Cai stood and turned around. She'd heard the conversation, had to deduce that something was wrong and still she showed no fear.

"What's up?" she asked.

"Someone's broken into my house, and the page with Ron's address is gone."

She buried her fingers in her hair and scratched her scalp. "Well, I ran once. I won't run again."

Chris released a heavy sigh. "You ever heard the statement 'pick your battles'?"

Her hands fell to her waist. "Yeah. This would be the one."

CHAPTER 10

Several hours later, Cai stretched and then clicked on the CNN Web site. It couldn't hurt to check the site. Having a famous sister should have some fringe benefits.

She'd read everything she could find on Honor. Her baby sister was all grown up and had just had a baby herself, named Nicola after her daddy, Nicolas.

After catching her up to speed on everything he knew—her memory from when she first arrived at Chris' was still sketchy—Chris had suggested he check the neighborhood for anything suspicious. She'd pointed out that because the guy obviously knew him, it might be better to let Ron peruse the area on his way home from work.

This was a military installation, protected by a perimeter fence that required a code to enter. The only way this person could get in was if he were affiliated with someone who lived there.

Frustrated at his inability to do anything, Chris had gone to check on Melana, and Cai had turned back to the Internet to get reacquainted with her fully grown and famous model sister.

The last thing Cai remembered was Honor entering her freshmen year worried about her baby fat. Her older sister, Mia, had been miserable because she and dad weren't speaking, except to yell at each other. Cai remembered feeling caught between them and torn by the anger she'd felt from being ignored by her parents, but not why they'd fallen out. So, Honor had grown out of her baby fat. Had Mia and Dad reconciled?

Cai clicked on the Columbus, Ohio, white pages and typed her parents' names. No listing. Why? Chewing on her bottom lip, she tried to recall. Chris wouldn't want her to push herself, but she wanted to talk to her family.

Her mother was a veterinarian! What about her dad? Their home number was unlisted so clients couldn't call at all hours, but what about her office? Cai deflated. She couldn't recall the number or the name of her mother's practice.

She was so close!

With a quick glance at the clock on the bottom of the screen, Cai went in search of Chris and Melana. They were both asleep, Melana in her usual position and Chris stretched across the bottom of the bed.

Cai stared at the little cherub. Was Ashanti Naja her daughter? Would she be as beautiful and affectionate as Melana? Were they close? Cai couldn't imagine loving any child more than Melana.

Her eyes fluttered open as if she could sense someone watching her. She smiled, then her face fell. Chris stirred, too, then sat up slowly.

"I thought we could fix dinner together," Cai told them.

Melana piped up at that and ran over to Cai. "Just like a real family?"

"You didn't think you were getting rid of me that easily, did you?"

The little girl threw her arms around Cai's waist. "Nope, me and Daddy would miss you too much."

"Is that right?" she asked, looking over Melana's head to Chris. What had they been talking about?

Grinning, Chris approached the two of them. "Who can argue with female logic?"

Chris' phone rang about an hour after dinner. Ron and Melana were in the kitchen "sneaking" a second piece of cake and Cai was beside him on the couch trying to remember her parents' number.

He pressed the talk button. "Hello?"

"Is this Chris St. Clair?"

"Yes?"

"This is Tyrone, Kim's ex. You left a message?"

Chris saw Cai's curious expression and mouthed, *It's Tyrone.* "Yeah, I'm trying to locate her brother Jace?"

"I haven't seen Jace since the divorce in ninety-four."

"Ninety-four? Melana wasn't born until ninety-six."

"That's her daughter? I heard a few years back that she adopted a little girl."

"Adopted?" If this guy wasn't going to be upfront about paternity, he probably wouldn't be of much help.

"She couldn't conceive and her obsession with having a baby destroyed us. I was sorry to hear she died. Kim had some serious issues, but she was basically a good person. Sorry I couldn't give you any info on Jace."

"Thanks anyway." Chris disconnected the call and let his head drop forward.

Cai slid her arms across his shoulders. "Chris? What's wrong? What did he say?"

Could he actually say the words out loud? "He said Kimmy couldn't conceive."

Amber exhaled. "Well, obviously he's lying. You were there, weren't you?"

"I adopted Melana when she was two," he explained. Cai wouldn't remember he'd already told her. Why would Kimmy lie to him about Melana being adopted and worse, allow him to believe *he* couldn't father a child?

"So you never knew Kimmy adopted Melana? Why would she keep that from you?"

Ron stopped halfway into the room, Melana several steps behind him. Chris and Cai looked at each other before turning to Melana, who didn't look as if she understood Cai's statement.

Still, Chris knew Melana would sense something amiss, and he needed time to regroup before trying to explain any of this. "Ron?"

"Why don't I get Mel out of here?" Ron suggested. "We need to walk off that cake."

"Sssh! Uncle Ron. We were sneaking," she whispered loudly.

Ron chuckled, though it sounded forced. "Can you grab the lotion from my bedroom before we go?"

She skipped off apparently unaware of the adults' tension. The moment she was out of earshot, Ron said, "What's that I overheard? *Kimmy* adopted Melana?"

Chris rubbed his forehead. "She never told me. Seven years and she never said a word." Unable to bear their pitying glance, Chris stood up and headed toward the kitchen.

Ron put his hand on Chris's shoulder as he walked by. "For what it's worth, I'm sorry."

He strode through the kitchen and dining room and outside to the patio. He needed time alone to think, to figure out how he could marry a woman he obviously never knew.

It was chilly and he shivered at the sudden cold. Sticking his hands in his jeans pockets, he leaned against the rail and looked to the sky.

"How could you do that, Kimmy? Why did you feel you couldn't tell me the truth?" he wondered aloud.

For years, he'd wondered if Tyrone would show up to play daddy one day. Now he had to worry if two other parents would show up out of the blue to claim parental rights.

What about Melana? How would he explain any of this to her?

Cai stepped onto the patio, interrupting his thoughts. She started to place a throw over his shoulders, but he shrugged it off. She caught it and placed the thick material around him again. "Please? It's cold."

When he didn't resist, she brought the material together against his chest and leaned into him. "What do you want me to say to you?"

He looked into Cai's dark eyes and knew she was hurting for him. "Tell me why a woman who professed to love me would lie to me everyday of our married life? Why would she allow me to believe I had the problem?"

Cai shook her head with a helpless expression on her face. "I can't explain it, Chris. It's . . ."

"Evil." He would've never thought he'd used that word in relation to Kim, but how else could he explain it?

Cai touched his cheek. "You couldn't love a woman who was evil. I wish I knew what to say. *I'm sorry* seems so inadequate."

Attempting to justify Kim's behavior had to be as difficult for her to try as it was for him to hear. Amber had never met her and still never liked her.

He pushed her back a little with his body and eased away from her. "I just want to be alone."

"Chris—"

"Amber—Cai. Please."

He turned away and waited several long seconds before he heard the patio door open and close.

Cai was drying off in the bedroom after a hot bath when she remembered Melana had taken the lotion into the front room. She wished Chris had allowed her to comfort him. He'd taken such good care of her. Besides, she loved him. When he hurt, she hurt.

She'd decided to watch TV in the bedroom to give him time alone. After a twenty-minute struggle between her heart and mind to go to him or do what he'd asked, she thought a long hot bath might distract her.

It hadn't, of course. So now what? She still didn't know what to say to Chris. The news that Kimmy had lied to him had rocked him.

Slipping out of the bedroom, she peeked into the kitchen to see if Chris was still on the patio. He wasn't. She turned toward the living room and saw him on the sofa with his head back, his eyes closed. Tiptoeing into the room, she reached for the lotion, trying not to disturb him. His left hand snaked out and he caught her by the wrist. His eyes opened. "I'm sorry. I shouldn't have pushed you away."

"You're hurting. I understand."

His thumb pressed against the pulse in her wrist.

His skin was warm so he must have been inside for a while.

"Are you afraid?" he asked.

"No." Her pulse was beating rapidly for another reason. Desire. She didn't need Chris to tell her that.

His hand left hers to trail down the length of the towel. There, he slipped his hand beneath the cloth. The towel hiked a bit to allow him access, or, uh, she hiked it to give him access. He tugged her closer, and she straddled his hips. The last time he'd been dreaming of Kimmy, but this time, he was seeing Cai.

His hand trailed lazily along the crease of her thigh and stopped just above her center. She bit her bottom lip to keep from pleading with him to touch her.

"Don't hurt yourself like that," he told her, pulling her lip free with his other hand. He combed his fingers through her hair and watched it rise and fall onto her shoulders. "Are you ready to tell me why you were upset the other day?"

She hid her face in his chest and shook her head.

"Please, Cai. Tell me. As it turns out, I don't like secrets very much."

Tell him her most embarrassing moment or go the way of Kimmy. What a choice. Cai sighed. "The other night I came out here to watch TV, and I lay down with you. You . . . touched me but only because you thought I was Kimmy."

"I'd never mistake you for Kim, Cai. I thought I was dreaming of you and I was afraid if I opened my eyes you'd disappear."

"But you said her name."

He sighed. "I felt guilty. Kim never made me feel the way you do, and I thought it was wrong to feel the way you make me feel."

Drawn by his words, she finally raised her face to his. "How do I make you feel?"

Even as he lowered his lips, she closed her eyes, anticipating the sensual weakness that would invade her at his touch. He cupped the sides of her face and held her still as he kissed her deeply, making love to her with his lips.

She groaned deep in her throat as anticipation burned between her thighs, and she pressed against him, feeling his desire for her.

He broke the kiss but kept his hands on her face. When she opened her eyes, his gaze met hers. "Cai, I want to touch you. I want to be inside you so bad it hurts. But if you belonged to me, I wouldn't want any man looking at you, let alone touching you."

The possessiveness in his voice made her belly quiver and she knew more than anything that she wanted to belong to this man. Tonight.

"Chris, if I were married, I'd know it somewhere inside. I'm sure of it. I want to be with you."

His eyes didn't leave hers as his hands dropped to her shoulders. He paused, giving her time to change her mind, but Cai knew she would never regret this moment.

He kneaded her shoulders and she could feel the heat of his hands even through the thick material. With each outward circle, her robe spread farther apart, revealing first the valley between her breasts, and then her breasts.

His gaze lowered and his hands followed. Slowly, he pulled the material apart until it fell off her shoulders and pooled around her waist. Her breasts grew heavy and full, her nipples, still damp from her shower, drew into tight beads of desire.

His mouth roamed the swells of her breasts, leaving a damp path behind. He licked, nibbled and sucked until she gasped for air, wanting to rip the robe off and experience his mouth all over her.

She gripped his shoulders, pulling him closer. His mouth was everywhere, on her face, her lips, her throat. His lips closed over hers and his tongue tangled with hers as she matched his passion. Running her hands beneath his shirt, she dragged her nails across his back, yanking him closer until their bodies meshed and she no longer knew where she ended and he began.

His hand eased across her hip, her thigh, then curled behind her knee and moved upward, hauling her against him. His lips never left hers as he ground hard against her center, making her gasp as a sharp stab of need flared in her lower belly.

Her mind emptied of everything except the sensations invading her body. His thighs opened, spreading her legs wider. She felt his fingers just above her apex and she pressed into him, her body seeking the pleasure she knew he could bring.

His fingertips brushed her center and she arched against him, her body shuddering. She felt Chris spread her open. He paused again, but she was too weak. "Please," she moaned.

He appeased her with a thumb against her sensitive nub that had her writhing and grinding her hips. She felt a mounting pressure at the heart of her sex and bore down on Chris instinctively. Pleasure ripped through her and she froze, her head thrown back, her mouth wide open.

Chris brought her lips to his, ravaging her mouth as wave after wave of sensation coursed through her body.

She fell against him, limp. Gently, he laid her down

on the sofa and grabbed the bottle of lotion from the end table. He poured the creamy liquid into his hand and began to massage her body, starting at her shoulders. Her body was alternately hot and cold as he used long strokes down and across her skin until she was teetering on the edge again.

Chris crawled between her thighs, but didn't rest his weight on her. His fingers returned to her center, twisting, pulling, teasing her. As if her body had a will of its own, her legs automatically spread, welcoming his touch. She waited for him to plunge his finger deep inside her. She arched her hips, pleading. Instead, he squeezed her sensitive nub just enough to send her over the edge.

She bore down again as the pressure swelled, her hips thrusting wildly to the beat of her heart. Chris lowered his mouth between her legs and she cried out, expecting the pleasure to be too intense.

His mouth was no less relentless as he licked, nibbled, and tasted every part of her. Cai gripped the armrest as her thighs trembled from the onslaught. Weak now, her body could only jump sporadically.

Pressing his tongue to her nub, he gripped her hips and suckled like a baby. She flipped up so fast she almost fell to the floor, and would have if Chris hadn't been holding her. She screamed, panted, pleaded, tried to push him away and bring him closer until she couldn't fight it anymore.

She held his head as she ground her body against his mouth until fire started and spread from her belly, scorching her inside and out. Chris moved over her and when she opened her eyes, she could see a light film of her sex on his lips.

He kissed her and the taste of her own body lingered on her lips. "You are so beautiful, Cai. I love the way your body responds to me."

His hot breath on her mouth made her tremble, and she blindly reached for him. Scooping her into his arms, he carried her to the bedroom and lay her in the center of the mattress.

"I'll be right back," he told her.

Cai rolled onto her stomach and buried her face in her arms. She moaned, her body on edge with anticipation. Chris knew just where to touch her, just how to touch her.

Out of the corner of her eye, she saw Chris pulling his shirt over his head as he strolled back into the bedroom. A picture of his muscular chest, in another room, appeared before her eyes. She'd seen him undressed before.

He sank one knee into the mattress and she rolled toward him.

Leaning over her with one arm close to her head, he kissed her slowly, teasing her with his tongue. She cupped his length through his jeans, tracing the hard bulge with her fingers.

Capturing her hand with his, Chris placed a small silver packet in her hand. "Whenever you're ready," he whispered next to her ear.

She was ready. Her hands trembled as she ripped the packet down the middle and spread the condom across his length.

Chris lay beside her, facing her, his gaze locked on hers. She threw one leg over his to straddle his hips, but he pinned her with his hand. He found her center of pleasure with his fingers again and her body bucked against him seeking its third release.

His eyes flared with pleasure as he watched her response to him. Again and again he brought her to the brink only to snatch her back for more.

The ache in her lower belly deepened, the pressure increased. She felt the explosion of heat start at her center and a shudder tore through her body. Chris guided her on top of him and he plunged deep inside, fully embedding in her in one thrust. Her feminine muscles flexed all around him, squeezing, pulsating.

She heard his breath hitch in his throat, and she watched ecstasy explode in his eyes, felt it pulse through his body and warm her hollow cavity. Her own rapturous sensations tore through her, leaving only pleasure behind. She dropped onto his chest and Chris crushed her to him, holding onto her as if he never wanted to let her go.

"Don't be afraid, don't be afraid," she whispered again and again.

Chris rolled over, bringing Cai with him. His kiss was slow and deep as her body came down, her heartbeat slowed. She buried her face in his neck and inhaled his all male scent.

"I don't want to lose you, Cai. I can't."

"You won't. I prom—"

His lips closed over hers before she could finish her promise. "Don't let me be afraid," he murmured against her mouth.

Dressed in Chris' T-shirt, Cai stood in the kitchen watching his hand as he guided a knife through his birthday cake and lifted a piece onto a saucer. His smoldering gaze met hers as he handed her two forks and her insides clenched. She'd lost count of how many times Chris had made love to her over the last hour, but she'd never forget the pleasure, the closeness.

He brushed his lips across hers as he picked up the saucer and carried it into the living room. Before she could curl up beside him on the sofa, he pulled her onto his lap. "I could get used to this," she admitted. He fed her a piece of cake and she chewed slowly. "Any regrets, Chris?"

He didn't answer immediately and Cai's heart felt like it was about to split right down the middle. She had sensed his fear of losing her earlier and had hoped their lovemaking would help ease his apprehension.

He brushed his knuckles across the line of her jaw. "How could I ever regret making love to you? No, Cai. Never."

They fed each other cake and shared kisses until she realized she'd better get dressed before Ron and Melana returned. "I'll be right back, okay?"

His arms tightened around her before he reluctantly let her go. As she turned to leave, she saw the TV flicker on. A flash of a black-haired woman crossed the screen as Chris flipped through the channels. "Was that—?"

Chris quickly switched back and Cai saw a picture of herself. "It's me," she breathed.

He turned the volume up so they could hear the anchorwoman.

"In an ironic twist, child-finder Cai McIntyre has been reported missing. Her disappearance is considered suspicious."

A podium had been set up in the background and the camera panned in on a couple and a light-skinned young man. "Mom? Dad?" Cai leaned forward, staring at the screen. "They look older than I remember."

Her mother looked tired and drawn in a gray two-piece suit, her father strong and distinguished with silver peppered through his hair.

A reenactment video of a karate-wielding woman fighting off one guy after another began to play. "A source close to the family," a voiceover in man's nasal tone said, "who wishes to remain anonymous has indicated that Cai McIntyre is the elusive 'Bounty Hunter with A Vengeance' who has spent the last seven years . . ."

"Bounty Hunter with a Vengeance?" she heard Chris echo.

"Cai's been relentless in her pursuit of missing children," the man continued, "heralded as an angel by families who have, out of gratitude, kept her identity a secret, and a vigilante determined to retrieve a child by any means necessary. Things seemed to take a turn for the worse when she failed to reach a child who drowned in a river four years ago."

Another reenactment began and, her stomach churning, Cai turned to Chris to avoid the dramatic replay. "Am I good or bad?"

Chris sighed heavily. "Who's the man, the other man?"

The camera closed in on the podium again, and Cai studied the pretty-boy features of the man dressed in a black suit. "I don't know."

"Three packages turned up at District Attorney Daniel McIntyre's office as well as police stations in Florida and Ohio exposing an extensive black market adoption ring," the voice continued. "Renowned attorney Michael Turner has been charged with the kidnapping of Cai's daughter, Ashanti, and has been extradited to Ohio for questioning."

The press conference began and her father stepped up to the microphone. "Our daughter, Cai McIntyre, was last seen in Hampton, Virginia two weeks ago. We're concerned for her safety and we're asking anyone who's seen her to please come forward with any information you may have concerning her whereabouts."

Her mother broke down in tears and her father stopped speaking to comfort her. The young man stepped forward and cleared his throat.

"Cai, we love you and miss you. If you're out there, please know that we're doing everything possible to bring you home."

The camera panned back and the caption *Cai's Husband, Jason Taylor* appeared on the bottom of the screen.

Husband? Cai blanched at the thought. She turned to Chris to say something but the words died in her throat. The haunted look on his face said it all.

"Does seeing your parents *or your husband,*" he said through his teeth, "help you remember any more?"

She shook her head, then realized he couldn't see her with his gaze riveted to the TV. "No," she croaked.

He didn't say anything, didn't even look at her.

"Is your daughter the BHV?" a reporter asked.

A muscle in her father's jaw flexed. "Our concern is the safe return of our daughter. Please, anyone . . . if you have any information, call." Her father didn't directly deny that she was the bounty hunter, which meant she probably was. He wouldn't tell a direct lie, not with his strong principles.

Chris finally looked at her. "We need to decide where we go from here."

"You mean together, right? We can't shut each other out, Chris."

"I just made love to another man's *wife.* We're not together."

Cai knelt beside him. "You're upset. I am, too, but I committed myself to you, and we'll make this work."

"Yeah? How?"

She raised her hands in a helpless gesture. "Somehow."

"Someway?" he asked sarcastically. "It's already been done in song."

It was an inadequate answer, she knew that, but her head was spinning with so many thoughts. Could she really be this vengeful person the newsman had spoken about? Was she a fifth degree black belt? Who was this Michael Turner who had kidnapped her baby? And where was her baby?

"Chris, my dad didn't mention Ashanti. Do you think I didn't get to her in time, either?"

Chris's anger seemed to drain out of him with her question. "I don't know, Cai. If you're her, this bounty hunter, then I'd put my money on you every time. She's done a lot of good."

"A lot of bad, too?"

"She was angry and hurting. No one can blame her. If anyone even tried to take Melana from me . . ."

"But if I am her, then I hurt people. I don't want to hurt you."

"You wouldn't purposely hurt anyone, sweetheart. It's not in you." He pulled her into his arms and held onto her. "We should call the police, Cai. Let your family know you're safe."

"No." Standing, she rejected the suggestion outright. They still didn't know who was after her. If she were the bounty hunter, then she'd probably made many enemies over the years, even of the police, if she were the BHV.

She turned toward Chris. "How long have I been with you?"

His gaze traveled the length of her body, beginning at her bare feet. "Eight days. Why?"

"And the last contact I had with my family was fourteen days ago." She tapped her bottom lip as she grasped at a distant thought. "I'd rather not involve the police on this end. Not yet. We know someone is after me, and we know a powerful attorney is behind the kidnapping of Ashanti. If I go home now, I'm no safer. In fact, I'm more vulnerable."

"But your family—"

"They're worried," she interrupted, pacing back and forth, searching for that elusive thought. "The eight-hundred number will be set up to trace calls. If we call, the police will be at the door in fifteen minutes, and if Taylor has people on the inside, they'll be here in ten."

"You sound different."

Cai stopped pacing to look at Chris. His expression was cautious, reserved. "Do I?"

CHAPTER 11

Cai pushed the ten digits on the phone pad and waited. Last night had not been very restful. After Chris had walked away from her, she'd turned to the TV to discover she'd missed the last part of the segment. She thought she'd catch it the next hour, but Ron and Melana had come home, and Cai didn't want Melana to hear the report.

She'd gotten up twenty minutes ago and while anxiously flipping through the channels, she'd remembered her father's private number at his office.

"Hello?" His warm but strained voice came over the line.

"Dad." Even if she hadn't heard his voice yesterday, she would have recognized it immediately.

She heard a shuddering sigh. "Thank God! I've been here all night waiting for your call. Where are you, Cai?"

"I'm safe. How're Mom, Mia, Honor?"

"Frantic. Give me the address and we'll be on the next flight out."

"How did you know I'd call you at your office?" she asked, going back to his first statement.

"That was what we'd planned, if anything ever went wrong."

His voice dropped with the second part of his sentence causing her stomach to knot with dread. "Dad . . . so I am the Bounty Hunter?"

A long silence followed her question. The thought had plagued her all night. If she recalled correctly, Mia had taken an interest in martial arts her freshmen year and Cai followed in her footsteps.

"You don't know?" he finally asked.

"I have amnesia. I've been staying with a man named Chris and his daughter, Melana. They've been taking care of me." She didn't want to talk long. Her father's line probably hadn't been bugged and it was more difficult to trace a cell phone, but she didn't want to endanger her family, her natural family or her new one.

"Tell me where you are." He sounded urgent now.

She heard a noise, like a movement, then the tapping of keys against a keyboard. Knowing she couldn't keep them away, she typed Ron's address into an email and pushed the send button.

"Got it. We'll be there around noon," he said in a gruff voice.

"Dad—"

She heard the sound of movement again and then static. "I've got to leave now if I'm going to catch this flight. Your mother and Mia will have to meet me there. Cai?"

"Yeah?"

"I love you, sweetheart. Hold on, okay? We'll be there."

The line disconnected and she stared at the silver phone a moment, glad that she hadn't allowed them to worry any longer than necessary.

She Googled her alter ego to put together a time line of her activities. The answer to whoever had hurt her had to be there.

Her interest grew as she tracked her movements over the last seven years. She'd started with small cases close to home, then branched out across the United States. The families were usually poor, limited only to the local police's time, ability, and money. Cai didn't charge a fee for her service but took whatever donation the family could afford.

Maybe she was a good person after all.

She was printing the timeline when Chris walked into the living room.

"Hey," he mumbled.

"Good morning, Chris. You'll be happy to know I spoke to my father."

He paused in the process of sitting down. "You remembered the number?"

"Yes. He confirmed that I'm the bounty hunter."

"Did you speak to your husband?" His voice was neutral as he settled into a cushion, but his body looked as taut as an electrical wire.

"I didn't think to ask," she admitted with a sheepish feeling. "My parents will be here around noon."

"So you'll be going back with them?"

Chris didn't look at her. "Is that what you want?"

"My marriage vows said 'Entreat me not to leave thee, or to return from following after thee: for whither thou goest, I will go; and where thou lodgest, I will lodge: thy people shall be my people, and thy God my God.' What about yours?"

Cai rolled her eyes. "You know I don't remember."

"You should be with your husband." He nodded, his jaw flexing.

"How can you be so cold after everything we've shared? You made love to me just last night, Chris."

"But you belong to someone else."

"No more than you do," she retorted.

Chris jumped up. "Don't bring Kimmy into this."

Cai leaped to her feet as well. "Why the hell not? She's all over it in every nightmarish nook and cranny." She threw her hands up. "Oh, that's right, she's Miss Perfect. I'd better not forget that or heaven help me. Well, you can have her because I'm done. Is that what you wanted to hear? I quit. I'm finished."

Chris watched Cai storm out of the room and took a steadying breath. They weren't going to get anywhere tearing into each other. He didn't want her to leave, but how could he ask her to stay?

Melana hurried into the room, still wearing her nightgown. She rubbed her eyes as she tucked her legs beneath her on the couch. "Miss Cai's upset again."

Chris leaned back into the cushion. "Did she say why?"

"No. Is she mad at you?"

"Yeah. I need to talk to you, Mel, and it's important." He hesitated. How much should he tell her? "Cai spoke to her father this morning. Her parents are on their way here."

"To take her away?" she asked in a small voice.

"I don't know, honey. Cai has a family, a husband and a baby girl named Ashanti. We have a picture of her in a locket back in Mississippi and Miss Jasmine's going to mail it to us. Should be here today."

Melana's lips turned down, and Chris knew she was about to cry. She wasn't ready for this conversation and probably never would be. "How come she forgot them?"

"She took a pretty hard hit to the head. She wouldn't have forgotten them if she could help it."

Tears began to leak from Melana's eyes. "So I'm not going to have a mommy, a real mommy?"

"What do you mean?"

"Miss Cai did stuff with me like Olivia's mom does with her."

Kimmy never did was the unspoken part of Melana's statement and Chris couldn't deny it. He'd watched Melana become the child she was by loving and being loved by Cai, but what could he do? "Maybe . . . maybe we can visit her . . . in Ohio."

Melana shook her head. "It won't be the same."

She uncurled her legs from beneath her and trudged toward the kitchen. Chris let her go, knowing he'd never find the words to comfort her. He'd spent the night trying to decide if he should tell her Kimmy had adopted her. Would she want to meet her birth mother? What if they tried to find her and she wasn't interested? What if she was deceased? He'd never realized how much Melana craved having a real mother–daughter relationship. What if he found her mother only to lose his daughter?

Cai strolled by with her nose in the air and he couldn't help the small smile playing about his mouth. She was a temperamental individual, wasn't she?

Ron staggered into the living room from the kitchen carrying a steaming cup of coffee. How'd he get into the kitchen? The scent of bacon and eggs followed. He straddled the chair across from Chris. "How'd things go between you and Cai last night?"

"Apparently she's the Bounty Hunter with a Vengeance. Heard of her?"

"Who hasn't? She's fast becoming a legend."

After Cai had gone to bed, he'd read every article he could find online. Her exploits hadn't reached Germany, so he'd never heard of her. From what he had gathered, she was a force to be reckoned with. "Her parents are on their way. Her husband, too."

Ron offered him a pained expression. "Wow. Sorry, man."

"We always knew there was a possibility." Of course he'd *hoped* otherwise.

Now he had two regrets. It would've been hard enough saying goodbye to Cai without having made love to her, but he had. She was in his blood and he needed her like his body needed water.

"But it must hurt like hell. I know you were falling for her."

"What makes you say that?"

"That question, for one thing. Not to mention the way you look at her. Maybe it's a bad marriage, and she'll want out."

Chris tried to not to cling to that dream, refusing to get his hopes up only to have them dashed when she remembered her husband.

Cai swaggered into the room carrying two plates piled with bacon, eggs and pancakes. Smiling brightly, she offered one to Chris. "Hungry?"

Cai showered and changed into the pink dress Chris had bought her. She brushed her hair in the bathroom. Melana had on her dress, as well, and Cai thought it might make the little girl feel better.

Chris had retreated big time, but the pain in his eyes when he looked at her staved off any anger she could muster at his stance. He was a good man, a commitment-type man. When he gave his heart, it was forever, and he'd never betray his vows or want her to.

She heard the doorbell ring on her way into the living room. Chris met her near the sofa, carrying a sealed box in his hand. The mailman must have come early today.

Melana's expression soured. "I guess that's the picture of your precious Ashanti."

Cai glanced at her curiously. Chris must have told Melana about her baby. Possessive little thing, wasn't she?

Chris handed her the package and strolled over to the window, glancing outside.

Ron offered her an encouraging smile and her guilt eased. Surely, Chris and Melana knew she loved them!

Cai sat next to Melana, hoping their closeness would reassure her. Her hand began to shake even before she could rip the tape and she closed her eyes to concentrate. This hadn't happened since their arrival. Sighing, she offered the package to Melana. "I can't open it."

With a sulky pout, Melana tore into the package and removed a black bag Cai didn't recognize. Melana pulled the strings apart and pulled out the gold locket Cai's mother had given to her.

Cai gripped her hand to still the shaking as Melana opened the clasp and thrust it toward her without a glance.

Cai stared at the baby, her gaze roaming over her black hair and her closed eyes, her little nose and bow-shaped lips.

"You remember?" Chris asked softly, brushing his thumb across her cheek. She hadn't even realized he'd moved closer.

"I remember carrying her. We—me and Jason—
were so happy." Cai blinked. "I waited months, years.
Then I decided to find her myself. I was so angry,
bitter. Hard."

"How long has she been missing?"

"I . . . don't know." She paused, thinking frantically.
"The Bounty Hunter came on the scene seven years
ago, so it has to be at least that long."

Melana's little arms closed around her and Cai
laid her cheek against her hair. "Can I see her?"

Cai's hand trembled as she showed Melana the
picture.

"That's me," she said simply.

"What?" Cai looked at the photo again.

"That's a picture of me when I was a baby."

"Melana," Chris began, "you know all your baby
pictures were lost during our move to Germany."

"Uncle Ron has one. He showed it to me. Look."
She reached for a photo album on the table and
opened it toward the back. "See?"

Beneath the plastic cover, there was a picture of a
baby identical to the one in Cai's locket.

"There's another one further back," Ron said,
turning more pages. "I found them tucked away in
a drawer when we were packing Kim's belongings,
Chris. Mel was such a cute little baby I couldn't resist,
especially this one."

"This one" was a picture of Melana lying on a fluffy
bear rug eating her toes. On her upper left thigh was
a small heart-shaped birth mark.

Cai stared at the tiny heart. "That's *Ashanti's* birthmark. I have one just like it," she whispered.

"Kim must have had it removed from Melana
before you met her," Ron offered into the silence.

Cai stared at Melana, her heart beating wildly. "*You're* my Ashanti?"

Melana looked up at her with wide eyes. "That's what you called me before you fainted."

Cai reached out to touch Melana but stopped. So many times when she'd reached for her baby, she'd disappeared and she didn't—couldn't—bear it if Melana vanished. "I've been looking for you, for so long," she cried.

"So now what?" Chris' deep voice shattered the peace invading her heart, peace she hadn't felt in nine long years. "You want to take her away from me? Well, why not? You've taken everything else that means anything to me. You destroyed my and Kimmy's car. You proved how shallow my marriage was, my wife's insanity. And now you're going to take my daughter away from me."

His last accusation caught Cai off guard, and she staggered as she stood.

Ron stepped in front of Chris and pushed him back with his body. "Lay off, Chris. None of this is Cai's fault."

She couldn't blame him for his reaction, though. The thought of losing a child could undo the strongest person, but he had to know she wouldn't take Melana away from him. "Of course I'd never take her from you. You're her father. Chris?" she said, giving him a chance to say he believed her.

He turned his back to her. "Just get away from me before you do any more damage."

She turned her stunned gaze to Ron. "I wouldn't . . ."

"I know," he told her with a sympathetic smile.

Chris spun toward the front door and without even a glance in her direction, left.

Cai deflated. Even now, he chose Kimmy over her.

Ron slipped away as Cai turned to her Ashanti, tears flowing freely from her eyes as the hurt from Chris's defection faded in the wake of being with her daughter again. Ashanti's desperate gaze switched from the door to Cai as if she were torn between the only father she'd ever known and the woman she'd known as Miss Amber, Miss Cai, and now her birth mother.

Cai wanted to count her fingers and toes the way she had when she'd first held her so long ago, kiss her forehead, her eyes, her cheeks. But all she could do was stand there and look at her. Her baby girl was all grown up.

Chris wasn't out the door before he realized the two people he loved most were inside the house. He paced the driveway trying to figure out how his life had been turned upside down in one short week.

Had he *ever* known Kimmy? He thought back to how quickly they'd gotten married, at her suggestion. Had he only been a ticket out of the States? No wonder she'd vowed to never return. She must have been petrified of getting caught, especially once "the Bounty Hunter with a Vengeance" hit the news circuits.

What an idiot he was. She'd played him for a fool. Now he understood why she never argued with him or appeared to be angry. She would've been petrified of any possibility of his seeking a divorce because she would have had to return to the States.

Her family must have known about the kidnapping, or at least been suspicious, and disapproved. That would explain "the falling out" and why she rarely talked about any of them, except for a comment here and there about Jace.

Now, once again, he'd hurt Cai. Yes, she destroyed

his car, but it was only metal and any emotional significance attached to it was based on a fake marriage. Good riddance to it! His own feelings for Kimmy couldn't have been too deep if he compared them with what he felt for Cai. He hadn't taken care of her because she was weak. During the worst of her pain, she'd always been strong and outspoken and honest. No, her strength had drawn him.

But how could he trust what he thought he felt? He'd thought he loved Kimmy after a whirlwind few weeks and he'd known Cai even less time than that. He knew one thing. Cai would not take Melana away from him. He should've never allowed the words to leave his mouth. Unlike Kimmy, she didn't have an evil bone in her body, despite the news report. Plus, she'd experienced the hell of losing a child herself. She wouldn't put him through that no matter how many stupid things he said.

He'd go inside, apologize. Hopefully, she would forgive him.

Just then, he saw a black car slow and stop at the curb in front of Ron's house. Cai's parents and a small woman with short black hair, who had to be Mia, flew out of three different doors, looking both excited and apprehensive.

Chris met them halfway down the sidewalk, his hand extended toward Mr. McIntyre. "You must be Cai's family. I'm Chris. She's been with me and my . . . daughter for the last week or so."

"It's good to meet you, Chris," Mr. McIntyre said. "This is my wife and my daughter, Mia. Cai explained everything to me, and we owe you a debt of gratitude."

"No, you don't. I'm just glad she's safe and that her memory's returning."

"Where is she?" Her mother, a petite woman who

looked like she could never have given birth to two almost six-foot women, rushed passed even as she asked the question.

Mia was right behind her.

He managed to beat them to the door to hold it open, then stepped aside to let everyone inside.

Mrs. McIntyre's sweeping glance around the living room stopped on Cai who was holding Melana's fingers to her lips, tears pouring from both their eyes.

It was like a train wreck as Mr. McIntyre, Mia, and Chris stumbled into the back of each other. Then Mrs. McIntyre said, "Cai?"

Her mother rushed over to Cai who held onto Melana with one hand as she spun around to hug her mother close. "Mom!"

Melana looked at Mr. McIntyre with wide eyes as the two women spoke softly to each other. He winked to reassure her and she smiled. It was so much to take in, even for an adult. Melana's little mind and senses had to be reeling.

Mrs. McIntyre finally released Cai and Mr. McIntyre stepped up to her. Brushing the tears from Cai's face with his thumbs, he cupped her cheeks with his hands. "Hi, baby," he whispered.

She slid her free arm around his neck. "Hi, Dad."

"Can I get a hug, too?" Mia asked from behind her father.

Cai glanced around her father's shoulder and saw Mia and her whole demeanor changed. Laughing, she pulled the smaller woman into her. "Mia! I didn't see you hiding back there."

Grinning, Mia shook her head. "Don't even start. Just because I'm shorter than you doesn't mean I can't take you should the need arise."

Cai hugged her tighter. "I've missed you so much,

and I have someone I want you to meet." She pulled Melana closer. "This beautiful girl is our Ashanti Naja. She's home, Mia."

The humor faded from Mia's face as her gaze shot between Cai and Melana. "Ashanti?"

Mrs. McIntyre collapsed against her husband who caught her and guided her to the sofa. Mia hugged Melana, her tears flowing unchecked. "I'm so sorry," she whispered over and over again as Mrs. McIntyre cried into her husband's chest and Cai's tears returned.

Cai closed her arms around her sister and daughter. "It was never your fault, Mia, but we have her back now. Let's be thankful for that."

Why did Mia blame herself? How would they react once they realized he'd had their Ashanti all these years? How in the world would he explain it when he didn't understand himself? Chris wondered confusedly.

Cai brushed her hand over Melana's hair. "Honey, my mom and dad are your grandparents and my sister's your aunt. They've been waiting a long time to see you, too."

Sighing, Chris started to turn away. With this whole new family, where did that leave him? He felt little arms slip around his waist and paused.

Melana grinned up at him with bright eyes. "Now I have a mommy and a daddy and a grandma and grandpa and an aunt, just like Olivia!"

"Two aunts," Mia told her. "Aunt Honor couldn't come because she just had a baby."

"And a cousin, right, Daddy?"

"That's right, but honey . . ." He broke off. How did he go on? How did he explain about Jason? "Remember I told you Cai's married—"

"She's not married," her father interjected before

turning to Cai. "You got an annulment on grounds of abandonment."

"That's right." She spoke slowly, as if she were remembering something. "But he came back . . . didn't you tell me that, Mom?"

Mrs. McIntyre nodded. "He told me he wanted another chance, he wanted to make things right."

Cai looked doubtful. "Then why isn't he here?"

"We got a lead from a woman in Alabama who claimed she'd driven you to Selma, and he wanted to talk to her personally. He seemed genuinely afraid for you," her mother added.

Cai's father looked equally doubtful, but it could be he'd never forgiven Jason for abandoning his daughter.

Melana looked up at Chris with an adoring expression. "You're my dad," she told him emphatically, making his own eyes burn with tears.

"Cai . . ." he said, speaking to her for the first time. "Do you think we could talk, alone?"

She glanced at her family, then nodded. "Okay, let's go outside."

"You'll be okay?" he asked Melana, sure she'd jump at the chance to get to know her extended family.

"Yep!" She darted over to her grandfather and hugged him. "You know what? You're taller than me!"

Cai had obviously gotten her height from her father and by extension Melana had, too. Mrs. McIntyre and Mia were much smaller. Chris sighed. How had he ever bought Kimmy's story? What a fool he'd been.

Chris handed Cai a light jacket from the front closet and she slid her arms inside as she walked out ahead of him. It was a little chilly, but not too bad.

Her heart was so warm, nothing could chill her, not even the prospect of this upcoming conversation. Chris didn't look angry anymore, only remorseful. She knew he would regret his harsh words. They were at a crossroads now. No matter what had gone on before this moment, they both wanted Ashanti.

They walked side-by-side, not touching, but Cai felt so close to him. Second to her worst fear, that she'd never see her daughter again, was the fear that Ashanti had been mistreated, but Chris had taken excellent care of her, even knowing she wasn't his biologically. For that, she would always be grateful.

"I said some terrible things earlier, and it just wasn't right. I'm sorry I hurt you."

"You owed me that apology, so thank you. But I knew you were working from pure fear. Fear I've lived with nine years. I can't hold it against you."

They walked in silence as she grappled with what to do next. She didn't doubt her feelings for Chris. She loved him. Talking about Jason a few minutes ago, she'd remembered jumping into a relationship before and she didn't want to do that again.

"Why does Mia blame herself for the kidnapping?" Chris asked.

"Mia and my dad were having some serious issues and a lot of my parents' attention went to dealing with that, leaving me and Honor emotionally starved. I was lonely and desperate to feel loved. That's when Jason came into my life."

"What happened?"

"I'd gone to the library after school. Something I normally did because I didn't want to go home. I caught him watching me. He didn't speak to me that first time or even the next, but he would watch me until I was anxious for him to approach me."

She laughed at her naivety. "I was seventeen, my inexperienced body excited by the sight of this older, handsome, worldly man. He finally spoke, and I thought I'd faint, my body was so infused with heat, my cheeks flushed. He took his time getting to know me at first. He'd stare into my eyes and speak softly about his college courses and other mature insights. He seduced me. He carried me to the brink of lovemaking, only to back away proclaiming he respected me too much to make love to me before we were married."

They followed the sidewalk around the curve and continued walking.

"So when he proposed to me the evening of my eighteenth birthday, I said *yes* almost before he could finish the question. He suggested we fly to Las Vegas that very night and get married. I wanted to wait, to tell my parents, but they didn't approve of Jason. At twenty-one, he was too old to be dating a teenager. As far as they were concerned anyway."

Cai hadn't listened and her parents had been distracted. He'd crushed her body to his in a deep kiss and the next thing she knew she was saying "I do."

"We made love that night and it wasn't all I'd hoped, but I was a virgin, so I wasn't sure . . ." Cai trailed off, shying away from the painful memory. "My parents' shock and disappointment sent me into a tailspin of regret. Pride kept me from admitting my mistake and by the time I was ready to confess, I began to feel nauseous. Jason was ecstatic about the pregnancy, my parents were furious. We'd planned to live with my folks until I graduated a few months later, but we may as well have been living in two different homes."

Despite the turmoil, Cai had looked forward to the birth of her daughter. She'd fallen in love with this new life that had forever changed hers. On the day she was to take her baby home, Cai handed her Ashanti to a small woman with a doughy figure wearing a nurse's uniform and never saw her again. Until a week ago.

She'd known Jason for almost a year and thought she loved him. She'd known Chris for less than a week and thought she loved him. Would the pattern of later regrets follow as well?

"He abandoned you?"

"I was frantic to find her. Depressed. Consumed with guilt. After about three months, he said he couldn't stand to see me like that and left. A year later, I filed for an annulment."

They came upon a huge football field and by silent mutual agreement headed in that direction. Another product of Mia's guilt was Honor's eventual slide into anorexia, but Cai owned some of that blame as she'd gotten her parents' attention in a big way, making Honor feel even more isolated.

Chris straddled a bench and motioned for her to sit beside him. "I'm sorry you had such a rough time. A weaker woman would have stayed down. When did you decide to become a child-finder?"

"About a year after Jason left. I stayed at the police station studying every report that came in. They just didn't have the resources to stay on top of a cold case. And there were so *many* missing babies and kids. One day I stopped feeling sorry for myself and decided to find Ashanti myself. I kind of fell into helping the others, but I thought each case would give me the experience I needed to find her."

He nodded. "Then the Bounty Hunter with a Vengeance was born."

"It took time to get there. The press was intrigued,

especially when I decided to work anonymously. I saw so much ugliness, Chris. Adults who once claimed to love each other snatching their kids away to hurt each other. I didn't make it to one child. Ryan. He was a beautiful, bright butterfly. You just knew he had a gift to share with the world. When his mother, his *mother*, realized she was going to be caught, she threw him into a river and he drowned before I could reach him."

A shudder tore through her body as she remembered her frenzied search for his lifeless body. She'd tried to resuscitate him until the paramedics had to literally haul her away from him.

"It changed me," she confessed. "And not for the better."

CHAPTER 12

Cai allowed Chris to pull her into his warm embrace. They sat in silence for a while as she glanced the length of the football field.

She'd spiraled quickly, in fact. The news that Honor, who had never hurt anybody in her life, couldn't conceive had been her undoing. She was mad at the world. God, too. She had determined to never lose another child, and she never did. She began to skirt the law and have run-ins with cops who were embarrassed when she solved a case before they could. Through it all, her whole focus of living had been finding her daughter. Now she had. Honor had her baby, and Cai had her Ashanti back. Once Mia put her guilt aside, their family would be healed.

"I'm not quite sure how to proceed from here," Chris admitted. "As far as I'm concerned, Melana's my daughter."

Melana. Everyday for the last week, Cai had held her, reassured her. The baby girl she'd loved and missed for nine long years. "First, we'll have to ask her what she wants to be called. It should be her decision, right?"

Chris nodded. "She'll probably want me to call her Mel, and I'm fairly sure she'll want to be called Ashanti. She and Kim were close, but more like friends than mother–daughter. I can't imagine she'll feel much of a connection to the name. Did you explain what Kim did?"

Kim. Not Kimmy. Were his feelings changing for the other woman? "I couldn't talk for the lump in my throat. All I could do was stare at her."

"That's how I felt when I first met her." A faint smile touched his lips. Then he sighed. "I guess Kim destroyed her baby pictures sometime before or after the move. By then, she probably knew you were the BHV. But I can tell you everything I remember about your Ashanti."

Cai carried his hand to her cheek and closed her eyes so she could visualize everything. "Tell me," she whispered, her voice breaking.

"She could already walk when I met her. Even then she was tall. The doctor said she would always be taller than her classmates. She didn't like wearing dirty diapers, so Kim was already potty training her. She was always a neat freak but a cute one."

Chris chuckled and Cai couldn't help grinning. Ashanti had definitely gotten that from her. She opened her eyes. "Was she a happy baby?"

"I don't believe she was *unhappy*, but she was always so stoic—"

Cai gasped. "That's what Naja means, stoic and strong!"

"Then you named her well. Since you've been in her life, I've seen her exhibit more emotion than at any other time. Kim needed *her*, but your Ashanti needed *you*. She's a little girl now. It's like she's . . . whole."

Cai felt tears burning her eyes again. "There were

so many times when I wanted to close my eyes and never wake up, but the hope of seeing her again kept me living and now I feel alive."

"Which brings us to what we want to do, I guess. Ultimately, *legally*, you'll have the final say."

She heard his cautious tone and spoke quickly to dispel his fears. "Ashanti would be torn apart if we tried to share custody living in two different states. Since you're in the military, and my job allows me the freedom, it would be easier for me to move."

"So we'd live in two different homes, and you'll be willing to move every time I receive orders?"

She danced around his question by posing one of her own. "Would that be okay with you?"

"Who would she live with?" He continued the dance.

Cai lapsed into silence. More than anything she wanted to shout, *with me! You've had her seven years!* But she couldn't be that selfish. Of course, it wouldn't be fair to leave the decision to Ashanti. She was too young to make that choice. Either one could leave her guilt-ridden for years.

"You want her to live with you," Chris said flatly.

"Yes I do, but it's not right. She needs a family, a mom *and* a dad."

"You could go home, with us."

"As what, Ashanti's mother or . . . why am I skirting around this?" she asked, suddenly frustrated with her own game. "Where do *we* stand, Chris?"

"You told me you love me. Has that changed?"

"No, but I don't want to rush into a second marriage, especially a marriage of convenience."

"I'd be committed to you, Cai."

Because of the type of man he was, not because he loved her. "Out of love for me or a desire to hold onto your daughter? I don't think I'd be very happy watching you pine after a woman who kidnapped my baby."

Chris bolted up, towering over her. "I can't believe you said that."

Cai leapt to her feet, too. "Why not? For at least as far back as I can remember, you've done nothing but declare your love for her."

His nostrils flared as he stared at her hard. "I'll be leaving in the morning, and I'm sure Mel will want to go with me, so you can go with us, or we can drag this thing through the courts because I'm not giving her up."

Cai grabbed his arm as he swung away from her. A court may give her custody, but she'd never have Ashanti if Cai forced her away from Chris. "Listen, Chris. I'm sorry. I shouldn't have said that. I'll go with you, of course, I will." She could hear the desperate edge in her voice but she couldn't lose her daughter again. She'd never survive. "Truce? For Ashanti's sake?"

She extended her hand toward him, searching his hard expression for any signs that he might be willing to meet her halfway.

"We should get back," he told her.

Cai's heart sank. Did this mean he wasn't willing to compromise?

They didn't say another word to each other as they walked back to Ron's place. Chris couldn't care less about breaking the silence, refusing to pander to Cai as he'd done with Kim.

It wasn't like he wanted to marry Cai anyway. He'd already decided he didn't want to rush into another marriage. Then why was he so ticked off? Because he *could* see himself spending a lifetime loving and arguing and making up with her. Only she wasn't interested because of some punk kid who had obviously taken advantage of her innocence.

Chris sighed. Still. Spouting off about taking her to court wasn't a good idea. Melana would probably want to go with him, but legally Cai held all the strings, and they both knew it. She was only going back to Biloxi for her daughter's sake, and he'd do well to remember that.

He entered the house ahead of her and Melana— it would take time getting used to thinking of her as Ashanti—raced over to him. "Guess what? Uncle Ron went to the commissary to buy lots of food. We're going to have a big family dinner!"

"That's great, honey," he told her, looking beyond her to her new family. It was hard not to feel a little possessive. For so long it had been him, Kim, and Melana, and now she had this family of grandparents, aunts and uncles, cousins. "I think I'll check in at work."

She looked crushed by his statement, and Chris relented. He wasn't really a part of this family and didn't particularly want to have dinner with them, but Melana didn't want to leave him out, which meant a lot to him.

He heard a horn blow and sighed at the reprieve. "That's Uncle Ron. Want to help bring the groceries in?"

Mr. McIntyre stood. "Why don't we all help?"

Mr. McIntyre, his wife, Mia, and Cai filed out ahead of them and as Chris turned to follow, Melana caught his hand.

He stopped. "Everything all right? How'd you like meeting your grandparents and aunt?"

"They're cool. They look like me. But you're still

my dad, right?" she whispered, leaning forward so no one would hear her.

Chris knelt down to her eye level. "I'll always be your dad."

She frowned. "How come Kimmy had me?"

Of course it would have only been a matter of time before he'd have to explain, but it would've been nice to have more time to prepare. "She stole you from Cai when you were a baby. She really wanted you, but what she did was wrong."

"So she was a bad person?"

When he thought about the pain she caused Cai and her family and the time Melana had lost with her birth mother, he wanted to say, *yes*, but was it right to destroy Kim's image altogether? There was just no way to know how to handle this situation. "Not bad. Sick . . . mentally sick. Do you understand what I'm saying?" How could she? "Listen, Mel—do you want to be called Melana or Ashanti?"

"I like Ashanti, but you can call me Mel."

"Okay, Mel. It's hard to understand all of this. I don't get it myself, but tomorrow me, you, and Cai are going home together. We're going to be a family just like you wanted."

"We're going to keep her! Oh, yeah, oh, yeah," she sang, dancing around.

Chris laughed, his heart nearly bursting at the sight of her unrestrained joy. This was definitely Ashanti.

Cai was helping her mother butter a hot batch of homemade biscuits in the kitchen—all of her daughters had inherited her love of cooking—when she caught her mother's wondrous expression. "It's good to have Ashanti back, isn't it?"

"It's good to have you back, too," she responded tearfully.

"Oh, Mom." Cai wiped her hands on a dishcloth and then hugged her mother.

Her mother held her tight, but it didn't have the claustrophobic feel of these last years. They held each other for a long time despite the crushed atmosphere. Eight people in one kitchen was a bit much, Cai thought with an indulgent smile.

"If we're passing out hugs, I'd like one myself," her father said next to her ear. Her mother released her and Cai turned into her father's embrace. "Congratulations," he whispered into her ear.

"For what?" she whispered back.

"Finding Ashanti. As scared as I was imagining you in all sorts of dangers, I never doubted you. You're one of the strongest women I know and one of my three best girls," he added with a teasing smile.

Cai chuckled, her vision blurred with tears again. He called all of his daughters his best girls. *Keeps the jealousy down,* he used to tell them.

Taking her hand, Mia pulled Cai toward the living room. Ashanti, who was helping Chris make a salad to go with the vat of spaghetti Ron was cooking, stopped to give Cai a kiss on the cheek. Her gaze met Chris's and he glanced away.

He had been so distant since their return, but she'd seen him and Ashanti talking, and the little girl was so happy. He couldn't have told her Cai wouldn't be a part of her life. He wouldn't be so cruel no matter how angry he was.

Mia plopped onto the couch and pulled her close. "You look happy, baby sis. I can't begin—"

"Then don't," Cai said gently. She knew exactly where this was headed. "Don't blame yourself anymore, you hear me, Mia?"

Mia smiled her first guilt-free smile in a long time, and it went a long way as a balm for Cai's embittered heart. "How's Honor and the baby?"

"More in love everyday. She's already talking about having a little Nicky."

"I can't wait to see her again."

"So what's the plan with Chris and Ashanti?"

Short-term or long? Either way, the answer was a little tricky. "We're going back to Biloxi tomorrow. Ashanti needs a family," Cai rushed on. "And it'll be easier for me to move than Chris since he's in the military."

Mia offered her a wry expression. "You said family. Are you and Chris getting married?"

Cai hesitated. Would her parents disapprove of her plans? What was she thinking? Of course they would. "I don't want to rush into a second marriage, Mia. Look how the first one turned out."

"So you're going to shack-up?" Mia shrieked before quickly covering her mouth with both hands. "Are you looking to start round two with the folks? The first one was bad enough."

On the level of a war wouldn't be an exaggeration. But she was older now, more mature. "We didn't discuss our living arrangement. Maybe we'll alternate on the sofa for a while. I'll talk to him, but I'm sure both of us want to provide Ashanti with the best example possible." Ignoring Mia's dubious expression, Cai changed the subject. "So how's everything with you and—"

"Dinner's done!" Ashanti shouted from the dining room.

"We'll talk soon," Mia told her, hugging her. "We have plenty of time now."

They met the rest of the family, including Ron, in the dining room. Ashanti took Cai's hand and led her to the chair beside Chris's before sitting between her grandparents.

At first Chris and Ashanti seemed overwhelmed by all the noise of a large family. Nobody could stop looking at Cai's little girl, but she seemed to take it all in stride.

"Ashanti tells us you'll be heading back to Biloxi tomorrow?" her father said.

Cai looked to her big sister for help and only received a knowing smile. Her father was pretty predictable.

"We thought that would be best . . ." Cai trailed off. She was almost twenty-eight, not eighteen. Surely, her parents would know she'd grown in ten years.

Her mother turned to Ashanti. "We bought you presents for every birthday and Christmas. You'll have to give me your address so I can mail them to you."

"Cool," Melana said, wide-eyed. "How many presents is that?"

"Well, let's see. There are five of us and you've had nine birthdays so that's forty-five right there. You have even more Christmas presents. That's a lot, huh? Maybe you and Mommy and Daddy can visit us for Christmas and you can open all of those."

"Can we, Daddy?"

Chris glanced at Cai who nodded. "Sure. We'll have to rent a truck to bring everything home."

Melana giggled.

Cai's father set his fork on the plate with a clink and Cai's heart sank at the familiar firmness in his face. "Cai—"

"Mr. McIntyre," Chris interrupted. "I'd like to have a few words with you after dinner. Perhaps we can talk then?"

Her father hesitated. What did that mean? What did Chris want to talk to him about?

He waited patiently for her father's sharp nod and then winked at her. "No worries, okay?" he said to Cai.

Cai's heart melted. How did he know? How did he always know?

"Need me to referee this challenge?" Ron quipped, blocking Chris's path toward the patio.

Now that dinner was over, it was time to talk to Mr. McIntyre. "What challenge?"

"The one you offered Cai's father to take over the role as the man in her life," he said dryly.

Chuckling, Chris brushed his friend aside. "Nah, I got this."

Mr. McIntyre was standing on the patio with his legs slightly apart, his arms folded across his chest. Chris could well imagine taking that same position in another few years when young men would be coming for his daughter.

"You wanted to talk," Mr. McIntyre began.

The sun had gone down since he and Cai had talked earlier. The darkening earth made her father look menacing. "I wanted to let you know that I have the best intentions toward you daughter. I love her."

"Then you're planning to ask her to marry you?"

Straight from the hip, Chris thought. At least now he knew where Cai and Ashanti got their straightforwardness. "Apparently, she was pretty burned by Jason. She's afraid of jumping into another marriage."

Her father relaxed a bit, and even seemed a bit surprised. "I thought she'd put that behind her. She rarely mentioned his name after the annulment."

She had probably been embarrassed, which Chris could well understand. He felt like a fool for letting Kim get over on him. Ron had sensed something was off. Who else had? He'd gone on and on about loving Kim when she had obviously never loved him. Hell, she'd probably laughed at him every day.

He shook his thoughts away. That was the past and he didn't want to let it rule his present and future with Cai.

"Melana mentioned that she and Cai have been sharing a room here. That's how it'll be in Biloxi, or do you have a guest room?"

Subtle, Chris thought, suppressing an urge to smile. "It's a two-bedroom house and during the hurricane we took turns sleeping on the couch." Except for the one night Cai slipped into his bed, but he didn't think her father would want to hear about that. "That should work for us."

"I saw the way she looks at you. She trusts you . . . and that, as well as how well you've taken care of my granddaughter, says a lot about the man you are."

"Thank you, sir. I'll get Cai down the aisle one way or the other, maybe even by Christmas."

Mr. McIntyre chuckled. "I like you, son, so I'll give you a bit of advice upfront. The McIntyre women don't like to be told what to do. You'll have a lot less gray hairs than I do if you just let them have their way from the start."

Chris had already learned that lesson from raising the next generation of McIntyre women. Hadn't he bought Ashanti a cell phone in Alabama?

No, he wouldn't tell Cai what to do, but he knew exactly what he had to do.

* * *

Cai wiped at an errant tear with her fingers as she, Chris and Melana drove away shortly after dawn the next morning. They'd said goodbye to her parents and Mia who were in the car behind them but would go a different route outside the gate. They'd said goodbye to Ron, who put the whole family up last night. His wife would be home later today, so he was probably glad to see them go.

Through the rearview mirror, she saw Melana waving out the back window. She was totally in love with her new family.

Chris handed Cai a tissue. "We'll see them again in a couple of months, maybe even less," he assured her.

It would be the first time she'd looked forward to going home in a long time. Right now, she had a new home to go to.

Last night, after Chris and her dad had talked outside, he'd caught Cai up to speed on the case against the attorney she'd turned over to his office. He'd been extradited to Ohio to face charges as reported, and her dad said there was enough evidence to put him away for a long time, even without her testimony.

Quietly and quickly, before the press could get wind, he would arrange for Cai and Ashanti to test their DNA to prove maternity, and he'd seek to have Jason's parental rights relinquished and have Chris's adoption request processed so they would both be Ashanti's legal parents. Then he'd surprised her by giving her his blessing to make a new family with Chris and Ashanti. That had led her to wonder what the two men had talked about, but neither had been forthcoming.

Also, she'd gathered from talking to her father that she was still missing a week of her life. She'd gone over the timeline of her activities, but they stopped cold shortly after visiting Honor in the maternity ward.

Cai remembered going to Florida to investigate a tip about a baby-stealing ring that might have something to do with her daughter, but the rest of it was a blank. All she remembered was waking up at Chris's house, hurt.

They figured Turner, the attorney mastermind, must have sent someone after her, and now that he'd been arrested and she wouldn't have to testify, there would be no more trouble.

"There they go," Ashanti said, waving furiously out of the window.

Cai waved one more time, too, then turned to Chris. "Let's go home," she told him.

As they headed toward Biloxi, Cai thought about her future as a child-finder. She didn't want to leave Ashanti ever again, not even for a weekend, but being a child-finder was all she knew.

She'd asked her mother to send whatever mail there was in her post office box and then close it. Over the years, she'd gotten into the habit of sending copies of evidence to herself so it wouldn't get lost as she traveled. If she'd sent anything from Florida, it'd be there by now.

Her hand began to shake and before she could stick it under her leg, Chris placed his hand over hers.

"What are you thinking about?"

"My job. I've only ever been a child-finder. I don't know what else I'm qualified to do."

"Do you still *want* to be a child-finder?"

"I don't ever plan to miss another day of Ashanti's life." Cai didn't miss the flash of relief in his eyes. Her job could be dangerous, so she could imagine his worrying. "Chris . . . I don't think I could go back to it if I wanted to."

"What do you mean?"

"I'd have to have complete control of my body to be successful and my hand . . ."

"You probably just need more time to heal, sweetheart. It's only been a little over a week."

He was probably right, but a little voice in the back of her mind told her not to get her hopes up too high.

Chris pulled into the driveway around one o'clock that afternoon, the trip from Georgia—thank heaven—was much less stressful than the trip to Georgia. Ashanti managed to stay awake through most of the drive, but at the last stop Cai had gotten into the backseat with her and Ashanti had dropped off to sleep with her head on her mother's lap.

They were all climbing out when Olivia ran across the street. The girls jumped up and down and threw themselves into each other's arms like they'd been apart for a year instead of a week. Cai smiled as she watched their interaction.

Once they settled down, Ashanti walked over to Cai and said, "This is my mom. My *real* mom."

Olivia's lips formed a perfect O as she stared in surprise.

"Hi, Olivia. My name's Cai, and it's very nice to meet you."

"Hi, Miss Cai." Olivia turned to Ashanti, frowning. "I thought your mom died?"

"I have a lot to tell you," Ashanti said, sounding very grownup.

Chris couldn't fathom how that discussion would turn out.

"Can I go to Olivia's house, Daddy?"

"Okay, but stay there until I come for you, or ask Miss Jasmine to walk you across."

The girls ran off together and he and Cai smiled at each other. "They're a pair, I tell you," he said, grabbing their luggage from the trunk.

"I can't wait to get to know her friends. I want to volunteer at school, throw her a big birthday party, take her shopping, get her ears pierced—if she wants to—oh, and what else? I have so much time to make up for," she said as she followed him toward the door.

She and Ashanti would thrive on every minute.

Cai stopped at the sight of Righteous Red parked in the driveway behind her covered rental car and Chris felt like a fool all over again.

"Is this the infamous car? I have insurance. We'll get it repaired, Chris."

He started to tell her he didn't give a damn about the car, but she'd never believe him. Not after the way he'd carried on.

"It's a beauty."

He unlocked the front door and went in first, flipping on a switch as he entered. The light flickered on though it illuminated very little in the daylight.

The garage door was indeed busted up. He set the bags down and strolled through the front room toward the dining room. Michael must have straightened up the furniture when he'd patched the door.

He left Cai in the front room as he walked through the rest of the house. The other rooms looked untouched, so the guy must have quit looking once he found the address book.

Chris came back into the living room and saw Cai with her legs braced and her hands straight up in a type of karate stance.

When she saw him, she broke the stance. "I can't do it anymore. I've lost it."

He didn't know the first thing about karate, but if she were a fifth-degree black belt, it seemed like it would have taken years of training and self-discipline to reach that level.

Not wanting to make matters worse with empty platitudes, he simply closed the distance between them and put his arms around her.

She rubbed her forehead back and forth across his chest. "I deserve it, to lose my ability, I mean."

"Why do you say that?"

"I turned against the teachings of karate, which is to be used only in self-defense and as a last measure. There were more times than I care to admit when I should have walked away, and I didn't. I was wrong."

Chris didn't know what to say. He wanted to help her, but he just didn't know how. Cai had been worried about Mia's guilt, but it looked like she was carrying a load of her own.

Chris called housing maintenance to have the door replaced. To avoid filing a police report and bringing attention to Cai, whose name and face had been plastered across America, he'd blame the destruction on the hurricane. They dispatched a handyman immediately and Cai waited in the bedroom until she heard him leave.

Chris was closing the door when she strolled into the front room. "The kitchen's empty, so I'm going to get some groceries. You want to stay with Jasmine while I'm gone?"

"Why would I want to do that?" Because she was

crippled physically and mentally and couldn't take care of herself anymore?

"So you won't be alone."

"I don't need a baby-sitter, Chris."

"I know you don't *need* a baby-sitter. I would just feel better if you weren't alone today."

"Don't worry. If someone was after me, they'd have gotten to me by now."

He stopped before her and she could see the genuine concern in his eyes, and a stubbornness she'd seen on at least two other occasions.

"I shouldn't be too long," he told her. "If you need anything, Jasmine's number is on the fridge along with my cell phone number."

He cupped her cheek with his hand and slowly lowered his mouth to hers. He hovered near her mouth and she waited, heart thudding, her body flushed with heat. Making love to Chris would be tantamount to making a full-time commitment, but nothing had changed. She wasn't rushing into a second marriage.

At the last second, she turned her head and Chris's lips brushed against her ear. "I won't be long," he whispered.

Her body trembled as his warm breath flowed into her ear and down her neck. He left and she stood there, her lips tingling with the desire to taste him, her body heavy with need.

She'd spent years in karate training, honing her body and mind, determined to get control of both, and now she had control of neither.

The doorbell rang and she walked over to the door to answer. Peeking through the peephole, she saw Jasmine, Olivia, and Ashanti on the porch.

As Cai opened the door, she planted her right hand on her hip. "I take it Chris asked you to come watch over me."

Jasmine laughed. "I told him you'd see right through this, but I really wanted to see you again."

Cai welcomed the other woman with a hug as the girls raced off to Ashanti's bedroom.

"How are you? Chris said some of your memory's returned?"

"Everything except the week prior to my coming here. I know I was in Florida on a case, but it's fuzzy from there."

"Well, don't rush it. If you're meant to remember, you will. I can't believe we've had a star in our midst and didn't know it," she said, sitting at Cai's invitation.

Cai almost didn't catch the star reference but then she remembered her secret was out. "I'm not sure I've reached star status," she demurred.

Jasmine peeked around the corner where the girls had gone before turning back to Cai. "Melana told us that her name is Ashanti and you're her real mother. Is that true?"

"Yes." She heard the pride in her voice. Ashanti's mother. "Kim couldn't have children, so she stole my baby, the thief."

Cai bit her lip to keep herself from calling her a liar, too. Chris loved the woman, and even though Ashanti never talked about her, Cai assumed she loved her, too.

"That's amazing. Are you going to take . . . Ashanti away?"

"We've decided to raise her together."

Jasmine's left eyebrow shot up. "Together? So does that mean you two are going to get married?"

Cai groaned. *Not again!*

CHAPTER 13

Something was wrong. Chris could tell.

Cai opened the refrigerator door and dropped a gallon of milk onto the bottom shelf. She was nervous and trying to hide it. How surprising. He'd grown fond of her openness.

He reached for the package of spaghetti in the bag on the floor and their arms touched. Cai stiffened, then quickly moved away.

"What's Ashanti's favorite dinner?" she asked, a little breathless. "I thought I'd cook that for her tonight."

He saw her glance down at herself and followed her gaze to the taut nipples pushing against her shirt. She turned away from him.

What could have happened in the hour he'd been gone? Maybe he shouldn't have left her. He'd known she was feeling vulnerable, so he'd asked Jasmine to visit with her, then rushed through the aisles trying to get back as fast as he could. "Beans with hot dogs on toast," he told her.

Cai chuckled, though it sounded strained. "That should be easy enough. Jasmine came by. Right after you left, in fact."

"Is that right?" he asked blandly. Was Cai upset about that? The threat of attack might be gone but her inner demons were surfacing with a vengeance. Despite her philosophical approach to losing her martial arts ability, it had been a vital part of her, and she didn't need to be alone right now.

She rinsed off a skillet. "So you're fairly easygoing but determined when you want to be. I'll remember that."

Chris reached for a couple of cans of fruit as she opened the beans and dumped them in the skillet. He noticed how she went out of her way to avoid physical contact with him. The way she'd turned from his kiss earlier hadn't escaped his attention either. Now that almost all of her memory had returned, she seemed like a different person. Amber had been open and honest, uninhibited. Cai was more reserved, cautious to the point of being afraid. Of what though?

"What's wrong?" he finally asked her.

She tried to laugh off his question but failed. She leaned against the counter, then began to play with the lock on the sugar canister as if she couldn't be still. "I'm just anxious, I guess. This is the first time I'm cooking a meal for my little girl. I want it to be perfect."

No doubt she'd prepare the simple meal with the same joy she'd exhibited cooking with her family yesterday. The woman had some serious cooking skills . . . But there was something else going on. He wouldn't push her. Wouldn't let her pull away from him altogether, either.

Offering him a tomato, she said, "You want to help me make the salad?"

Her eyes lifted toward him and then lowered, revealing just a hint of shyness. How could she be shy with him after they'd made love?

He took the tomato, deliberately brushing his hand against hers. He felt her tremble and smiled. "I'm not sure I know how to cut it properly. Will you show me?"

She looked doubtful. "I'm not sure there's a proper way to cut a tomato."

"But we don't want to take a chance and possibly ruin the meal you've fixed for Ashanti."

A grin played across her lips and his chest expanded. *There she is,* he thought. "Where's the cutting board?"

Chuckling, he fished the plastic board from a drawer and laid it on the counter. He stepped up behind her and was immediately distracted by the softness of her body, the scent of her hair.

"We should rinse it first," she told him.

She turned on the water and her body jiggled a bit as she adjusted the knobs, bouncing gently against him. He closed his eyes and swallowed hard.

He felt her satiny hand close around his and carry it beneath the water. She washed the tomato, running her fingers around and through his. He pressed closer to her and buried his face in her hair.

"A-are you p-paying a-attention?" she stammered.

He barely recognized her voice it was so thick. Moaning, she rotated her hips and he dropped the tomato to grasp her waist. No, she couldn't do that.

He heard the patter of little feet approaching and backed away to adjust his jeans. He'd almost forgotten that Ashanti—he just couldn't get used to that name—was in the house.

"I didn't know you were back, Daddy." She rushed to Cai's side without giving him his usual hug, which was a good thing right now. "That smells good!"

Cai turned off the water and scooped up the

tomato from the sink. "It's your favorite, right? Why don't you wash your hands while I toss the salad? Chris? Can you set the food on the table?"

He could try. His body was so on fire for her, he could barely string two thoughts together. "Yeah, I can do that."

Grabbing a large ladle from the drawer near Cai's knee, he paused to look at her, but her gaze was trained on the cutting board. Guess they were back to square one. Sighing, he spooned the beans into a serving bowl and carried it to the table.

Ashanti followed, gingerly carrying a pitcher of lemonade. "School reopens tomorrow, kiddo. You ready to go back?"

She set the salad on the table beside the beans. "Sure."

Why did he even ask? He playfully tugged on her French braid, her favorite style at the moment. He figured it'd last as long as any of her other fads.

"I'm not sure if we'll have the spelling test," she continued, "but I'll study just in case."

Cai strolled into the dining room carrying the salad and a saucer of toast and they each fixed their plates. He sat down with Cai on one side and Ashanti on the other. Cai winked at Ashanti from across the small table and the little girl giggled.

Ashanti took a bite of her beans and Chris glanced at Cai, feeling the sudden tension emanating from her direction.

"This tastes different," Ashanti said with her usual candor. "Mmm . . ."

"I added a touch of cinnamon," Cai said quickly. "Do you like it? If not, I can cook it the way you're used to . . ." she trailed off looking both guarded and hopeful.

Ashanti grinned. "Nope, I love it!"

For good measure, she ate another forkful. He saw a sheen of tears in Cai's eyes before she lowered them to her plate. She really was anxious about pleasing Ashanti.

The beans were good, the salad, too. Normally, he just dumped a ready-made bag into a bowl and poured dressing on it, but Cai had added cucumbers, tomatoes, bell peppers, boiled eggs, and sprinkled it liberally with cheese.

Ashanti dug in and he grinned at her bent head. He hadn't been exaggerating when he told Cai she'd brought a new dimension to his little girl.

Cai, on the other hand, was too busy fidgeting with her fork to eat. "Honey?" she said, her lips curved in just about the most endearing smile he'd ever seen. "Would it be okay if I walk with you to the bus stop?"

Ashanti's head snapped up, a stricken look on her face.

"Never mind," Cai said, retreating. "You're too old and it would be embarrassing."

If Chris had known this was coming, he would've spared Cai. Ashanti had claimed public mortification as early as first grade. There was no way she'd want a parent—even a newfound mommy—walking her to the bus stop in the third grade.

"No," Ashanti said, a little stilted. "I won't be embarrassed."

Poor kid. He could only imagine what it took for her to say that.

Cai shook her head. "I shouldn't have asked. It's okay, I won't."

"No!" Ashanti said more forcefully. "I want you to."

"You do?" Cai's guarded and hopeful expression returned.

She did? Ashanti hadn't budged for him and Kimmy, but she loved her mommy something fierce. He was so proud of her for putting Cai's feelings first. The newness of it would wear off soon enough.

Cai relaxed, and her smile was breathtaking. "Okay, but just once . . . well, maybe for this year. But definitely not next year."

Ashanti nodded. "Yeah, because I'll be too old next year."

The irony in her voice went *way* over Cai's head as she mopped at her tears with her fingers.

Chris chuckled inwardly. Living with these two was going to be very interesting.

Cai perched on the edge of the sofa beside Chris, forgetting her plan to keep her distance until she could get her physical reaction to him under control. "I put her on the spot by asking to walk with her to the bus stop, didn't I? Do you really think she minds?"

"You're asking me? She's *your* daughter."

His words touched her to the core. It was still so hard to believe sometimes. Ashanti was her daughter. "Is she a lot like me?"

She knew she sounded desperate, latching onto everything little thing . . . but she needed every little thing to latch onto.

Chris leaned back and stared at the ceiling. "I'm not sure anymore," he admitted. "She knows what she wants and she's outspoken about it like I thought you were, when you were Amber. Now that you're Cai, you're different."

Her heart dipped at the accusation she could hear in his voice. "Different good or different bad?"

He shrugged, nonchalant. "Just different. Before you were *un*guarded, now you're *guarded*."

"But it's not always best to say and do what you think or feel in the moment. It's good to have some self-control."

"It's not always an issue of good or bad, Cai, but I get the feeling you're talking about something specific. Care to elaborate?"

She backed off, unwilling to lie and unable to tell the truth. She found it easier to talk to Chris than she ever had Jason. Jason had always seemed so mysterious and larger than life, there but just out of reach, whereas Chris was generally unflappable. He'd had that moment when he'd realized what he'd married, but even that burst of anger hadn't lasted long.

Cai heard the shower shut off. "Ashanti asked me to help her study her spelling words after her shower. My first," she said, overwhelmed at the opportunity. "Then I'm going to braid her hair."

She put her hands on the cushion to push herself up and Chris placed his right hand over her left one. "Have fun, but we're going to talk about this eventually."

Using his other hand, he brought her mouth down on his for a brief kiss that left her wanting more. She stared at him in confusion before hurrying away. Why was he suddenly touching her, initiating kisses? What about his great love affair with the perfect Kimmy?

Ashanti was waiting for her in the bedroom, and when Cai walked in, she looked up with an eager smile. "Ready?"

Her confusion cleared, at least temporarily, as she concentrated on her daughter. Kim wouldn't have kept a baby book and Ashanti was too old for one, but

Cai could put a scrapbook together to remember all their firsts.

She'd enjoyed watching Ashanti interact with her family and she was grateful for Ron's hospitality, but she was so glad to have her baby all to herself.

Cai peeked at the last word on the list hidden beneath her hand. This was a challenge word so she wasn't sure if Ashanti would get it right or not. "Okay, one more. Spell imaginary."

Ashanti looked less than impressed. "I-m-a-g-i-n-a-r-y."

Laughing, Cai grabbed Ashanti and they fell back on the mattress together. "You know you got your genius from me, right?"

"Daddy said I got it from him, through os . . . osmos . . ."

"Osmosis." Cai laughed. "I don't mind sharing with him. He's been good to you?"

"He's the best dad in the whole wide world! I've been thinking about what you said."

"About what?"

"Kids teasing me because I'm so tall. I don't care about it anymore. And I don't even have to wait until I'm a WNBA player for them to look up to me. They already do!"

Even though Cai's words of advice were probably forever lost in the wasteland of her mind, she laughed and hugged Ashanti close, happy that she'd helped her daughter in a way Kimmy never could've. "You're such a special girl. I love you so much."

Ashanti turned in Cai's arms. "I love you, too, Mommy."

Fresh tears filled Cai's eyes as the envy she'd felt for

the other woman drained away. She was Ashanti's mother and no one could ever take that away from her.

Cai kissed her daughter goodnight and turned off the light on the dresser. She stood in the doorway for a few minutes, partly to avoid Chris and his cryptic statement, but mostly she just didn't want to let Ashanti out of her sight. Even though she hadn't raised her, they were so much alike, down to how they wore their hair. Still, Ashanti was so much prettier and smarter. She was perfect.

At the most, Cai figured she had nine years of daily interaction, then Ashanti would be off to college. Maybe she'd want to attend school close to home and live with them. No, she couldn't hold onto Ashanti forever. She'd have to let her little bird fly. In the meantime, she'd treasure every moment.

Cai reluctantly left her baby and headed back to the front room. In another nine years, she'd have no reason to stay with Chris either, she realized. The thought left her feeling unsettled.

He glanced up from the newspaper spread across his lap. "How'd it go?"

"Great!" Cai breathed, instantly distracted from her grim thoughts. "She is so perfect. She—"

"What?" he asked with an indulgent smile.

Cai covered her face with her hands. "Nothing. This is all so new to me, but you've been with her most of her life."

His hand slipped through her hair to massage her neck and her eyes rolled back in her head. "Doesn't feel real yet?"

"The fear is real. I can't lose her again. I'd never survive." Her heart pounded at the possibility. During her pregnancy, it never occurred to her to even consider the prospect. Now the thought was a reigning terror. "I'm afraid to close my eyes. What if I wake up and it's all been a dream?"

He used the hand massaging her neck to turn her head toward him. "If making love to you the other night was part of the dream, then don't ever wake up."

Cai's body responded instantly to Chris's words. His determined gaze met hers but he didn't lean forward to kiss her. "I think I'll go to bed, too. Did you want me to take the sofa since you have to get up early for work?"

"I'll be okay. Though I don't intend to sleep out here indefinitely, Cai."

She recognized and rose to the challenge in his words. "Whenever you're ready to switch, let me know."

Her head held high, she walked purposefully from the room, his rich laughter mocking her every step of the way to the bedroom. She gazed at the huge bed and knew the joke was on her. She hated being afraid, but once again fear ruled her.

"Cai?"

Cai heard her name being called and slowly opened her eyes in the darkness. Chris was sitting on the bed beside her dressed in his military uniform. She'd never seen him in a uniform and he filled it well with his broad shoulders.

"I'm on my way out, and I didn't want to leave without saying goodbye."

She smiled sleepily, touched that he'd take the time. "What time should I wake Ashanti?"

He offered her a lopsided grin. "You're kidding, right?"

"She wakes up by herself without the alarm?" She

laughed but her laughter quickly dissolved into tears. Covering her eyes, she said, "I've missed so much."

"I know, sweetheart. But you have the rest of your lives."

She nodded through her tears. "I swear I've turned into a big baby. I *never* cry!" she wailed.

"Then I'd better buy a mound of tissues because you must have a lot of tears stored by now."

She laughed. He was teasing her, trying to make her laugh, and she appreciated that.

"That's better," he told her. "I'd better go. You'll be all right by yourself? I'll call you when you get back from the bus stop. I have a feeling I'll need to cheer you up again." He started to get up but stopped. "Oh, don't forget the tow trucks will be here for both cars sometime this morning, okay?"

He kissed her on the mouth, a brush of their lips that invited her to pull away or deepen the kiss. Last night before she went to bed, he'd given her the option of a first move and she'd chosen to wait him out. Apparently, she wasn't going to get another first move option.

She reached out to draw him closer, but pulled back, refusing to set herself up for the disappointment sure to follow. What did this cat and mouse game mean?

"Chris, I'm not sure what your intentions are—"

"You've forgotten?" he asked with a challenging lift of his left brow.

She shook her head. "No, it's just that I—"

"I'm not Jason, Cai," he said softly.

"I know. But we haven't known each other very long." Definitely not long enough to know if they could spend the rest of their lives together.

"And somehow I feel like I've known you forever."

Now it was her turn to issue a challenge. "Yeah? What's my favorite color?"

"Two days ago, *you* didn't even know that. I know you love your daughter, and you'd do anything for her. I know you're passionate and giving. I know somewhere in there is a fierce defender of the innocent, but right now, fear of being abandoned has resurfaced and you haven't conquered it yet. I also know you will. Should I continue?"

So much for challenging him, she thought with a reluctant smile. "I guess not."

His right hand dropped to her side just beneath her breast. The touch seared her despite the shirt blocking skin-to-skin contact. She waited for him to cup her breast, to tease the nipple into a tight bud the way he had the night they'd made love. Her breasts grew heavy as she remembered the heights to which he'd taken her.

But he remained still.

Then his left hand slid up the back of her scalp and twisted in her hair. He made circular motions with his thumb behind her ear that made her groan out loud. Of all the places he could touch her that had to be one of the most sensual.

She closed her eyes and heard the raspy sound of her own breathing.

"Will you kiss me goodbye, Cai?"

Her immediate thought was a resounding *no!* but she opened her eyes and one look into his chocolate depths and the follow-through fell apart somewhere in the execution.

She pulled Chris toward her and their lips meshed in a whirl of lips and teeth. Her tongue delved into the hot cavern of his mouth, ran across his teeth, melded with his tongue. He tasted like coffee with a touch of sugar and milk, and she drank greedily, his kiss as potent as caffeine.

A low, throaty growl escaped Chris's lips, and he pressed his hand into her back, drawing her closer to him, deeper into the shelter of his body.

They broke apart, breathless. In an almost imperceptible glance, his sharp gaze raked over her, stripping her with his eyes. It felt like a physical caress and her body trembled.

"I should go," he told her.

She nodded, afraid if she opened her mouth she'd find herself pleading with him to stay.

He left and, groaning, she buried her face in the pillow. *You've done this before, Cai. Love does not always equate to happily ever after. Remember that.*

Cai was a wreck. She cried over the bowl of raisin bran she'd fixed for Ashanti—the little girl wasn't a heavy breakfast eater and preferred cold cereal and a piece of fruit. She cried when Ashanti reached for her pink backpack, which somehow reminded Cai of the pink baby blanket she'd wrapped her newborn in all those years ago. Was she ever going to get off this emotional rollercoaster?

Realizing she was staring at Ashanti, Cai spun toward the door, forcing herself to stop before she scared the child to death.

"We'd better go, Mom."

"Okay." It was time for Ashanti to catch the bus, and Cai had been looking forward to this moment all morning.

Opening the door, she automatically reached up to pull her hat down, then remembered she didn't have one. "Honey, does your dad have any hats?"

None of them needed the exposure a media storm would provide if someone identified her.

"On the shelf," Ashanti said, pointing at the closet by the front door.

Cai opened the closet door and grabbed a Miami Heat cap from the shelf, stuffed it on her head, and pulled the bill low over her eyes. Circumstance would force this on her only a short while longer. Soon enough she planned to tell the world—or at least the people in this housing area—that she was Ashanti's mother.

The bus stop was at the end of the block and she could easily see it from the house.

She and Ashanti walked side-by-side downhill. It was a nice fall morning, a little nippy, but not cold. Kids were already playing, chasing after each other, throwing footballs. Bookbags were lined up at the curb. Several parents were grouped together talking, two still in their bathrobes.

Several of the children waved at Ashanti as they approached. Cai nodded at the other parents, but kept her face averted so they wouldn't recognize her.

She'd cautioned Ashanti not to tell anyone else about her new name or her new mommy until they'd gotten everything squared away legally. Once that happened, she would go to the school to meet Ashanti's teachers and sign up for the PTA.

Cai heard the rumbling sound of a bus and the kids began to line up.

Ashanti didn't vie to get first in line like the other kids but waited until everyone settled down to get in the back. "Are you going to come to the bus stop after school?"

She was indeed taller than all the kids. Cai remembered those days, but she'd had Honor to share her plight with. "Did you want me to?"

Ashanti glanced around with a pained expression. "Are you going to be crying?"

Cai chuckled. "I might have myself together by then. Are you going to miss me?"

"Yeah." She grinned. "You gonna miss me?"

Cai hugged her and Ashanti sighed really loud. "Definitely."

"Hi, Mel! Hey, Miss Cai." Cai turned to see Olivia running toward them with her bookbag flopping up and down her back. "You ready for the spelling test today, Mel?"

"Yep. My mom helped me study."

Tears began to trickle from Cai's eyes at the pride in her daughter's voice and Ashanti shook her head.

Olivia's backpack slipped off her shoulder and she straightened it. "I have to go to the dentist, so I'll be leaving school early today."

The bus chugged to a stop, puffing out black soot and a lot of noise. Cai hugged both girls, then watched them crowd the stairs as each child tried to find a seat.

The other parents waved once and walked off, but Cai waved until the bus drove out of sight. On the day she would've started kindergarten, Cai had imagined walking her to the bus stop, camera in hand, letting her little girl go off into the world. Nothing she'd envisioned could compare with this moment.

Tears were falling unchecked as she made her way back up the hill. She counted how many hours it would be before she saw Ashanti again, then thought about the baby blanket she'd quilted during her pregnancy. It might take a little time, especially if her hand didn't cooperate, but she would love to make Ashanti a bedspread and matching curtains for her bedroom.

Her footsteps quickened with her excitement and she wiped her eyes. Hurrying into the house, she grabbed the phone. She had plenty of money for a sewing machine in her purse. She'd call Chris and—

The phone rang and she pushed the talk button. "Hello?"

"How'd it go?"

Chris's sexy voice came over the line and she melted onto the couch. "Let's just say I had to promise not to be crying when I meet at her the bus this afternoon." His chuckle was soft and warm, the way he made her feel. Sharing these moments with him made them even more special. "I thought I'd sew Ashanti a bedspread and curtains for her room. Do you think she'd like that?"

"I'm sure she'd love it. What will you need?"

"I can find a pattern online. I'll need a sewing machine and . . . I'll make a list for you. What time will you be home?"

"Around five. Maybe we could all go to the store together. Get out of the house for a while."

It would be nice to get out for a short break. After seven years of living on the go, Cai would've thought being housebound would bore her, but it didn't. "We should go to the mall, then. I'll blend in easier there."

"Sounds like a plan. I'll see you later."

"Okay. Hey! What's Ashanti's favorite desert? I thought I'd have something ready when she gets home."

"Oatmeal-raisin cookies."

"I know the perfect recipe! Thanks!"

"My favorite color is blue, by the way. In case you need to know for some reason."

Cai smiled, recalling their earlier conversation. "I'll remember that," she said softly.

* * *

Cai was waiting for Ashanti at the bus. As the little girl rounded the corner to come down the stairs, she saw her mother and her face lit up. Tears flooded Cai's eyes.

Ashanti hurried down the stairs and threw her arms around Cai and her tears fell harder. "Tomorrow," she promised. "I'll be better tomorrow." She kept her arm around Ashanti's shoulder as they walked toward the house. "How was school?"

"Great! We're going to have the spelling test tomorrow, to give everybody a chance to study. What did you do today?"

"I baked you some oatmeal-raisin cookies. Your dad said that's your favorite?"

Cai released her and Ashanti opened the front door. "Yep. Will you teach me how to cook?"

"I sure will." Cai followed her inside. "I can teach you to sew, too. In fact, I thought I'd quilt a blanket for you. Would you like that?"

"Sure, but . . ."

A slight frown marred her pretty face and Cai's heart sank. "What's wrong? You don't want a blanket?"

Ashanti's shoulders drooped. "I do, but how come you just didn't do it? Olivia's mom wouldn't have asked. She just would've done it."

Cai scratched her scalp. She couldn't say she'd seen that coming. "Mmm. Well, I picked out a pattern so we'll go with that—unless you really, really don't like it, okay?"

Ashanti threw her hands up. "Mom!"

Cai captured Ashanti's hands and pulled her around so they were facing each other. "I'll work on it. I promise." Work on being a mom. Was there any such thing? She pushed Ashanti over to the table. "I'll pour you a glass of milk."

She strode into the kitchen, grabbed the milk from the refrigerator, and poured the cold liquid into a glass. If she couldn't handle the easy stuff, how would she deal with the tough stuff, like discipline? How would Ashanti respond to that? What if she decided she didn't want to be mothered after all? The thought terrified Cai.

She carried the glass into the dining room and sat down beside Ashanti.

"Do you want to sign my agenda?"

"Agenda?"

"We write our homework assignments in it and a parent has to sign it each night."

A parent. The word still managed to catch her off guard. "I'd better not sign it just yet, but may I look at it?"

Ashanti pulled the spiral notebook-type agenda from her backpack and for the first time ever, Cai looked at her daughter's *agenda*.

"I guess I'd better do my homework. I always do before I go outside, so I won't forget."

"That's a good idea," Cai told her, marveling at her offspring. Her mom used to drag her in the house kicking and screaming to do homework. In an effort not to smother the child, she forced herself to stand up. "Let me know if you need any help."

Smiling, Ashanti pulled a math book from her bag, and Cai reluctantly left her. She padded down the hallway to Chris's room and stretched out across his bed. Picking up the phone, she called *her* mommy.

"Hello?"

"Hey, Mom," Cai said forlornly.

"Cai! What's wrong, darlin'?" she asked in a tender voice.

"I'm terrified of my own daughter! I feel like I did the first time I held her. Remember how scared I was that I was going to drop her?"

"I remember. But I also recall that you didn't. Most first-time parents are nervous, honey, and normally your experience and comfort level increase as you interact with the baby. You were stuck at the infant stage for nine years while Ashanti continued to grow, but you'll catch up with her."

That made sense. She guessed. "How long will it take?"

"You'll get the hang of it, but you'll always be in wonder of the life you brought into this world. I have had no greater joy than seeing my girls grow into the strong women you've turned out to be."

Cai buried her forehead in her hand. She didn't remember her mother being so poetic. "That's lovely, Mom. But right now I need practical advice on how to deal with a nine-year-old."

Her mother laughed. "Just love her, darlin'. The rest will come."

"Maybe I'll call Dad," Cai said wryly. Feeling better, she decided to change the subject to a happier topic. "Have you mailed Ashanti's gifts yet?"

"They should be there in the next few days."

Cai couldn't wait. Ashanti's birthdays had been the most unbearable over the years. She'd spend an entire day shopping for the perfect gift, then she'd lovingly wrap it and pray that one day she'd be able to give it to her. Now she finally could.

Of course with the past always come thoughts of Jason. "Have you heard from Jason?"

"No, he's disappeared off the radar again. The

notice of parental relinquishment has been posted in the newspaper. If he doesn't come forward in thirty days, he forfeits his rights to Ashanti."

In nine years, he never showed interest in finding her, so Cai didn't know why he'd bother to claim his rights now. How curious that he would show up out of nowhere proclaiming he wanted another chance, present himself as a devoted husband on national TV, then disappear. Of course, he was good at disappearing.

CHAPTER 14

"We're here!" Ashanti screeched scrambling out of the seatbelt before Chris could pull into a parking space.

Cai smiled at her enthusiasm. Ever since she'd told Ashanti they were going to the mall, the little girl had been so excited, confessing that Jasmine had often invited her to the mall with her and Olivia, but it wasn't the same. She'd wanted to go with her own mother and now she could.

In one quick glance, Cai assessed the turquoise and white one-story Edgewater Mall. Three glass entrances. A Dillard's and JCPenney located on opposite ends with probably a hundred stores between. It was small compared with malls in Columbus, which worked for her. The less people there were to deal with, the less chance of being recognized.

Opening the door, Cai climbed out of the car and inhaled the salty, sandy air. The mall was located across the street from the shore of the Mississippi Gulf Coast. She met Chris at the back of the car, and they followed Ashanti as she skipped ahead.

He tapped her arm with his elbow and she glanced

to her left. His lips parted in a sweet smile and she felt a tug at her own lips. She hadn't quite known how to greet him when he'd come from work earlier. Despite the intimacy they'd shared and the fact that she was nine years older than the first time she'd made love, she still felt like the gauche teen Jason had seduced. Feeling silly and out of sorts, she'd launched into a conversation she couldn't even recall while he'd watched her with a patient expression on his handsome face.

Chris opened the door and Cai followed Ashanti inside. The mall was bright with shops on the left and the right and farther down, a huge carousel.

The little girl spun toward them. "Daddy, we'll meet you right back here in an hour, okay? *Please*, dad."

Cai saw the relief spreading across Chris's face and bit her lip to keep from laughing. When he'd suggested they get out of the house, he'd probably meant a quick run to Walmart, not a mall-length shopping spree.

He took his wallet from his pocket. "Let's meet at the food court."

Cai placed her hand over his. "We don't need any money." She didn't want to hurt his feelings or seem ungrateful, but her first trip to the mall with her daughter was on her.

He didn't argue but slipped the black leather wallet back into his pocket.

Bouncing with excitement, Ashanti grabbed Cai's hand and dragged her off. They passed several stores—a My Oh My, a beauty salon, Merle Norman—until Ashanti came to a stop in front of an outrageously expensive fashion boutique. "Olivia and her mom shop here all the time. Do you want to get matching outfits?"

Cai looked into Ashanti's eager eyes and couldn't

resist. "Oh, yeah." Chris had bought them dresses that were the same color but they weren't matching outfits, so they were about to do this up right.

A smiling salesclerk approached them. "Good evening, ma'am. May I be of some assistance?"

Cai captured Ashanti's hand. "No, thanks. We know just what we're looking for."

Cai spotted the dress section and headed that way. They'd get some jeans and tops, too, but first she wanted to buy her princess some pretty dresses.

She saw a lovely red flounced dress with a three-tiered flared hem she knew Ashanti would *love*. They were the same complexion and the color was perfect.

"Look, Mommy." Ashanti held up a hanger with a beautiful tan ballet neck sweater with a wide neckline—to be worn off the shoulder—and a full flowing skirt with a shell belt to compliment the outfit.

Her daughter definitely had Honor's eye for fashion. "It's gorgeous, but no off-the-shoulder for you, young lady." She said that in her best I'm-the-mother-tone and felt quite proud of herself.

Ashanti grinned. "How about the skirt? We can probably find another top that's the same color."

"Deal." Cai breathed a sigh of relief. Maybe she'd have this parenting thing down in this lifetime after all. "Let's try these on, then go buy some jeans!"

Ashanti gave her a thumbs-up. "Yeah!"

Standing in front of a mirror at the Hat Shack, Cai tucked her hair beneath the black Gypsy hat she'd just bought and lowered the bill over her right eye.

Through the mirror, she saw Ashanti tuck her baby blue Gypsy hat between her teeth and try to put her hair up the way Cai had. As she reached for the hat, her hair fell and she grunted in frustration.

"Why don't you wear your hair down? It's so pretty." Cai stepped behind her and spread her hair down over her shoulders and put the cap on in a cute side style. "Perfect."

Ashanti turned her head from side to side, admiring the hat. "How come you wear yours up?"

"To hide my identity, the way I look."

Her gaze met Cai's in the mirror. "How come?"

"So people won't recognize me. In my job, my old job . . . I used to find missing children and I worked undercover for my safety and for the kids' safety."

Ashanti turned around, her gaze earnest. "How come you don't work anymore?"

Cai tapped her upturned nose with the tip of her index finger. "Because I found the one baby I've been looking for."

Ashanti's eyes widened. "Me?"

Cai nodded, close to tears. Each case had taken a small piece of her heart, but she couldn't regret even one of them because they'd given her the experience to find her Ashanti. Thank God she'd never given up.

Unable to resist, Cai cupped her daughter's cheeks. She sighed. Smiled. "I guess we should find your dad. He's probably wondering where we are by now."

They picked up their bags and as Cai followed Ashanti out of the store, she caught a glimpse of an undercover security guard trying hard not to look like one.

"The food court's this way," Ashanti told her, turning left. "Do you want to share a smoothie? Strawberry-banana is my favorite."

Cai trailed behind, distracted. "I'd love to."

With the hat on, she felt a little more secure. There

were more people than she'd anticipated for a week-night, but no one was expecting the BHV to be here, so she should be okay.

They reached the crowded food court. There were lots of food choices, from pretzels to catfish to pizza. Ashanti guided her over to Nezatsy, just outside the food court. Cai scanned the area as she placed their order. She noticed the security guard again and pinpointed the suspect under observation—a Caucasian male between eighteen and thirty, the average shoplifter.

The mental rush that always accompanied a new case hit her out of nowhere. The key to success was knowledge. Figure out the motive and the rest pretty much took care of itself. From his clean, professional look, it was obvious he could afford whatever he'd taken. He'd probably started as a teen and enjoyed the thrill. He'd chosen an inexpensive item, something he could pay cash for if apprehended. Thinking it not worth the hassle of filing a report, the manager would let him off with a warning.

Ashanti took the cup from the employee. "This is the most fun I've ever had."

"Me, too, honey." Cai paid for the drink and followed Ashanti to a table.

The guard approached the perpetrator and she watched. He'd go without incident, not wanting to be handcuffed and draw attention to himself. Too bad. The chase was half the fun.

The thought sank into her consciousness and she blinked. Those days were over for her.

She noticed Chris coming toward them, carrying a small bag in his hand. He was nibbling on a hot pretzel and she smiled absently at his penchant for junk food. He'd eaten three oatmeal-raisin cookies after work.

Ashanti jumped up and raced off in one smooth motion as Cai watched the two men walk away together. Her hand began to tremble.

Chris' dark eyes narrowed on Cai. "You all right?"

She held her hand beneath the table. "I'm fine. I see you've been shopping," she said to distract him.

He knew her too well.

"I bought a camera so we can take pictures of Ashanti and of you and Ashanti."

"And you, too, Daddy." Ashanti clapped her hands together. "There's a photo booth by the carousel! We should get our picture taken together."

Chris slid onto the chair beside Cai and captured her still hand. "How about it?"

"Sounds like fun." She forced a smile for their sakes. It really did sound like fun, but the adrenaline was beginning to fade, leaving her feeling somewhat at a loss.

She'd always thought when she found her daughter, she would be complete. When she saw Ashanti so happy, there was peace, but what about the other parents who might never know her joy? Was it selfish of her to walk away just because she'd gotten what she'd wanted?

"Mom? Are you ready?"

Cai glanced up at Ashanti's question and saw her and Chris's curious expressions. "I'm ready."

Chris released her hand to stand and she felt even more bereft. Her hand had stopped shaking so she reached for the bags. Chris stretched forward to grab them, too, and the clash sent shivers of awareness up her arm, reminding her of the desire she'd felt when he'd pressed against her in the kitchen yesterday.

Their gazes met and she knew by the look in his eyes that he was remembering, too. He wanted her. He'd made no secret of that, but how did he feel about Kimmy? Did he still love her?

He picked up the bags and they followed Ashanti who had run ahead. As they walked to the other side of the mall, Cai noted a couple of stores she wanted to visit the next time they came. One upside to early retirement was her choice of colorful clothes in place of the usual black outfits she wore.

Ashanti was impatiently waiting for them at the picture booth, her hand on her hip, her right foot tapping against the floor. "What took you guys so long?"

The booth was small, too small for three people.

Chuckling, Chris reached into his pocket for some change. "Sorry, kiddo. You ready?"

She slid inside and posed in a silly position. Laughing at the little girl's antics, Cai squeezed in beside her and they took the next two pictures together. Their first, she thought nostalgically.

"Come on, Daddy," Ashanti said. "We need one of the whole family."

Chris eyed the machine with a skeptical lift of his brow. "I don't think we can all fit in there."

Cai climbed out. "You just have to use your imagination. Okay, Ashanti. You come out first."

The little girl slid off the small seat, then Cai shooed Chris inside. Still looking doubtful, he settled inside, his big legs slightly parted. *What did she just get herself into?* Cai wondered. She took a deep breath and climbed onto his lap.

"My imagination just kicked in," he murmured in her ear.

His warm breath flowed across her cheek and down her neck, making her feel weak. Swallowing hard, she wiggled her fingers toward Ashanti and helped her shift her legs over Cai's until they were all inside.

Ashanti lifted her hand over her shoulder. "Where's the money, Daddy."

"In my pocket," he answered, laughing.

Ashanti burst into a fit of giggles and with a sheepish grin, Cai helped her out of the booth and shifted across Chris until she could reach his wallet. Trying hard, she might add, to ignore the bulge pressing into her back.

He took the money out of his wallet, Cai scooted back over—slowly—and Ashanti climbed back onto her lap.

Ashanti eased the bill into the slot. "Everybody ready?"

Cai nodded. "Ready."

Chris just groaned.

Cai put her arms around Ashanti just as the flash flickered. They couldn't change poses, but she moved a little to the right and leaned back toward Chris so their faces were close together. He smiled at her and the second picture snapped.

"Don't move," he whispered.

She couldn't if she wanted to—but she didn't want to. He lowered his mouth to hers and just as their lips touched she saw an explosion of light beneath her eyelids.

"It's going to take a few minutes for the pictures to print," Ashanti said.

Cai jumped, flustered. Did the machine already take the third picture?

Locking his arm around Cai, Chris offered Ashanti several dollar bills. "Why don't you ride the carousel, honey?"

She took the money. "Are you and Mommy going to have your picture taken?"

"Among other things," he said in a throaty growl that made Cai quiver. If he hadn't been holding her, she probably would've slid right off of his lap.

Ashanti skipped off, oblivious, leaving Cai and Chris alone.

His hand slipped beneath her top to rest on her belly and she sucked in a quick breath. "We shouldn't be too much longer. There's probably a line by now."

She glanced to the right and left and, of course, there was no one waiting to enter the booth.

"Let's take your hat off. You shouldn't hide your beautiful hair."

Just for a few minutes, she told herself. She slipped the hat off her head and allowed her hair to swing free. Hiding wasn't a choice she wanted to make. The media could be relentless and she didn't want any of them exposed to that.

Chris placed a dollar in the slot and she leaned back into him. "It's okay to smile. I don't bite . . . unless you want me to."

He gently sank his teeth into her neck and she laughed just as the bulb flashed.

Smoothing her hand over her mouth, she said, "Okay, let's get a serious shot."

Chris rearranged his face into a very solemn expression and she laughed again, completely ruining her own idea.

"I thought you wanted a serious pose?" he asked with a straight face.

He looked at the camera, grave face back on and she slowly turned forward. Suddenly his fingers slipped around her waist, and he began to tickle her.

Laughing, she tried to get away from his hands. The

camera clicked, taking the photo, and she tapped his arm with her fist. "You play too much!"

He chuckled. "I couldn't resist."

Their humor faded and she leaned into him. Neither of them moved as they waited for the finished product to slide out.

Chris' fingers trailed up her sides, skimming the edges of her breasts. Easing across her shoulders and up her neck, he buried his hands in her hair. She closed her eyes and waited, her mind and body on the precipice, ready to fall at his command.

Sighing, he gathered the long strands in one hand and put her cap back on her head. His fingers trailed back down her neck and across her shoulders, lingering for a moment. "We should go."

Her eyes flew open. "Chris—?"

He took a deep breath. "Cai—"

"Yeah, we'd better go," she interrupted, refusing to let him be the one to reject her.

Jason had left her and she would not give Chris the chance. He was physically attracted to her, but he'd told her time and time again that he loved Kimmy. She needed to remember that.

Something was bothering Cai. To date, she hadn't told him what, but he'd seen the confusion and despair in her eyes at the mall a week ago. She did not like to share her feelings and she was damned good at hiding them, at least with him. She couldn't be less uninhibited toward her daughter.

Besides the sewing machine and a bunch of fabric she was miraculously transforming into a blanket, she'd bought a scrapbook where every mother–daughter first was lovingly notated. Her enthusiasm for simple things, like walking the child to the bus stop or having a warm after-school snack prepared, hadn't waned, and may have increased.

Cai and Melana had developed a nightly routine that mostly excluded him, but he didn't mind, knowing how much alone time with her baby girl meant to Cai. She was a good mother. She'd started a little rocky, questioning herself, asking his opinion on the smallest thing, even calling her mother every other day, but her confidence was growing.

Ashanti was thriving in a true mother–daughter relationship. She wasn't even much of a stickler for cleanliness anymore, but that probably had more to do with the fact that Cai was a neat freak, too, and kept the house spotless.

He'd indulged Cai for a week, but now it was his time. He'd suggested they ask Jasmine to keep Ashanti so the two of them could go out to dinner. Ten emphatic *no*s later because "she wasn't ready to leave her baby," he'd asked her to meet him in the living room at nine o'clock, which would be more than enough time for Ashanti to be asleep.

At the exact hour of his request, he heard his bedroom door open. Even though they weren't fully alone, this was the closest they'd come since they'd gotten back to Biloxi, and he was looking forward to it.

Cai was wearing the night-shirt he'd bought her in Georgia. At the time, he'd opted for something that covered her, and he couldn't regret it as he imagined uncovering the treasure beneath.

She stopped in the entryway, her gaze darting around the room until it settled on him. He hadn't bothered to hide his desire for her, so she'd probably expected a full-blown seduction scene. He wasn't going to seduce Cai because that was what Jason had done. No, Cai needed to come to him fully aware of what she wanted and ready for it.

If she needed a nudge, though, he'd help her along. "Want to watch a movie with me?"

She hovered in the entryway. "It's been a long day . . ."

"Yes, it has." Every day was a long day when he began each morning with a goodbye kiss that would have to last him twenty-four hours.

Teetering from one foot to the other, she hesitated. "I'll . . . get my blanket."

She dashed out of sight and he allowed himself a small sigh of relief. He hadn't been sure they'd get this far. Other than those early morning moments when her resistance was down, she'd stoically kept as much distance between them as she could.

Chris heard the swish of fabric crossing the floor and glanced up. Cai had wrapped the thick comforter around her twice and could barely walk. Chuckling softly, he reached for the remote. He was in for a long night. When he saw her curl into a ball on the other end of the couch, his theory was confirmed.

He bypassed an NBA basketball game and she spun toward him. "Want to watch the game instead?"

"All right." The Wizards were playing the Nuggets. He was a Heat fan himself, but this would probably be a good game. "Rooting for any particular team?"

"I haven't had a chance to watch a game in . . . years. I used to play in high school."

"What position?"

"Shooting guard. Ashanti, too, right? I've seen her out there. She has game."

"You should give her some pointers."

"It's been so long. Mia was into karate and I wanted to be just like my big sister, so I started getting into that. Playing basketball requires commitment and self-discipline, but karate took me to another level. Good thing, too. I needed that type of focus later."

Chris studied her for a moment. Was that Cai's problem, a lack of focus? She was going through so much right now, learning how to be a parent, fighting her feelings for him, giving up her career, unable to control her body. "Now that you've retired, maybe you can relax a bit. You must have stayed on edge in that line of work."

He saw her massaging her left hand.

"Yeah, but . . . I still have to be able to depend on me."

"It must be lonely depending only on you," he said softly.

"Sometimes," she confessed.

As if to punish him—or herself?—for admitting to that much, she turned her back to him to watch the game while he continued to watch her. Mr. McIntyre had suggested letting Cai have her way and Chris wasn't about to force her to do anything. In the first place, he wouldn't be successful. Cai was fiercely independent and used to working on her own timetable. Prodding her along wasn't the answer either. So what, live with her for the next nine years sleeping out here on this damned couch? That just wasn't an option.

"I was so tired just before I left for Florida," she began in a small voice. "Honor asked me to stay with her, to be a part of the family again, and shower all the love I'd stored for Ashanti on them. I was so tempted."

"That's because we were *designed* to be in relationships. My parents were only children and I'm an only child, so when they died, I was alone. I think that's why I jumped into marriage so quickly. After Kim died, I thought I'd never fall in love or want to get married again, so I cut that part of me off. But I was only partly alive, Cai. Existing. And that's not enough for me anymore."

Cai turned toward him, her ebony eyes liquid in the moonlight. "Do you still love her?"

Chris took a deep breath. "As much as I hate to admit it, even to myself, I never knew her."

A lone tear slipped out of the corner of Cai's eye and traveled down her cheek. When they'd first discovered Kim's deceit, he'd mistaken the look in Cai's eyes for pity. Now, he saw understanding. She must have felt the same way about Jason.

Slowly, she allowed her head to lower onto his chest, and Chris was overwhelmed by the trust she was placing in him. He leaned back against the arm rest, bringing her with him. Maybe a little prodding mixed with patience worked after all.

With a quick glance at the clock on the stove, Cai touched the peanut brittle cooling on the counter. Ashanti's bus would be here any minute, and if she didn't leave now, she'd be late.

Grabbing a jacket and her hat, she stuck the hat on her head and slid her arms through the sleeves, then hurried out the door. Last night she'd fallen asleep in Chris' arms, her heart relieved of its burden as she'd confessed how lonely her life had been before him and Ashanti. Today, she felt jittery, out of sync.

As she jogged to the bus stop, she saw the bus chugging along. They were a little early today. There were a couple of parents off to the side on the sidewalk, so Cai waited in the street near the curb. They waved and she raised her hand in acknowledgment. She'd gotten an update from her father today. The lab had received the cotton swabs of DNA she and Ashanti had submitted last week. It wouldn't be long now before they confirmed maternity.

The bus rumbled to a stop and the door opened. Cai glanced around uncomfortably as kids filed down the stairs. She saw Ashanti hurry down the stairs, then jump off the bottom step. "Hi, Mommy!"

"Hey, sweetie. How was your day?"

"Great! We had a substitute teacher and . . ."

Cai felt strangely divided as Ashanti chattered. Something was definitely wrong. She glanced over her shoulder, then in a semi-circle. So sure the threat had been eliminated, she hadn't taken stock of the area the way she normally would and wasn't sure what was out of place.

". . . so Olivia's dad picked her up. She should be home by now, though. Can I go to her house after I finish my snack? I don't have any homework today."

"Sure, honey."

"And guess what else? I might get a lead in the Christmas program. Can you sing, Mommy?"

"I couldn't carry a note in a bucket," Cai said absently.

Ashanti laughed. "That's funny! Can Aunt Honor or Aunt Mia sing?"

Cai picked up the whirring sound of a helicopter blade and began hurrying Ashanti along. "We have to get in the house, honey."

"Why?"

"Something's . . . not right. When I say go, run straight to the house. If we're separated, go inside and lock the door. Do you understand?"

"But, Mommy—"

"Don't argue with me, Ashanti!" she said more sharply than she'd intended.

Hugging the little girl to take the sting out of her words, Cai spotted a blue van two doors down on the other side of the house. Two people were inside, one behind the wheel, the other in the passenger seat. They were definitely out of place and that meant trouble.

She'd have to run interference. Timing was crucial. A moment's hesitation and the guy in the passenger seat would beat them to the door.

A swarm of cars descended from both directions and Cai groaned. "Go!"

She and Ashanti shot off and the men from the blue van bolted out the doors. Cai didn't recognize them. She matched Ashanti's stride but ran at an angle that would put her directly between the men and her daughter.

Ashanti ran up the hill, pumping her arms fast. "Mommy, mommy, I'm scared!"

The man sprinting toward them looked startled. Who was he? She noticed the other guy hoisting a camera onto his shoulder. Reporters! Damn. How had they found her? The first man stopped and even backed away as Cai veered back toward Ashanti and covered her face with her jacket.

Cai pushed the door open and hustled Ashanti inside. Breathing hard, she spun around and locked the door, then jerked back around to check on Ashanti.

She was jumping up and down and pacing back and forth, practically bouncing off the wall with adrenaline. "Let's do that again!"

Again? Cai's mind snapped, a clean clear break with reality. She fell back against the door and slowly slid to the floor, too numb to feel anything, but keenly aware of everything. Her senses heightened, she heard Ashanti gasp, heard her footsteps fade away and return, then she felt the little girl plop down beside her. She was crying, but Cai couldn't move to comfort her.

"I called Daddy. He'll be home in a few minutes. Don't cry, Mommy," she said between sobs.

Was she crying? Cai touched her cheeks and felt the wetness on her fingers but not on her face.

She heard the key twist in the lock and felt the door move. Even though she knew it was Chris, she couldn't move.

The next thing she felt was Chris's strong arms encircling her. "Take Mel to the bedroom, would you?" she heard him say.

"No, don't take her," Cai cried, reaching blindly for the little girl in the darkness invading her mind. "I can't lose her again. I can't . . ."

He squeezed Cai tighter. "She's safe, Cai. Nothing's going to happen to her."

Crying harder, she began to struggle against his hold. "Why weren't you here? You should have been here!"

His arms clamped around her, pinning her arms at her sides. She held her body erect, resisting the comfort he was trying to provide. No, no, no. Just last night she'd admitted how hard it was being a one-woman island. She'd confessed her need for help and Chris hadn't been here.

"I'm here now, honey. I got here as fast I could."

She went limp against him. With gentle hands, he pushed her hair away from her damp forehead. "You want me to go out there and kick their butts?"

He brushed his thumb across his nose and pretended to box and she laughed despite herself. "It's not funny," she protested.

He captured her hands and brought them together

against his chest. "They didn't mean to spook you like that. I think they'll leave you alone a lot faster if you give them a statement."

She let her forehead drop onto their joined hands. Go public? Wouldn't that only feed the frenzy? she thought, lifting her eyes to his. "How did they find me? Only my family and Jasmine know I'm here. I've only been outside to the bus stop. Oh, that one time at the mall, and I always wear a hat."

Chris shook his head. "There's no telling. I had really hoped this nightmare would be over for you."

Cai turned in the safety of his arms. Through the window, she could see about a dozen reporters milling around in the front yard. Chris was right. Her hide and seek game with the press had kept her in the news because of the sensationalism, the unknown. By coming forward, she'd dispel the myth. "Keep Ashanti inside, okay? She's off-limits to the press."

"I agree, and I'll go with you." His chin dropped to her right shoulder. "We're in this together, Cai. It's time you start depending on that."

Her heart softened at his words. "Let me check on Ashanti and splash some cold water on my face."

She hurried off, knowing but needing to see for herself that her daughter was okay. Stopping outside the little girl's bedroom, Cai peeked inside and saw a much calmer Ashanti chatting with Jasmine.

Backtracking, she slipped into the bathroom. Gripping the edge of the counter, she silently dared her hand to shake. Just last night she'd told Chris she had to be able to count on herself, but she hadn't even realized she was being watched. Not blocking the area was unforgivable. Know your environment—that was the first thing she'd learned in her business.

"I didn't protect her," she mumbled, her head bowed.

Her knees buckled at the thought but she caught herself. Taking a deep breath, she turned on the faucet and cupped her hands beneath the cold water. This wasn't the time for weakness, but a time for change.

Cai stepped outside ahead of Chris and the reporters began throwing out questions the moment they saw her.

"Are you the BHV—?"

"Why'd you keep your identity a secret—?"

"What's your next case—?"

Cai exuded a quiet strength as she waited for them to quiet down. Chris captured her hand and she smiled at him. She had to be the strongest woman he'd ever met.

"My name is Cai McIntyre. Nine years ago, my daughter was kidnapped from me. For the last seven years I've been a child-finder, and, in the process, I was dubbed the Bounty Hunter with a Vengeance. In recent weeks, I've had the good fortune of being reunited with my daughter, and I ask you to please respect our privacy as we strive to be a family again. Thank you."

A young woman thrust her microphone toward Cai. "Will you testify against Mr. Turner in the case?"

"The District Attorney has informed me that there is enough evidence without my testimony, but should I be needed, I will be available."

"What are your plans for the future?" another reporter asked.

"To raise my daughter."

"Is this the end of the BHV?"

"Yes, it is."

Cai didn't miss a beat, which surprised him. For

seven years, she'd dedicated her life to finding children. Giving it up would not be easy.

She nodded at him, signaling the end of the impromptu press conference. Chris positioned himself between her and the reporters, but they didn't rush her. Now that they'd done their damage and gotten their scoop, maybe they'd leave her alone as she'd requested.

He closed the front door behind them as he searched her for any signs of breakdown. "You okay?" he asked softly, guiding her toward the couch.

He couldn't have known she'd need him, but he still wished he could have been here for her. Jasmine had phoned him with an SOS, so he had already been on his way when Ashanti called. Thank God she'd kept her head. Instead of being afraid of the people outside, she'd been terrified for her mother. He couldn't blame her. Finding Cai cowering against the door crying had scared the hell out of him.

Her knees buckled and she dropped onto the cushion, her right hand shaking. He carried her hand to his lips and held it there until the trembling stopped. Cai was strong, but she'd reached her limit today.

Ashanti ran into the room with Jasmine behind her trying to catch her. The little girl flew into her mother's arms, throwing her backward.

Half-laughing, half-crying, Cai held Ashanti against her. "Oh, my baby," she murmured. "Did Mommy scare you?"

Jasmine shrugged and mouthed, *sorry.*

Nodding, Chris stood to see her out. "It's okay. Thanks for helping."

"No problem. Cai okay?"

Chris watched Cai and Ashanti speaking softly to

each other. Because of the initial kidnapping, she would probably always have a fear of her baby being stolen. Right now she had Ashanti in her arms and she looked happy. "She'll be fine," he assured Jasmine.

As he opened the door for Jasmine, he noticed that the reporters were gone, at least for now.

He closed and locked the door, then sat back down on the couch. Cai offered him a wobbly smile, her copper eyes bright with relief.

Ashanti straightened and glanced around. "I smell peanut brittle!"

Cai chuckled. "Made especially for you. Why don't you wash your hands, and then we'll break it up together."

"All right!" Ashanti skipped off toward the kitchen, easily bouncing back from a scare as kids do.

Cai watched after her, a soft smile curving her lips. "She's fearless, isn't she?"

Chris slid his hand beneath hers and entwined their fingers. "Just like her mother."

Cai shook her head. "Except she's the real deal. I was . . . terrified."

"Experience hasn't taught her to be more cautious yet."

"I'm ready, Mommy!" she yelled from the kitchen.

Cai's fingers tightened around his until her knuckles whitened. "I hope she never experiences that level of fear. I don't like being afraid. In fact, I hate it."

CHAPTER 15

Sweat dribbled down Cai's temple as she concentrated on executing a front kick in the middle of the living room. She'd almost given up twice in frustration, but she wasn't a quitter. If the time ever came, she needed to be able to protect her daughter.

Running away was not an option. Ever.

She'd made up her mind yesterday and this morning, after walking to the bus stop with Ashanti, she'd returned to the house with a new determination, a new perspective. She wanted her gift back. Of course, fate wasn't cooperating, as usual.

All it would take was a quick snap of her leg, but the command from brain to limb wasn't reaching.

"I was angry," she said to the empty room, her words echoing through the house.

She closed her eyes and concentrated hard, but her leg didn't move. *Come on leg, work.*

She broke the stance. "I did some things I shouldn't have. I admit that. I took risks. I endangered my life."

Exhaling, she repositioned herself. *Just snap, kick out and snap,* she told her leg. *Do it.*

Her leg shook and she stumbled to the left. Crying

out, she raised her fists into the air. "You let my daughter be kidnapped!" she shouted at the fates. "Now I have her back and I can't protect her? That is unacceptable."

Cai's hand began to quiver and she threw herself into the chair in front of the computer. What was she going to do? She couldn't give up. She couldn't.

Her gaze swept across the screen, then jerked back as the scrolling words with the yellow background caught her attention. Out of habit, she'd downloaded the Code Amber Desktop Ticker—a nationwide abducted-child alert system. During an active AMBER alert, the ticker changed to a yellow background and provided details of abductions.

She read the scrolling words.

A new alert, out of New Orleans, rolled by. Cai closed her eyes and took a deep breath. Yesterday, when the reporter had asked about her future plans, her retirement statement had flowed from her lips. It seemed like quitting would be so easy, especially when she had her family's safety to consider, but who was she without her alter ego, a broken-down shell of a woman? That was her legacy?

She clicked on the red and yellow link and read the report. A six-month-old, biracial male had been kidnapped from his Caucasian mother's home. The suspect? His father. Pictures of both the baby and his olive-skinned father were posted. Cai studied his last name for a moment before typing it into a search engine. Creole. They were a proud people and shared a strong bond with one another in a world and culture all their own that extended nationwide. Dad could easily go underground.

Cai felt a surge of energy and waited for her hand to begin shaking. It didn't. Reaching for the phone, she dialed the number listed.

"New Orleans Police Department. How may I direct your call?"

"I'd like to speak to the detective assigned to the missing child case. My name is Cai. I'm the BHV."

That was the first time she'd verbally claimed the title and it felt . . . right.

"I'll put you right through."

"Detective Landry here," a woman's harassed voice barked into the phone.

"Hello, Detective. My name is Cai McIntyre—"

Banging sounds erupted through the earpiece as the phone hit at least three objects on its way to the floor, a less than typical reaction. Detectives were usually too cool to show surprise, let alone admit their need for help.

"The Bounty Hunter?" she squeaked, the sound of her scrambling around breaking her words up.

"Yes. I'd like to offer my help, if you're interested."

A month ago she wouldn't have asked, but would have added one more enemy to the list by assigning herself to the case.

"What can you tell me?" the detective asked.

"He's Creole for one thing, so I'd look into his family, see how far they extend. If I were placing bets, I'd say all the way to the Caribbean."

"I'll do that. Let me give you my direct number so we can keep in touch."

Cai wrote the number down before hanging up. Heady from the adrenaline pumping through her veins, she turned to the Internet to do her own search. The BHV was back. Not in her original form but back. It felt good.

Cai's slick ponytail slapped the back of her neck as she ran through base housing. After she'd dropped

Ashanti off at the bus stop this morning, she'd stretched and begun her daily jog around the perimeter. A light sweat made the cool air against her skin cooler.

There were two gates. Outside the front gate was a body of water with several wooden piers dotting the border. The second gate opened into the base during set hours. Every yard was well-kept with short, edged-up grass, weeded gardens, and manicured bushes.

Three days later, she still couldn't perform a front kick, but she would. Her hand hadn't been shaking, but that usually came with some type of emotional up-heaval. Chris, heaven help him, was getting on her last nerve. His early morning kisses were driving her to distraction, keeping her body on the edge and aching for fulfillment.

In the evenings when she would be fighting the urge to throw herself in his arms with the complete abandonment he loved, he'd smile knowingly. He knew because she practically oozed sex whenever he entered a room.

He'd confessed to not loving Kimmy, so what was holding her back? Did she really believe Chris would leave her the way Jason had? Chris was a good man, but she'd thought the same thing about Jason. The problem wasn't Chris. The problem was her.

She jogged the perimeter twice before heading back to the house. On their block alone there were twenty houses, ten on both sides of the street. One person ran an in-home daycare center, there were three cars parked in driveways, two on the street. She noted the makes and models, filing them in the back of her mind.

Her thoughts turned to the case she'd helped Detective Landry with. Cai knew she'd find the father through his Creole roots, so it didn't take long to figure out that he'd planned to smuggle the child into the Caribbean through his family where strong familial ties would protect him.

She'd wondered if she might feel a little bittersweet not being there when they found the baby, but she hadn't. The chase wasn't important, only the safe return of the child mattered.

What a change, she thought as she slowed to a brisk walk and began her cool down. Could anyone really make so fundamental a change?

Enticed by the lapping water, Cai felt her way along the rickety pier with her foot two days later. The first, fifth and seventh logs were loose. Too much weight and the whole thing would collapse into the cold, murky water below.

Still unable to execute a strong front kick, she'd decided to practice balancing with a basic kata routine. A kata was normally a very formal, prearranged routine combining blocking, kicking, striking, and breathing techniques to demonstrate methods of defense, attack, and counterattack, but in Cai's case she was severely limited.

Breathing deeply, she spread her arms wide and began a sequence of fundamental karate techniques, her movements jerky and uncoordinated instead of beautiful, controlled and perfect.

She let her arms fall to her side, and then gingerly made her way to the end of the pier. "Is this it, then?" she pleaded to the fates. "I abused my gift and this is the punishment?"

The last three logs were also weak. Carefully, she sat down and allowed her legs to swing over the edge. Cool water sprayed her cheeks and soothed her flushed skin. Guess this was where anger and resentment got you . . . sitting on a pier contemplating your life.

What was her problem? She'd lost this one thing but she'd gained so much more—her parents and sisters after so many years of estrangement, Ashanti, who adored her and wanted to be just like her, Chris who loved her. He hadn't said the words, but he'd made his feelings clear in everything else he said and did. Why couldn't she let that be enough? How long would she punish herself for a mistake she made when she was eighteen?

Cai heard a musical tone and reached into her pocket for Ashanti's cell phone. They weren't allowed on school property, so she'd graciously offered to let Cai use it during the day. She glanced at the caller id and saw *Dad's Cell*. She pushed the talk button. "Hi, Chris."

"Are you okay?" He sounded worried.

"Yeah. What's wrong?" Her heart leapt into her throat. "Is it Ashanti?"

"No. I thought you'd be home from your morning jog by now, so I called the house. When I didn't get an answer, I got a little concerned."

"I'm sitting on a pier looking out at this endless pool of water and you know what I was thinking? I'd like to spend a day with you, just the two of us. Can you take off tomorrow?"

"What did you have in mind?"

"I want to make love with you." The realization settled softly in her soul. It was time to let love in, completely.

"What? Cai! What did I tell you about saying whatever you feel?"

Cai heard the smile in his voice and grinned. "You know you secretly love it."

"Yeah, well, your timing stinks."

Laughing, she pushed herself to her feet, paused when the logs shifted, and started back down the pier. "I'm looking forward to tomorrow," she whispered into the mouthpiece.

She heard him swallow. "Me, too," he croaked.

"I'm on my way home. I'll see you later?"

"Definitely."

Cai pocketed the phone, stretched, and began the jog home. She turned onto her street, saw an unfamiliar car with a Louisiana license plate parked several houses from theirs, and slowed. Keeping her face straight ahead, she made a quick sweep of the clean, empty interior out of the corner of her eye. Probably a guest, she told herself, noticing a rental car sticker on the driver's side window.

Still, remembering her slip-up with the reporters, she couldn't take a chance. She'd call Detective Landry to see if she could find out the name of the renter.

Cai was working on Ashanti's blanket when she heard the sound of a truck and glanced out of the living room window. A big UPS truck was parked in front of the house. Perfect timing. Cai had just taken a shower and changed into a dark brown turtleneck and beige mini-skirt. She'd also called and left a message for Detective Landry, who was out of the office.

Quickly folding the material, she rushed to the door and pushed the screen open and locked it in place. A tall, muscular guy was hoisting boxes onto a trolley and she waited anxiously. Ashanti was going to be so excited, and Cai couldn't wait to see her response as she opened each gift.

The young man pushed the trolley up the driveway

to the door, smiling broadly. "Afternoon, ma'am. I have a *lot* of boxes for you."

Chuckling, Cai swept her arm the length of the living room. "You can put them in here."

He shoved the trolley through the door and rolled it over to the far wall. She followed, trying to read the description on the top of the box. There would have to be at least twenty of them.

He pushed the trolley back through the open door and she searched for the box labeled *mail*. He returned with another load, shifted the stack onto the floor, and she went through them.

Finally, Cai spotted her box. Ripping off the tape, she pulled the cardboard pieces back and yanked out a large yellow envelope addressed to herself in her handwriting. The postage stamp was marked Florida.

It didn't look familiar, which really surprised her. Why couldn't she remember that week? What could have happened?

Tucking her legs beneath her on the sofa, she tore into the package. Several bulging legal folders were inside. The first section consisted of a typed bio on which she'd made notations. No surprise there. Knowing the enemy was crucial, and she looked for patterns in their business and personal associations to figure out their M.O., modis operandi.

The evidence she'd gathered against Turner was organized and very easy to read. She didn't remember any of it, though. His minions were an organized group; Turner wielded all the power. He wasn't greedy, which explained why he'd thrived so long. The adoptive parents were rich, desperate couples, so they probably hadn't asked many questions.

The birth mothers were scattered across the country and thoroughly researched. Because of the differing locales, it would be harder to connect the dots and form a pattern.

"Ma'am?" Cai glanced up into the delivery man's sweaty face. "That's everything."

She glanced around the packed room. So caught up in her reading, she'd forgotten he was there.

"Oh! Uh, okay, thanks." Standing, she skirted several layers of boxes on her path to the door. Was it proper to tip? Twenty boxes seemed to warrant a little extra something. Reaching into her purse, she grabbed a ten dollar bill and slipped it into his hand.

He mopped his face with a handkerchief. "Thanks."

She closed the door behind him and reclaimed her seat in the corner of the sofa. Rubbing her hands together, she shifted the file with her name typed on the label onto her lap. What would she find here? she wondered.

Before she could lift the cover, the front door flew open and Chris barreled in. Grabbing her hand, he pulled her up against him, oblivious of the papers in her lap. "Come here," he growled.

When his lips came down on hers, she forgot . . . everything. She twined her arms around his neck and kissed him back, her lips parting greedily. Their tongues met, meshed, and danced to the beat of their hearts.

Chris kissed her harder and deeper as his hands cupped her thighs and brought her up against him. She straddled his hips and thrust into him, craving the pressure of his hardness.

He carried her to the bedroom and laid her on the bed. They finally broke the kiss and she gulped air into her deprived lungs. "I thought we were going to wait until tomorrow," she said with each exhale.

Chris tugged her turtleneck over her head and

his deft fingers immediately latched onto the bra's front catch. "We still can," he told her, his breath harsh and uneven as it exploded from his body.

"Uh? No."

He tossed a small plastic bag onto the bed and a pack of condoms spilled out. She pulled at the buttons on his uniform, and he leaned back to strip the shirt off. It dropped to the floor even as he made quick work of removing the T-shirt beneath.

Cai snatched him back down on her and his weight crushed her between him and the mattress. Chris pushed her loose hair away from her face and planted soft, moist kisses on her forehead, her cheeks, and the sensitive areas behind her earlobes. His lips were everywhere, his fingers, too, as he finally released her breasts from their confinement.

He played with her nipples, pulling and pinching until they stood erect, the pleasure-pain almost sending her over the edge. He didn't favor either one, but lovingly lavished attention on both, going from one to the other and back again, sucking, nibbling.

She arched her back, moving her breasts closer to the pleasure of his lips. When he dipped lower, pressing his firm lips to her belly, she unzipped her skirt. Pushing her hands away, Chris hooked his fingers beneath the top of her skirt and her panties and slowly drew them down her legs, exposing her freshly shaved apex.

Chris traced the triangular outline with gentle fingers and like a flower opening to the sun, Cai's legs spread outward seeking the heat of his touch. His lips joined his fingers and he bared her pearl to his hungry eyes. His lips settled over his newly found treasure and he drew her into the hot cavern of his mouth, flicking his tongue back and forth. A jolt shot from her belly and she nearly leaped off the bed.

"Chris, Chris . . . oh my . . . Chris!" she screamed, exploding all around him as she crashed back onto the bed. Waves of pleasure surged through her body, and she clung to him as he buried his face in her neck.

"I'm weak," she told him, breathless.

Chris chuckled and she felt the soft rumble against her throat. "Let's see if we can find a little more energy."

He rose to his full height, towering over her, his broad chest glistening with sweat. He unbuttoned his pants and that was about all it took. She sank to her knees to untie his boots, her fingers fumbling with the strings as she watched him push his pants over his hips.

He sprang free from his underwear and she gulped. "Can I touch—?"

"You can do whatever the hell you want," he groaned.

She abandoned his boots to grasp his hot silky length. She used her fingertips to trace the veins from the base to where they stopped beneath the mushroom shaped head. Her saliva thickened as she imagined tasting him.

Chris kicked his boots off and stepped out of his clothes and he stood before her—strong and power-ful and . . . hers.

Grabbing a condom from the bed, Cai pulled Chris down to her and kissed him slowly and deeply, over-whelmed by her love for this man. She pressed her body into his, pushing him back on the floor.

The curly hair on his legs tickled her nose as she kissed her way up one leg and then the other. Moan-ing, Chris twisted beneath her. She traced his length with her tongue and nibbled the stretched skin with her teeth.

Her hair fell like a sheet between them and he grabbed a fistful in each hand and guided her toward the tip of his sex. The sexy scent of his arousal filled her senses and she drew him into her mouth, eliciting a groan and several slow thrusts of his hips.

Closing her eyes, she flicked her tongue across the tip and circled him with her tongue as he filled her mouth. He tasted *so* good.

Quickly slipping on the condom, Cai continued her journey along his body, stopping to tease his nipples into hard buds before reaching his lips. Still gripping her hair, he held her against him and made love to her with his mouth.

Their eyes met and held as she straddled his hips and slowly lowered herself onto him, teasing him.

"Don't play with me," he whispered.

Sinking her teeth into her bottom lip, she eased up and rotated her hips around his sensitive tip. A groan tore from Chris' lips and he latched onto her hips and brought her down as he thrust up. The air left her lungs in a whoosh as he filled her completely.

Falling forward she clutched his shoulders as he lifted and plunged and lifted and plunged, her body bathed in sweat, the aroma of their lovemaking permeating the room. With one final thrust, her name tumbled off his lips as he reached his climax. She dropped onto his chest like a rag doll, her body vibrating with tremors of pleasure. Chris continued to move deep within her, keeping her body in the throes of passion until she pleaded for another release. His hand slipped between their bodies and he teased her pink pearl with his fingers until she tensed, squeezed him, and released a flood of juices all around him.

* * *

Cai stretched and rolled over to stare at Chris. She must have fallen asleep on top of him because she'd awakened in bed beside him and couldn't remember how they'd gotten there.

Why had she ever been afraid to trust her own feelings? Even if she'd only known Chris one day, her heart had recognized him as her soul mate. True love. That was what she'd found with Chris.

Brushing her lips across his firm jaw, she slid out of bed and slipped on her panties and his T-shirt. She padded barefoot into the living room to finish reading the file.

Cai gathered the papers that had fallen unheeded to the floor and curled up on the couch again. Ashanti would be home shortly, so she didn't have much time.

Though her name was typed on the label, she still expected to find information about her family. With her father's position and Mia publicly stepping forward as an alibi for her boyfriend, it was easy to get information on the family, but the plan unfolding before Cai's eyes centered on her. Banking on her feeling abandoned, Turner had purposely targeted Cai for a special case. His daughter, Kim, had come to him desperate for a baby, and he wanted to make sure there'd be a legal tie to the baby since Cai's father was the DA. As a result, he recruited the perfect, familial candidate. Kim's brother.

Cai stared at the paper, seeing but refusing to believe.

Jason? Jason was Kim's brother?

"Chris!" Cai ran into the bedroom and dived onto the bed. "Chris, wake up!"

He jumped up, his head jerking around the room until his gaze clashed into hers. "Cai? What's wrong?"

"Jason is Kim's brother!"

"What?" Chris rubbed his eyes. "They're brother and sister? You remember this?"

"The boxes came today. Remember my mom was sending the mail from my post office box? It's not unusual for me to send copies of evidence to myself but this is the original. I must not have sent copies to my dad, or he would have had Jason arrested, too."

Chris's hand dropped to the mattress. "So he had an agenda all along."

"I guess so." It suddenly explained so much. His rush to marry her, his adamant desire to use condoms instead of birth control pills. Why he contacted her before she went to Florida. "How could he steal my baby? How could he watch me die a little every day for three months, and then leave me?"

Chris raised his hands in the air as if it to say isn't it obvious? "Clearly, he was a damned nut. It must run in the family."

Cai laughed. "Oh, God, there is nothing funny about this! No wonder I blocked it out. I was a fool."

Chris slid his arm around her and pulled her close. "Don't say that. You were young and vulnerable, and he was working for a professional."

Still. She couldn't help feeling the fool.

Chris leaned back but kept his arm around her. "I wonder why no one connected him to Turner."

"He goes by his mother's last name, or so he told me. He never mentioned a sister, and I never met his mom." Cai glanced at the clock on the nightstand. "I'd better get dressed so I can go get Ashanti." Cai tried to smile, tried to find a little of the joy she'd felt earlier. "She's going to enjoy opening all her gifts."

Chris touched her cheek with his finger. "I'll get dressed, too. What are you going to do about Jason?"

She shrugged. "I don't know. If I hold onto the evidence and he decides to fight for custody, I could use it as leverage against him, or I could send it to my dad. Do we really want Ashanti to know her birth father?"

The phone rang and Cai broke off. Chris answered as she grabbed a pair of jeans and her shoes from the closet.

"Hello?"

She slipped into the pants and sat down on the bed to put her shoes on.

"Yes, she's here. Hold on a second." He held the phone toward her. "It's the detective."

Cai quickly tied her shoes and took the phone. "Hello?"

"Hey, Cai. I checked on that rental for you. It looks like a guy named Jason—"

Cai dropped the phone. "Oh, my God." She shot off toward the door. "Jason's going to grab her, Chris! Tell Landry to call the local police!"

She heard Chris scuttling around as she bolted through the house and out the front door. Her gaze shot to the end of the street and she saw Jason forcing Ashanti into the car, kids screaming and running in different directions.

Cai sprinted down the street and was halfway down the hill when he sped off. She skidded to a stop, almost falling, spun in the opposite direction, and started running.

Chris ran out the front door but she didn't slow down to explain. "I've got to stop him."

"He has her?"

"Yeah . . . take the car. I'll see if I can head him off."

Cai sprinted through the yard and ran between two houses. She knew the kids would slow Chris down, but this was between her and Jason. He must know she had the evidence, but how? How could he know?

Thank God she'd learned the housing area inside and out. She hopped a fence, raced across the yard, and jumped over the other side. She had to beat him to the gate.

Out of the corner of her eye, Cai saw the silver car come around the bend. He must have seen her because he sped up. There was only one way to stop him.

She dashed into the street and the car swerved. She heard Ashanti scream and ran back toward the car, raising her fist to smash the driver door's window. The car swerved sharply to the left, throwing her backward.

The car sped off just as Chris pulled in front of it, forcing Jason to stop. She saw Ashanti struggling with Jason, but he quickly subdued her and dragged her out of the driver's side. Cai scrambled after them as he dragged the little girl toward the pier.

"Mommy! Daddy!" Ashanti cried.

"Jason, you don't want to do this," Cai said in as soothing a tone as she could muster. Her heart was pounding so hard she could barely hear the waves crashing against the embankment.

"You gave me no choice. I tried to tell you, but you wouldn't listen!" He sounded hysterical.

Chris jumped out of the car and headed straight for Jason.

"Get back!" Jason warned.

She saw his quick glance at the dark, churning water. He backed Ashanti up toward the pier. The wooden slats could never hold all of them.

Cai grabbed Chris' arm. "Wait. Let me talk to him."

Chris plowed ahead and she struggled to hold him. "The pier's too weak, Chris."

He stopped, but his gaze never left Ashanti.

Cai turned to Jason who miraculously bypassed the first step. "I don't remember the last time we met. Will you tell me what happened?"

"I already told you! But you didn't want to hear it. All you wanted was revenge."

Cai searched her mind for any memory. All she could recall was her mother telling her he wanted to meet with her and Cai refusing. Did she change her mind once she realized his part in Ashanti's kidnapping? "I don't remember, Jason. Tell me again. This time I'll listen."

He stepped on the fifth slat and the pier shook before stabilizing. "You made me hurt you, Cai. I didn't want to, but you made me."

"I—?" What was he talking about?

"You only agreed to meet me here because you wanted revenge. You wanted to kill me, but I was ready for you."

Cai's hand flew to the now permanent scar on her left arm and Chris cussed under his breath. She and Jason had met here and he'd left her to . . . die? "No, Jason. No."

"Daddy!" Ashanti whimpered.

"Beruhige dich! *Er wird*—" Chris began in what, German?

"Don't say another word," Jason ordered.

Chris raised his hands in compliance. "I was only telling her to calm down, that you won't hurt her."

Jason's gaze whipped back to Cai. "Why couldn't you leave well enough alone, Cai? You had my father jailed, but you wanted to take me down personally."

Cai glanced at Ashanti whose tawny eyes were

pleading with her to save her, then to Chris. Was Jason telling the truth? Had her anger gotten so out of control?

Chris placed a gentle hand against Cai's cheek, and she allowed his warmth to seep into her skin and soothe her soul.

"I told my father I couldn't go through with it," Jason rushed on. "At first it was business. Or it was supposed to be. I wanted to stop the whole thing, and I would've if Kim hadn't run off with her. We didn't know she was in Germany until she died."

Cai didn't know what to think anymore. "I believe you, Jason, and we can work something out. I was very angry, but I'm not like that anymore. Chris and Ashanti, they taught me how to love again."

"Just give me the file, Cai. Her life for mine."

Cai raised her eyes from Ashanti's tear-stained face. "You sent the reporters, didn't you?"

"One for the BHV. How'd you guess?"

The sound of sirens shattered the silence and Jason snatched Ashanti closer. "You called the police!" he shouted.

"I didn't!" She glanced around trying to locate the vehicles. It sounded like four of them, at least. "They're on their way, Jason. Let Chris take Ashanti back to the house, and we'll talk to the police together. I'll explain everything."

She saw the desperation in his eyes, the confusion. He reached into his pocket and pulled out a knife. He flicked it open and Ashanti screamed. Oh, God.

Cai felt Chris lunge and blocked him with her body. *Please, God. Just one hit. Let me save my daughter, and I promise I'll never use karate again.*

Cai slid into a front stance, pivoted on her left leg, and snapped her right leg around for the strike.

Her foot connected with Jason's temple and he reared back, releasing Ashanti.

Cai caught Ashanti as she stumbled and then deliberately pushed her into Chris to keep him from running onto the pier. With a sharp blow against Jason's wrist, she disarmed him and yanked him toward her by his shirt. "I don't remember our last meeting, but if I'd wanted to kill you then, I would have. And if I wanted to kill you now, I could."

She released him with a shove, knowing the revenge she'd craved over the years wasn't the answer. He teetered on the edge, swinging his arms wide to balance himself. She lunged forward to catch him and the whole damned thing caved. Gravity yanked at her and she fell—hard.

She saw Chris and Ashanti drop as she hit the cold water with a splash. The flood swelled over her head, stinging her eyes and rushing into her nose and mouth. Sputtering, she kicked her arms and legs until she broke the surface. Trying to catch her breath, she treaded water as she looked for Ashanti through burning eyes.

Chris erupted through the water beside Cai and spun her to the right. A trickle of blood was oozing from a small cut on his forehead but other than that he didn't appear to be hurt. "Get Mel! I'm going after Jason."

Cai grabbed Chris's arm before he could take off. "Don't hurt him, okay?" Her plea was not for Jason's sake but for Chris's. Revenge would only leave a bitter taste in his mouth.

Cai dove into the water and kicked hard, using long strokes to reach their daughter. Ashanti's eyes were closed and she was screaming and fighting the water. Cai tried to grab her arms and Ashanti forced them both under the surface. Cai exploded out of the water, her lungs burning. "Ashanti, stop fighting, honey." She went under again and Cai dove in to get her. She clamped her arms around Ashanti and lifted her to the top. "Hold on, sweetie. I have you."

Ashanti coughed and gasped. "Mommy?" She looked at Cai as if she just realized she was there, and then fastened her arms around her neck. "I don't want to do this again," she cried.

Cai swam toward the embankment with her daughter in her arms. "Me, either, my love."

She saw Chris emerge from the water with Jason just as the police arrived.

Chris slipped an arm around Cai's shoulder as they followed Ashanti toward the house. She laid her head on his shoulder, absorbing his strength. They'd given their statements to the police at the scene before making their way home. Jason would be charged for his crimes and, hopefully, spend many years behind bars.

Ashanti stopped in the doorway. "My presents came?"

With all that had happened Cai had never had a chance to tell her. "Why don't you take a hot shower before you dig in?" she suggested. "Get out of those wet clothes."

"I bet I know what they are. Dolls!"

"And carousels, a jewelry box, a diary. Everything a princess deserves."

"I'm a princess?" she asked, sounding awed.

"You're our princess," Cai assured her.

Ashanti threw her arms around Chris's waist and hugged him. "You're still my dad, right?"

Chris knelt to Ashanti's level. "I'll always be your dad, honey. You don't have to worry about that."

Cai's eyes filled with tears at the tenderness in his eyes and voice. They hugged each other before she skipped off, her little world back on an even keel.

He straightened and pushed several boxes out of his way. Sitting, he stretched his legs out in front of him and pulled her onto his lap. Their clothes were wet, too, and she shivered a little. "You've been awfully quiet. Did Jason say anything that jogged your memory?"

"I think that week is lost to me forever." Her gaze dropped to her lap. "Do you think I met him there to kill him?"

Chris tipped her face up to his with a finger beneath her chin. "Honey, you don't have the heart. I'm sure you wanted to confront him. Who wouldn't? He probably panicked knowing you had the evidence to put him in jail."

She laid her head against Chris's chest and allowed the steady beat of his heart to comfort her. What she'd told Jason was true, loving Chris and Ashanti had changed her. In her heart, she knew she could never take another life, and that knowledge would have to be enough.

Lifting her eyes to Chris's, she said, "Earlier, I showed you what I feel in my heart. Now I want to tell you. I love you, Chris. Not the way I thought I loved Jason. That was infatuation. I love you in a way I've never loved any other man."

"I love you, too, Cai." He pressed his lips to her temple and she closed her eyes for a moment, enjoying the sensation of his cool lips against her skin. "I know you haven't known me very long, but will you marry me and spend the rest of our lives loving me?"

His deadpan expression made her laugh. "You got jokes, huh? Funny is all in the timing, you know."

"My timing has always been a little off. If I hadn't been running late the morning you crashed into my car, I could've missed meeting my one true love." He pressed his lips to the pulse in her throat, the sensitive spot behind her ear. "I don't know what I would've done if you'd been married, but you belong to me and I'm never going to let you go. Marry me, Cai, and we'll belong to each other—"

"Forever," she whispered.

He touched his lips to hers and his kiss was so gentle, loving. All those years ago, when she'd been devastated and heartbroken, Cai never imagined that the search for her daughter would lead to *her* one true love.

Maybe fate knew what she was doing after all.

Dear Reader,

Thank you for choosing to share in Chris and Cai's love story. There's a bit of intrigue in the plot I found fun to write. Add to that an amnesiac with short-term memory issues and I never knew what was going to happen. I hope you enjoyed the voyage as much as I did.

Sweetest Taboo is the second book in the McIntyre sisters' trilogy. You met Honor and her debonair hero, Nic, in *Honor's Destiny*. Next you'll meet Mia, the oldest sister. Mia's "indiscretion" set off the domino effect that had Cai running off to get married at eighteen and the subsequent kidnapping of her daughter, and Honor's eventual slide into anorexia. Let's hope Mia fared a little better.

I appreciate everyone's support. Your emails and guestbook entries on my Web site are truly a blessing to me. I definitely like hearing your thoughts on the sisters and their heroes, so please feel free to contact me at *yolonda@yolondagreggs.com* or via the USPS at PSC 80 Box 17623 APO AP 96367. I look forward to hearing from you.

Sincerely,
Yolonda J. Greggs

ABOUT THE AUTHOR

A native Ohioan, Yolonda Greggs has recently relocated to the beautiful island of Okinawa, Japan with her husband and children. *Sweetest Taboo* is her second published romance novel. As an artist, Yolonda enjoys creating characters and conflict in her stories that touch and inspire. She loves to sing and worship God through praise dancing as well as teach and speak in public forums.

SIZZLING ROMANCE BY

Rochelle Alers

__HIDEAWAY	1-58314-179-0	**$5.99**US/**$7.99**CAN
__PRIVATE PASSIONS	1-58314-151-0	**$5.99**US/**$7.99**CAN
__JUST BEFORE DAWN	1-58314-103-0	**$5.99**US/**$7.99**CAN
__HARVEST MOON	1-58314-056-5	**$4.99**US/**$6.99**CAN
__SUMMER MAGIC	1-58314-012-3	**$4.99**US/**$6.50**CAN
__HAPPILY EVER AFTER	0-7860-0064-3	**$4.99**US/**$6.99**CAN
__HEAVEN SENT	0-7860-0530-0	**$4.99**US/**$6.50**CAN
__HOMECOMING	1-58314-271-1	**$6.99**US/**$9.99**CAN
__RENEGADE	1-58314-272-X	**$6.99**US/**$9.99**CAN
__NO COMPROMISE	1-58314-270-3	**$6.99**US/**$9.99**CAN
__VOWS	0-7860-0463-0	**$4.99**US/**$6.50**CAN

Available Wherever Books Are Sold!

Visit our website at **www.arabesque.com**.